ZANE PRESENTS

D1378311

# THE Last EXHALE

## Dear Reader:

What happens when two people struggling in individual marriages decide to seek comfort in each other? Chaos, intrigue, drama, and ultimately, clarity. Sydney is married but not happy. She realizes that she made a mistake and was actually a rebound for her husband after losing the true love of his life. Brandon loves his wife but cannot understand why she has turned away from him—both physically and emotionally. When the two of them join a local gym around the same time and Sydney mistakes Brandon for his twin brother who teaches her daughter, they connect and then start making excuses to be around each other. That never works, especially when there is an instant physical attraction.

*The Last Exhale* is a novel that many will be able to relate to. When a marriage is on the rocks, some often find it easier to turn to a third party instead of trying to work things out with the people they promised to love throughout eternity. Julia Blues examines how things can fall apart when the realities of life intervene in a seemingly perfect situation. When illness, death, stress, and natural evolution change people. It is a riveting, engaging book that will bring many to the brink of tears in several scenes.

Thanks for supporting the authors of Strebor Books. As always, we strive to bring you amazing stories from prolific authors. We appreciate the love. You can find me on Facebook and Twitter @AuthorZane, on Instagram @planetzane and you can join our text service to be aware of upcoming titles and events by texting Zane to 51660.

Blessings,

*Zane*

Publisher
Strebor Books
www.simonandschuster.com

ZANE PRESENTS

# THE Last EXHALE

## JULIA BLUES

STREBOR BOOKS

NEW YORK  LONDON  TORONTO  SYDNEY

Strebor Books
P.O. Box 6505
Largo, MD 20792
http://www.streborbooks.com

ISBN 978-1-59309-497-3
ISBN 978-1-4767-1151-5 (ebook)
LCCN 2014931187

First Strebor Books trade paperback edition June 2014

Cover design: www.mariondesigns.com
Cover photograph: © Keith Saunders Photos

10 9 8 7 6 5 4 3 2 1

Manufactured in the United States of America

For information regarding special discounts for bulk purchases,
please contact Simon & Schuster Special Sales at 1-866-506-1949
or business@simonandschuster.com

The Simon & Schuster Speakers Bureau can bring authors to your live event.
For more information or to book an event, contact the Simon & Schuster Speakers
Bureau at 1-866-248-3049 or visit our website at www.simonspeakers.com.

*This book is dedicated to marriage.*
*This book is also dedicated to Barbara & Gary Williams, Sr.*
*Thirty-nine years of marriage and counting.*
*May you continue to be a walking, talking, living, breathing*
*testament to what marriage is all about.*
*Thank you, Mom & Dad.*

# SYDNEY HOLMES

My hand shakes as I unfold the letter.

I know the words by heart because I wrote them. Wrote them six years ago on the eve of my wedding day. Wrote them to my husband to tell him I wasn't going to meet him at the altar the next morning.

I made a mistake.

That night, I should have gone to his hotel and slid the letter under his room door like I had planned. Should've done that and taken the taxi to the airport, hopped on the flight I purchased a ticket for the night before, and flown to another life where nobody knew my name. Should've done all of that, but I didn't.

"Mommy, are you crying?"

I stuff the letter back in the shoe box, toss a worn pair of shoes on top of it. Shove it under the bed just like I did my heart when I stood in front of family and friends and God and promised to love a man for the rest of my life who I couldn't even love at that moment.

Before my son can see my face, I grab a tissue off the night-stand. "No, honey. Mommy's not crying. It's my allergies." I blow my nose to emphasize my lie.

I knew the moment the doors opened and I placed my feet on freshly sprinkled rose petals that I was making a mistake. My heart begged me to turn around, save myself before committing to a lifetime of insecurity. But my right foot betrayed me, then my left. Moments later, there was only a breath standing between us. I closed my eyes as his lips touched mine. Deep down, I prayed that when I opened them, it would have all just been a dream. A really bad dream.

It wasn't.

Almost seven years later, I'm still hoping to wake up and realize I'd been placed in the *Guinness Book of World Records* for the longest uninterrupted nightmare.

My son stands in front of me, stares me in the face to see if I'm really telling the truth. "Your eyes are red."

I pick him up and sit him on my lap. "Well, that's what they do this time of year, EJ. Let's just pray you don't grow up to be allergic to everything like your mother."

He shakes his head so hard it makes me feel like I have a bad case of vertigo, then runs his tiny finger down my nose. "I don't want to be allergic 'cause it makes you look bad."

Wow. I don't know if I should be insulted or laugh at his truth-telling innocence. I catch a glimpse of myself in the full-length mirror in the corner of the room. Bags under my eyes large enough to incur an overweight baggage fee. There's nothing laughable about my image. I put Eric Jr. down and pat him on the butt. "Go tell Kennedy it's time for bed. I'll be in to check on you two in a minute."

"But I'm not sleepy, Mommy."

I give him the look of looks, one that lets him know I mean business tonight.

He shuffles out of the room, yelling for his sister to go to sleep before she gets in trouble. Just like him to threaten his sister with his punishment.

Kids.

I go in the bathroom, grab a rag, and saturate it with cold water. Lay it over my eyes until it loses its cool. Rewet it with more cold water. Then I add a few drops of the liquid that promises to take the red out, let it marinate behind my eyelids. I do my best to get rid of any evidence of breakdown. Not that my husband would notice anything is wrong, I'm just not in the mood to tell any more lies. This might be the one night I set the truth free.

"Mom." This time, my daughter comes barging in the room yelling at the top of her lungs. "EJ just squeezed all my toothpaste in the trash."

"Kennedy, calm down. I've told you, no one can hear you when you yell. Now, what's the problem?"

Why do these kids insist on working my nerves tonight? Don't they know I'm near my breaking point? Don't they know that if either of them so much as sneezes, I will walk out that door and not look back?

My daughter repeats her distress and marches down the hall to their bathroom to show me the evidence. "See." She points to the trash. Pink gel with a ton of sparkles is splattered all in the trash and on the floor.

"Eric Thomas Holmes, Jr.," I call out. No response. I look under the cabinet and hand Kennedy a new box of her favorite toothpaste. "Brush your teeth and get in the bed." That seems to settle all her problems for now.

Heavy footsteps climb up the stairs. "What's all this noise up here?" the man of the house questions.

I tell him, "Your kids doing what they do best."

He pulls a smaller version of himself from behind his back. "This one was hiding under the dining room table."

I point to EJ's room door. "Bed. Now."

He scurries to his room like a dog with his tail tucked between its legs in its moment of chastisement.

"I'll have them asleep by the time you get downstairs." My husband kisses me on the forehead, tells me, "The dishes are done and I left the DVR up so you can catch up on your shows."

I stare at him momentarily. Do my best to convince my conscience that I did the right thing six years ago by not giving him that letter. And for a moment, it works.

I wink at him. "I'll be up shortly."

*D*ownstairs, I stare at a blank TV screen. Can't bring myself to scroll through the list of recorded shows. I'm so overwhelmed with my life, overwhelmed with the decisions I've made that have brought me here. It was my choice to keep dating Eric when I knew something was missing. I'm the one who chose to say yes when he proposed. And now I'm here, with two kids added to the equation.

In a way, it pisses me off that he can't see how unhappy I am. How can he claim to love me and not feel my pull in another direction?

Movement in my peripheral draws me from my thoughts, puts my attention on Forrester, our tabby cat, as he rolls over in front of the fireplace. He's so big, rolling seems to be all he can do. I watch him as he stretches his paws from the Atlantic to the Pacific, looks up at me, and lets out an exasperated yawn as if he's over-worked and underpaid. He gets up, turns around, plops back down, shuffles until he finds the perfect position to drift back into the wonderful world of chasing birds and squirrels, and probably in-dulging in steroid-filled Thanksgiving turkeys at will. The vet says he's severely obese, but if Forrester could talk, he'd have a different story to tell.

Watching him makes me think about my own life. Forty is a few blocks away, and I have no idea the last time I've had a genuine smile cross my face. This is not the life or marriage I imagined for myself. I always saw myself married to a man I'd travel the world with and create so many beautiful memories to share with our children and our children's children. Now, all I want to share with Kennedy and EJ is not to get married.

This is the bed I committed to when I agreed to take Eric's hand in marriage.

And this is the bed I have to lie in.

Long after the shows have gone off and my tears have dried, I make my way back upstairs.

I look in on Kennedy and EJ before heading to my room. Both of them are knocked out. When the kids are asleep or sick, I swear they're perfect angels. When they're awake, well...

As I open the door to the master bedroom, Eric staggers out of the bathroom. He says, "I was just about to come down and get you," his voice groggy.

"Why? You know how my insomnia can get."

He looks at the clock on his nightstand. "And you know how you don't like to get up in the mornings."

It's a few minutes after one a.m. In less than five hours, my world of wife and motherhood begins again. Sleep is the only time I feel like it's just me. I always dream I'm someone else, married to someone else, living somewhere else. Anyone but me, and anywhere but here. Sometimes, I swear sleep knows this, which is why it hides from me.

I go to the bathroom to empty my bladder before hopping into bed. I lean over and give Eric a goodnight kiss. His lips linger a little longer than mine. I pull away. "I don't like to get up in the mornings, remember?"

He rubs a hand up my thigh, suddenly wide awake. "What's a few more minutes?"

What's the point of avoiding this? Eric's manhood will spend the next few hours throbbing against my backside anyway. I shrug and let him kiss me again, let his tongue dance around mine until I feel the familiar tingle traveling down south. Eric's always been a good kisser. Had he not kissed me the way he did on our first date, I might not have gone out with him again.

My gown is lifted over my head and my breasts are sucked to erection. I rub my hands along a broad, muscular back, try to massage away the roughness of his skin. "We've got to get you some more exfoliant," I say.

"Mmm hmm," he mumbles with my nipples in his mouth.

The teasing way he licks my nipples makes me forget about exfoliating his back and focus on the wetness accumulating between my thighs. I let my legs ease open as his pelvis inches closer to mine. He eagerly slides into my womanly haven. His penetration has always sent my arousal to the umpteenth notch. I rock my hips to his rhythm, feel the groove he creates. Just as my eyes begin to roll their way to the back of my head, I feel warm liquid dripping down my thigh.

A few minutes indeed.

Luckily, I didn't marry Eric for earth-shattering bedroom skills. He does just enough to get my fire started, get me into it, but quickly douses my flames the moment he gets his jollies.

I turn on my side. He makes sure his alarm is set before scooting up behind me. He plants a tender kiss on my shoulder. "Love you, Syd."

Tonight, I can't form my lips to say it back.

I'm lying in bed.

The sound of water dripping from a recently shut off shower draws my attention to the woman I married nearly a decade ago.

I watch her through the cracked bathroom door. Her movements are calculated, methodical. So matter-of-fact. She gathers drenched jet-black coils, squeezes as much water out as she can, smoothes them into a ponytail with her hands. Braids up twelve inches of frizz, wraps it around itself until it can't wrap anymore. Forms a knot at the back of her head.

My warm feet find their way from under the covers and hit a cold floor. I wince at the change in temperature as I move to the space to join the love of my life.

I wrap my arms around her waist, lips touch her naked shoulder. I whisper, "Morning, love."

She moves away from my embrace.

I cut the faucet on, rinse my mouth out with water, then reach for my toothbrush. My eyes watch my wife through the mirror as she brushes down resistant frizz. She sees me looking at her, but deliberately keeps her eyes from making contact. I swish water and toothpaste around in my mouth while debating if I should tell her about our reservations for the night. Maybe things will be different.

She grabs her body oil, heads into the room. Leaves me in this space alone. Reminds me of how I've been feeling in this marriage as of late. Every morning, I awake with the hope things will be different. And every morning, I'm hit with the reality that nothing has changed.

I cut the shower on, put my mental anguish on hold. Step under the water headfirst, let the hotness beat against my bald head until I feel my scalp burn.

Rene's shadow reenters the bathroom before she does. Her presence makes the water feel Antarctic.

I can't take this anymore. The shower door swings open. I find myself standing on the outside, dripping wet, standing in front of my wife. "What's happened to you? What's happened to us?"

Still avoiding eye contact, she looks down at the bath rug.

"Enough with the silence, Rene."

Her stance is defiant, eyes on mine.

More silence.

We stand.

We stare.

"Nothing, Rene? You have nothing to say?"

Her eyes travel down from mine, give their attention to the area below my chest. She blinks, walks out of the bathroom with not so much as one word, but her look of disgust tells me everything.

All of a sudden, I become self-conscious. Grab a towel, wrap it around my expanding waistline. I follow behind her. "It's my weight, isn't it? I've gained a few pounds, I get it. But that doesn't deserve this."

Rene's lips part, a heavy sigh thrusts out. "Don't put words in my mouth, Brandon." She shakes her head and walks down the stairs to the kitchen.

My footsteps continue to mirror hers. "You haven't said much at all lately, so I fill in the blanks where I see fit."

She walks over to the sink, looks back at me, stares at me while she rinses out a glass. A lot is written across her face, but I can't read anything. Can't break the code. Need Robert Langdon to come in and read her like he did *The Da Vinci Code*.

"Tell me something, Rene. Tell me my breath stinks. Tell me I've gained weight. Tell me you're no longer happy. Just tell me something."

She just stands there, looks through me.

Inside the refrigerator is her lunch. I pull out the container of Caesar salad with garlic shrimp on top I made for her last night. Put it in her bag. Do that to gather my thoughts before I lose it and say some things to my wife I'll never be able to take back. I push her packed lunch to the side and stare at my wife. "What happened to us, Rene?"

Lips I haven't kissed for too long to remember tell me, "Nothing."

Her response isn't enough for me. "Do you still love me?" If she says yes, I'll fight to make this marriage work. If she says no, I'll give her hell. Either way, I have work to do.

She grabs her lunch, says, "Thank you," and heads for the garage.

Still wrapped in nothing but a towel, I watch her get in the car. She lets her eyes dance with mine long enough for me to see a glimpse of light behind them, a hint of a twinkle. It gives me hope for the future.

For now, my questioning is sufficed.


The security alarm chirps, signals I'm no longer home alone. Keys hit the countertop with a deafening thud.

"How was your day?" My warm lips try to give life to hers.

She takes off her shoes, carries them upstairs with her. Not in the house a good two minutes and her silence has already spoiled the atmosphere.

"Your bath water should still be warm. I'll get your wine," I yell up after her.

Sometimes, I wonder who's the wife in this marriage. Running bath water, fixing lunch, sending out holiday cards, doing the grocery shopping, washing clothes, changing the linen, paying the bills. The list goes on and includes working a full-time job. It hasn't always been like this. Three out of nine years of marriage is long enough, though.

Not only is the bathroom door closed, it's locked.

I lightly tap on the door, put my ear against it.

Nothing.

I tap again.

"I'll be out in a minute," she says in an exasperated tone.

"You don't want your wine?"

"Said I'll be out in a minute."

Throwing the glass of red wine against the door is very tempting. Very. I take it back downstairs and pour it down the drain instead.

While I wait on her to come back down, I go ahead and empty out her lunch bag. Put the dishes in the sink. According to the clock on the microwave, we have less than an hour to make our reservations. Doubt we'll make it. Wish I hadn't made them after all. No need in trying to prove my love and devotion to the woman whose finger I put a ring on and stood before God and pledged forever to.

She comes into the kitchen wearing a robe with frayed edges and a hole underneath the arm. An obvious romance killer. Her deep-set brown eyes search for her nightly drink.

I tell her, "Poured it out."

"Told you I was coming right out." She reaches up and grabs another glass from the cabinet, pulls the bottle from the fridge and pours her own drink. Takes a sip with closed eyes. "How was your day?" She shows a little interest in my life.

"Could've been better."

Time keeps ticking. No time for small talk. I go ahead and tell her about the reservations. I already know she's not going to want to go, her stiff shoulders tell me so.

"Why didn't you say something earlier?"

I shake my head. "Oh, no. Don't try that. You know I've been trying to talk to you all day to no avail."

"You still could've said something." She takes a smooth sip of her wine, displays her level of control.

Obviously, I'm the only one losing my cool at the moment. "Okay, you want to play that game." I rub a hand across my forehead, wipe away the beads of sweat that have formed in this cold room. "Plus, I wanted to surprise you. But you're too detached— Hell, I don't know what you're detached from. Me? This marriage? Life? I just don't know anymore."

She drinks the rest of her wine. "I'm going to bed."

I grab her by the arm when she passes me. "See, this is what I'm talking about. We're falling apart here and you're going to bed?"

Rene slides her arm from my grasp, moves a few feet away.

I raise my hands in apology. "Didn't mean to do that." I've got to get myself together. Mentally and physically, I've got to get control.

"What do you want from me?" Her arms folded.

Wait, was that a hint of emotion in her voice? Maybe all hope is not lost. Maybe she can still feel my love for her.

"I *want* my wife." I move close to her, pull her close to me. Feel her slowly thawing in my embrace. Doesn't last longer than a second before she turns back into ice.

She pulls away, heads back upstairs.

That's it. I've had enough. Every time I think she's relenting, she shuts me right back out. I grab my keys off the countertop. "Happy Anniversary," I yell and slam the door behind me.

*T*he chime of a soon-to-be empty gas tank transports me back to the present. I look for the next gas exit. When I grab the receipt, it tells me I'm in Montgomery, AL. Been driving for nearly three hours with Anthony Hamilton's *The Point of It All* CD on repeat. My thoughts were so caught up in what my marriage has become I hadn't realized I was in another state. I put the car in drive and get back on I-85 headed back north.

Just as the night prepares to clock off and switch shifts with the dawn of a new day, my truck pulls into the garage next to Rene's car.

Home.

The last place I want to be, but it's where I lay my head at night.

I'm dazed. Wondering what *is* the point of it all. This is not the way I planned to spend nine years of marital bliss. Maybe because it hasn't been that blissful. I take that back. The first six were great. Rene and I shared so much love.

We lived.

We loved.

We were one.

I knew what she was thinking before her thoughts could even form. She always knew what I wanted before I even knew. We were in harmony, in sync. Every day felt like the first day. We were amazed with each other, discovering parts of one another we had never discovered. Every day was like that.

Then, one day it all changed.

I remember the day like it was last night. We had just finished making love. Her head was on my chest and she was twirling the only five pieces of chest hair I had around her fingers. Her breathing was different. It was out of sync with mine for the first time. I noticed it almost immediately. She inhaled short and hesitant, exhaled hard and long, did that like she was on the verge of her last exhale.

"You okay?" I asked while rubbing her short-cropped hair.

"Just thinking."

"About?"

"Life. Love."

She talked freely. Didn't think about it. Just talked. Her breathing was still different, second-guessing itself.

"Okay, what about it?" I kept rubbing my fingers through her hair.

She continued playing in my chest hairs. "Do you love me?"

"Of course I do." My lips touched her forehead. "Why would you ask me something like that?"

"Just thinking."

Since she put it out there, I had to ask, "Do you love me?"

Her fingers released my hair. She lay there motionless. Only her lips moved. She said, "Nothing ever lasts. No matter what you do or say, nothing ever lasts."

The love of my life was starting to scare me. "Talk to me, babe. What's going on? Where is all of this coming from?"

Her head moved up off my chest, legs untangled from mine. She got out of the bed and went into the bathroom. Closed the door behind her.

I wanted to go after her, get to the bottom of her sudden despondence. I stayed in the bed, figured she needed a few minutes to herself to get her thoughts together. She would be out shortly and we would talk then.

A few minutes turned into twenty.

Twenty turned into an hour.

Moist sheets from our lovemaking were frozen underneath me. A chill ran through my body. I got up to close the window, knocked on the bathroom door. "Rene?"

Nothing.

I knocked again. "Rene," my voice louder. "You okay in there?"

Still nothing.

As I put my hand up to the knob to make sure it wasn't locked, the door flew open. She reached up and pulled my face to hers. Did it so fast I didn't have the chance to search her eyes for answers. Her lips touched mine with such a force it demanded me to kiss her back. I felt warm tears roll down my skin. I wanted to pull her away, separate my lips from hers and get to the bottom of what was bothering her. Her hunger for assurance in that moment kept me from pressing the matter.

We kissed.

She moaned.

She cried.

Hasn't been the same since.


The house is quiet when I make it inside.

Upstairs in our room, my wife sleeps as though our marriage isn't in trouble. She doesn't move when I walk in and sit down on the bed next to her. Doesn't flinch, not one bit.

My head falls into cupped hands. I just don't get it. I'm a good husband. Never cheated; never had the desire to. Never hit her, pushed her, disrespected her; never had a reason to. I've been here whenever she needed me, even when she didn't. None of this makes sense. My wife has lost sight of me and I don't know how to get it back.

I turn and observe her. Eyes closed effortlessly like all she had to do was lay her head down for sleep to pull her in the way an ocean's current pulls in an inexperienced swimmer. Her face denies worrying of my whereabouts.

I get up, grab my pillow off the bed. No point in sleeping in an empty bed even though there's another warm body lying there. Slowly close the door on my way out, watching her until I can barely see what's left of the moon's glow painting her skin a luminous shade of blue.

Her leg moves.

The door pushes open slightly.

My eyes peer back in on her, waiting for more movement. When hope fails me, the door closes.

If I weren't in my right mind, I'd swear I heard her exhale.

*I*'ve got on my little black dress and red belt to indent my waistline. I step into leopard-print stilettos. Spritz just enough peppered-violets in all the right places to make sure my scent is memorable. Take out the pins in my hair, fluff sandy-brown curls to perfection. As I grab my keys, I catch a glimpse of myself in the mirror. Despite the few pounds recently added to the scale, I must say, I'm looking good, and actually feeling even better. Feel almost like a single woman on the prowl. The sparkle on my left hand reminds me that I'm not. I blow my reflection a matte-red kiss anyway.

I'm meeting my girls at a lounge not too far from the house. It's Katrina's birthday. She's single and ready to mingle. Rachel's happily married and not ashamed to let the world know it. I'm stuck somewhere in between.

Eric pulled an extra shift for the night, so I thought it was the perfect opportunity to leave the kids with their grandmother. EJ and Kennedy will be just what she needs to keep loneliness from her pillow, while getting a break from all of them will hopefully keep regret from mine.

Surprisingly, there are quite a few people in the lounge. Unlike in my early years when no one came out until close to midnight. For it to be a few minutes to ten, I'm very pleased. These are the hours grown folks party, those of us with kids and real responsibilities.

Katrina sashays in shortly after ten. I wave her over to the bar where I've been standing long enough for me to no longer feel my toes.

"I was beginning to think I was getting stood up tonight," I say after we part from a hug.

"Forgot you're on borrowed time." She chuckles, but quickly stops when she sees the straight look on my face. "Rachel here yet?"

I shake my head. "Thought you two were riding together."

"We were, but she called thirty minutes ago to tell me she'd just meet me here. Said something about the zipper in her dress getting stuck and Michael helping her with it."

I look at Katrina and she looks at me. We burst into naughty giggles. "She's not coming," we agree in unison.

"If I play my cards right, I may be getting a little action tonight myself." She clinks her glass with mine. "Best way to celebrate this celebration."

A twinge of jealousy clogs my throat. I flush it down with pineapple-flavored tequila. I'm slightly jealous of both of my friends. One has the freedom to come and go as she pleases and the other doesn't want to come and go because she has a man she's madly in love with at home. I'd never let them know it, though.

I survey the room. Ask Katrina, "Anyone catch your eye yet?"

She shakes her head. "But I definitely see some eyes on you."

Two men sitting a few tables behind the bar raise their glasses in our direction. One of the men winks my way. I blush, but make sure I lift my glass with my left hand. Gold and platinum flash from their left hands. I quickly turn to Katrina. "Girl, they're married."

"A little flirting never hurt a soul," she says.

"I'm sure that's what someone was telling the woman who stole your husband."

My friend's eyes glaze over with hatred. The space between us grows hot. Feels like I'm standing face to face with the younger, fire-starting Drew Barrymore.

I grab her hand. "You know I didn't mean it like that."

She waves the bartender over, orders a shot of something clear. Downs it before he can sit it on the counter. "A girl only turns twenty-five once in her life. I'm not going to let you ruin my celebration." Then saunters off in the direction of salivating men.

Katrina hasn't seen her twenties in a decade. Every year, she celebrates the same age because she said that was the best year of her life. It was the year before she got pregnant and three years before her baby's father finally put a ring on her finger. Not a year into their marriage, she caught him in bed with their neighbor.

If twenty-five was the best year of her life, twenty-eight would have to be the age we'd celebrate for me. I met Eric two weeks before my twenty-ninth birthday. The rest is a blur.

The two married guys take their courage up a notch and ask us if we want to dance. Katrina tells Mr. Goldfinger, "Thought you'd never ask."

Mr. Platinum stands and waits for either a nod or a head shake from me. I toss back the rest of my drink. "What the hell," I say and take his extended hand.


My cell phone rings in my purse. "It's a great day to purchase a new home with Evans Realty. This is Sydney Holmes."

"You sound so different when you're in professional mode."

"Rachel?"

"Since the day I was born."

"Why are you calling my work number?"

"Because you're not answering your main phone."

I dig through my purse and see I have three missed calls and an unread text on my personal cell. It's on silent mode. I tell Rachel to hold on while I check out at the register of the sporting goods store I'm in. Two new pairs of running shoes, a few packs of sports beans, sports bra and a water bottle with a Velcro snap to put on my running belt. It's time for me to get the extra fluff off me I've packed on in moments of discontentment. Not that I'm an emotional-eater or anything.

"Sydney, you there?"

"I'm here." I put the items in the trunk. "What's so important that has you calling like I won the Mega Millions?"

"If that were the case, I wouldn't be trying to reach you by phone. I'd be camped out on your doorstep."

"Tell me about it," I say and start the car so I can feel the air. The rising temperature tells us spring went on vacation and skipped straight from winter to summer.

She wastes no time digging into my business. "So, I heard you ladies had a blast the other night without me, you especially."

"I was just trying to make sure Katrina enjoyed her birthday. As much as she tries to act like she's not, I can tell she's lonely since the divorce."

"That was her decision. I mean, she knew he was cheating before they got married and married him anyway."

"Yeah, that's true." I married Eric knowing what I was getting into. I know I can't be the only woman who's done so. My friend is proof of that. But still, to marry a known cheater and be okay with it is a different situation. "Now that you mention it, I can't see her divorcing him for that reason. Do you think something else happened that we don't know about?"

"Anything's possible, but she might not be the only person divorced if you keep dancing with random men like you're trying to make money to pay your mortgage."

I sigh. "It was a dance, Rachel. Why are you making it such a big deal?"

"I'm not. The guy you were dancing with is. He said you have some loose hips."

"How would—Did Katrina tell you that?" I parted ways with my friend after a few dances and drinks. I had a family to get home to. I was on borrowed time as she said. No telling what she did or better yet, who she did once I left. As liberated as she's been between the legs as of late, she might've taken both guys home to celebrate her birthday in style.

"I haven't talked to Kat." She lets that tidbit of information settle in before adding, "The guy you were dancing with is actually the supervisor over the fugitive unit Michael and Eric are in. You did know that, right?"

"How was I supposed to know that?" The one night I get out of the house and let my hair down, the whole world finds out. Such is my luck.

"Yeah, I guess you wouldn't, seeing as you never come to any of their get-togethers. We've played cards at his house a few times and he's been at the past two cookouts we've had over here. Now that I think about it, the last time you've been to any functions was at your house for EJ's first birthday. What's up with that?"

I pull out of the parking lot and get stuck waiting on a slow-moving train to pass. The temptation to roll down the window and toss my phone at the train to end this conversation grows the more Rachel grills me. "Enough about me. Why weren't you out celebrating with us?"

The smile in her voice can be heard on the moon. "Michael came home in one of *those* moods. Started the second he walked through the door, pinching me on the butt and nibbling on my ear. When I asked him to help me zip up my dress, he zipped it down instead. My dress ended up on the floor and we fell right on top of it."

"Ohhhh, spare me the details."

"You asked." She chuckles. "I know you two didn't miss me at all."

I can picture her sitting in a chair, head held back, mouth wide open, having a good laugh all by herself. "Still would've been nice to have you there."

"Let's plan something else soon."

The train finally passes and the light turns green. "Well, I'm around the corner from the office. Got a client coming in in about twenty minutes. Let me know when you ladies want to get together."

"Sure will. And I'll be sure not to plan it someplace where you won't be dry humping our husbands' boss."

"No, it *will* be a random guy next time," I say and quickly end the call.


Eric doesn't make a big deal of the dance when he gets in from work.

"Rachel made it seem like I was some stripper in a thong and pasties on my nipples."

"You know she likes to exaggerate. Don't take it personal, babe. It's not a big deal."

I rinse the cabbage and add it to the pan with chopped bell peppers and onions and olive oil. Add seasoning, give it a good stir before putting the lid on top to seal in the steam.

Eric says, "Next time you're feeling frisky, though, save it for me," then gives me a kiss.

I salute my husband. "Yes, sir."

He stops at the table where Kennedy is doing her homework and EJ is getting on her nerves. I'll be so glad when he starts kindergarten in the fall.

"Daddy, I'm glad you're home so he can bother you and leave me alone," Kennedy says.

"Be nice to your brother," he tells her.

"Can I hold your gun, Daddy?" Eric Jr. asks.

My husband looks back in the kitchen at me.

"That's your son," I say.

Eric Sr. puts a pencil in his hand. "Why don't you worry about holding this for now."

"Aw, Dad."

"Aw, nothing. Guns aren't for play, and they definitely aren't for little boys."

"Yes, sir."

I yell from the kitchen, "Get out of your uniform. Dinner will be ready in a few."

Kennedy brings a paper to me with clocks on it and the times she scribbled underneath. "I finished it."

I set the paper on the counter while I stir up the cabbage, unplug the rice cooker.

"Mommy, can I have a cookie?" she asks.

I hand the paper back to her instead. "One of these is wrong. Figure it out, then you can have a cookie."

EJ walks into the kitchen asking for a cookie next.

I shake my head. "After dinner for you, sir."

"No fair."

"Your sister gets a cookie before dinner, you get one after. You both get a cookie. That's very fair."

He huffs back to the table.

"Go upstairs and tell your dad dinner's ready."

He stomps up the stairs as if his feet are made of concrete.

Kennedy brings back her paper three times, figuring out which one she got wrong and making the correction. I give her the cookie as promised. "Great job, Kennedy."

I fix the kids' plates and set them on the table. Eric fixes mine and his while I pour us all a glass of lemonade. We grab hands as the head of this household blesses our food.

The dinner table is very quiet. It's so quiet I can hear Eric Sr. smacking on his food. I've never been able to understand why he feels the need to chew with his mouth open. While we were dating, I'd always try to find something to converse about, because his smacking would drive me crazy. He ate like he had no teeth. I told him about it once or twice and he'd stop, only to go back to it a few weeks later. Nothing seemed to work. Now, he has our son thinking it's a normal way to eat.

EJ fiddles around with his food.

I look across the table at him. "Cookie."

That one word straightens him right up. He smacks on the rice and chicken, does his best to work my nerves just like his father. The cabbage sits on his plate as he toys at it with his fork.

Kennedy pushes her empty plate in front of her. "Mom, can we go to the mall tomorrow? I want a pair of pink leggings."

My husband glances up at me, smiles, and shoves another bite of food in his mouth. He eats until his belly is full, without a single compliment to how the food tastes. Sometimes, I wonder if it's too much for him to let me know that the food is good. He could tell me it's bad and it wouldn't bother me as much as not saying anything at all. He's always been that way. He'll eat whatever I cook, as if an empty plate should say enough.

And this is how it goes every evening.

So routine.

There has to be more to life than this.

*D*ays have gone by since my failed attempt at celebrating nine years of marriage with my wife. Things are still the same. No talking. No lovemaking. Barely a touch in passing. Strangers sleeping on the same stale sheets.

Driving home from work, I decide to stop by the gym between the two places I spend most of my time. It caught my eye months ago, but I had no reason to go in and get in shape. Maybe this is what my marriage needs to get back to the way it used to be.

"Welcome to Pick Your Fit," a woman in jeans and a T-shirt bearing the gym's logo greets. "What brings you in today?"

"It's been awhile since I've seen the inside of a gym. Just wanted to see what you have to offer."

"Well, you've taken the first step. We have a lot to offer here. First of all, we're open twenty-four hours, seven days a week."

As she goes into the spiel that she goes over with every new person who walks through the doors, I can't help but feel like she sees my insecurity. Maybe it's part of her job description to read people, see who's serious about making a healthier life change and who's not. Then again, maybe it's just me being insecure, thinking everybody can see the same misery I see when I look in the mirror.

I ask, "Where do I sign?"

We step into her office, where she goes over the contract with me. I pull out my Visa, charge the full-year membership upfront. Get a full access passkey, T-shirt, water bottle, and an extra month out of the deal.

"See, now that wasn't so hard, was it?"

"Not at all," I tell her.

"If you have any questions or concerns about your experience here, my door is always open. This gym is all of ours." She reaches out, gives me a firm handshake.

"Glad to know that."

Since I had been eyeing the fitness center for a little while now, I knew today was the day to make the change. I packed a bag before I left for work this morning. I go back out to my ride, grab my bag and prepare to start a new life.


Time slipped away from me in the gym. I failed to notice day had turned to night. The manager's office light is out. I'm in here alone. I look up at the clock, see it's well after nine. I cut my MP3 player off, wipe the sweat off my face and neck. Refill my water bottle with fresh water, take a few gulps. Its metallic taste reminds me to get some fitness water tomorrow.

In the car, I pop in The Foreign Exchange. They're telling me to leave it all behind. That's exactly what I plan to do as I ride home with the windows down. Feel the warming breeze of seasons changing against my skin.

To my surprise, the aroma of basil, tomatoes, olive oil, garlic, and cheese permeate the room as soon as I open the garage door. I walk straight into the kitchen.

There's a single plate of lasagna and garlic bread at the table with a glass of wine. I notice a note next to the salad.

*Sorry about the other night. Come upstairs when you're done.*

I wash my hands, then touch the top of my food with my finger. It's still warm. I sit, say my blessings and dig in. Working out has given me quite an appetite.

Anxiousness almost causes me to choke as I toss the food into my mouth. Use the wine to wash barely chewed food down my throat. I put the empty dishes in the sink, wash them, and place them in the dishwasher to dry. Skip the stairs two at a time. Push open our bedroom door slowly. The wife's note in my hand.

"Rene?"

She's not in the room. I go in the bathroom, no Rene.

I check the office. No sight of her in there.

"In here," she directs me.

The guest bedroom. Trepidation creeps in.

I smell her.

Jasmine, amber, sandalwood, and wild berries with a touch of her own sensuality filters through my nostrils and swells my lungs. The scent teases me, plays with my emotions. I breathe her in, push open the door, find her leaning against the windowsill. A black negligee dancing with her curves in all the right places. Desire makes my manhood throb. I look down at my dank gym shorts. Don't want to enter my wife smelling like I've been wrestling camels.

Rene notices my disposition. Tells me, "I'll wait."

In a rush to get to the shower, I trip over my untied shoelaces and stumble on my way out of the room. "Damn." I find my composure before becoming twice the fool.

The water hits my skin, causes me to swim in my thoughts. As much as I want to—no—as much as I need to make love to my wife right now, I can't help but wonder what sparked her change of heart. Just the other day, she refused to acknowledge our anniversary, and now she's standing in the guest bedroom a fabric away from naked. I've been wanting this for a while now, but the thought slows my pace. Can't help it. It's the analyzer in me. It's what I get paid to do for a living.

I hop out of the shower in record speed, slather on a little lotion. Just enough to where I won't feel my skin cracking at the slightest movement. Throw on some boxers and look in the mirror on my way out the room. I backtrack, look again. Decide to remove the boxers.

Rene is in the bed when I push the door back open. Lying on her side facing the open window. She twirls a curl around her index finger.

I climb in the bed behind her, place my hand on her hip. Kiss the back of her neck.

She backs into me slowly, almost as if she's having second thoughts.

I rub her shoulder, plant kisses on it, try to get her to relax. It's been awhile since we've been this close. It's a little tense for both of us. Yet, not tense enough for me to let this moment pass, though. "Your skin's so soft."

She turns to face me. "No talking."

There's a lot I want to say at this moment. So much I want to ask. My hormones win as my wife straddles me. Her womanly part rests on my abdomen, my hands on her waist. Her eyes are on me, but she fails to look at me. Fails to look her husband in the eye as she lets me slip inside of her.

"Rene—"

"No. Talking."

I raise her off me, my manhood no longer inside her dry cave. This isn't about making love to her husband or about calming the seas in our marriage. I see that now. She couldn't even get wet for me. Who's the fool here?

She rolls over to an empty corner of the bed. Turns her face away from me. "Close the door on your way out."

"What's going on here?" I know she won't answer. She hasn't answered in the past few years I've asked.

"Not tonight, Brandon."

"When, Rene? If not tonight, when?"

Her shoulders raise as a mountain of frustration flows from her lips. "I just want to be alone right now. Can you give me that?"

"No, I can't. I'm tired of this."

My wife gets out of the bed, paces the floor. Pulls her hair over her shoulder, folds her arms across her chest.

I'm in the bed on my knees, watching her. I want to grab her and shake her until she loves me again, until the woman I married shows back up in this room. Feel like I've exhausted all possibilities. Don't know what else to say or do. Tired of having conversations with her silence. Tired of hoping, praying, wanting, wishing. What's the point of this? "I can't do this anymore," I hear myself say.

Her back and forth footsteps refuse to miss a beat as I climb out the bed and walk out of the room.

Something tells me her heart will do the same as I walk out of this marriage.

Andrew pulls up to the pool hall not long after me. He's on his cell when he gets out of his car.

I wait for him to finish before I get out of mine.

He taps my hood.

We embrace.

My twin brother. Been connected since conception. No bond like it.

"Ready to pay up?" he says.

"Do I ever?"

He smirks. "You will tonight."

We head inside. Order a couple Heinekens. Wait on a table to come open.

"How's Mel?" I ask.

He takes a big gulp of beer. I already know his answer. I'd respond the same way if he asked about Rene.

I move the questioning to one of his favorite subjects. "The school year been good to you?"

His face lights up. Totally different from the expression he gave at the mention of his wife's name. "Been real good. Hate that it's about to come to an end."

I sip my beer. "That's how you know when you love what you do."

"Can't imagine doing anything else."

"Yeah, you've always been good with kids."

Neither of us say anything for a minute. Both of us take a gulp of brew.

A table clears in the back. We grab our beers and pool sticks, head on over.

"You haven't said much about Rene. Everything cool?"

I hit the white ball so hard you'd think gunshots were being fired as balls roll around the table in a frenzy.

"Sorry I asked," he says.

We play in silence for a few.

To clear the air, Andrew asks, "You wanna talk about it?"

"Eight ball, right side pocket."

He gives me space. Puts a twenty on the table when I sink the game ball.

I sit on the barstool, sip on a fresh beer as he racks up the next game.

My brother, born fourteen minutes and some change before me, sits down next to me. Grabs his second beer. Tries to down it in one gulp. He drinks how I feel. One egg split in two.

"I'm leaving her," I finally say.

He feels my bitterness without me even having to say much. Nods. Gives me a moment to let reality sink in.

"You sure that's what you want to do?"

I put my beer down. "At this point, there's no other choice. Something's not right, and no matter how hard I try, she's not talking."

My twin chalks up his pool stick. When I look at him, swear I'm looking in the mirror. "Maybe you just need a little time apart. You know how women can get.",

"It's more than that, Drew. We've fallen apart."

He brushes some of the blue dust off his khakis. "Melissa and I aren't doing too good either."

"Figured as much. Is it the baby business?"

Andrew nods. Says, "I thought things would be a lot different, you know. Thought we'd have kids by now and be living life on a whole different level."

"Tell me about it."

I feel his eyes peering at me as I break the balls and get the next game underway. Tells me, "I'm sorry, man. I didn't mean to—"

I put my pool stick in the air, shake my head. Continue sinking solids in pockets. His frustration over not being able to be a father causes him to forget I'm no longer a father. It's not the first time. And until he has a child, I'm sure it won't be the last.

"For real, Brandon. I'm sorry about that."

"Your turn," I say. Grab my beer, guzzle down the remnants.

It's not really his turn. I'm just tired of playing.

Another twenty lands on the table. He's tired of playing too. Either that or he's lost his energy. Talking about lack and loss will do that to you.

My brother sits down next to me. "It's still hard to talk about, huh?"

I lean my head back against the wall. "Feels like it was yesterday."

Three years ago, my son passed away. He was only five. Wasn't sick. I could count the times he had been sick since birth on one hand. He went to sleep one night and never woke up. The doctors had no explanation. None at all. *"We're sorry,"* was all they had to offer.

Andrew flags down a waitress. Orders us a couple more beers.

"There are days I want to forget. Want to forget holding his stiff, cold body in my arms. Want to forget the pain in Rene's scream when she found him." My throat becomes dry. Wonder what's taking our drinks so long to arrive.

She finally comes. Andrew pays her with the twenty from the

table. She hands him sixteen dollars back. He gives her two bucks for her service.

I take a couple sips back to back before I say, "Sometimes I want to forget the day he was even born. Then it wouldn't hurt so much to remember him dying."

"Man, I can't imagine that feeling."

In a way, I know he can. We're cut from the same egg. What I feel, he feels. And what he feels, I feel.

"Do you think that's what's going on with Rene? You think she's just missing him?"

My answer doesn't come right away, need a second to let the thoughts marinate. "I mean, it's possible. She was a little despondent when he first passed, but she pulled it together to…you know, get him ready for the funeral. It was almost a year after that she started acting like a mute."

His mouth opens to respond just as his cell rings on his hip. "It's Mel."

"Tell her I said hi." I head to the bathroom to get a little relief. Beer runs though my kidneys like a leaky faucet at midnight.

When I get back, he tells me it's time to head on home. "Mel made dinner plans and I need to get the lessons done for the week."

"All right, man. Let's do this again soon. I could always use some extra gas money."

We end on a light note with a chuckle.

"You know I let you win." He grabs me by the shoulder. "In all seriousness, think about it before you walk out on Rene. Talk to her and make her talk back. Hate to see it all end like this."

"I'd hate for it to end like this too."

*I*n the glove box of my car is a gift certificate to a local gym I won in a drawing from the local radio station. I was going to give it to one of the other agents at the firm since I prefer working out outdoors, but right now, I need this for me. I grab it and walk into Pick Your Fit 24hr Fitness where I get to "pick my fit." The owner gives me a tour of the facility. Since the certificate pays for a year membership, there's not much she needs to sell me on. I fill out the necessary paperwork, proceed to the restroom to change. Find my way to the mat for some stretches.

Besides the owner and two guys spotting each other on weights, I'm the only other person in here. I could get used to a place like this.

It's been a while since I've run. Try to run at least three days a week, but work, the kids, and acting like a happy wife have worn me out lately. Running helps me put things in perspective, and that's just what I need.

Not even a mile in, my legs let me know they're rusty. Press the up arrow, increase to a six-and-a-half pace. Breathing is harder, heart pumping something serious. Feel my sweat pores open and pour out rivers of salt water, forms a lake in the crevice of my bosom. The burn in my legs calms down just a tad. Takes a minute or two for my breathing to settle to an even pace. Running slower aches more, especially when I go weeks without running.

As the two weightlifters leave the gym, another guy walks in. He causes me to lose my step. I step on the sides of the treadmill, take a breather. Use my towel to dry off my face and neck, sip on a bottle of electrolytes.

My daughter's first grade teacher hops on the treadmill next to me. He doesn't say anything when he looks in my direction.

"You don't know who I am, do you?"

He shakes his head while fidgeting with the buttons on the treadmill.

"And I only thought it was after a man sleeps with you that he no longer recognizes you." I chuckle.

He stares at me with one eyebrow raised. Not sure if he's trying to remember if I'm someone he actually did sleep with or if he thinks I'm totally off my rocker.

"I'm Kennedy—Kennedy Holmes' mom, Sydney."

His eyes widen as if I've just told him he has a child he didn't know about.

I relieve him of his confusion. "From school. Mr. Carter, right?"

He gives me a blank stare.

Maybe I'm the one confused. Or maybe my child's teacher has no manners outside of the classroom.

Out of nowhere, the guy laughs. "I'm messing with you. I *am* Mr. Carter."

I let out a hesitant chuckle while thinking about switching my daughter to another teacher. Not sure this is the kind of guy I want teaching my child.

He's still laughing. "You should see the look on your face."

I say, "Ah, didn't know you had quite a sense of humor." I shut my treadmill off, grab my towel, and proceed to the mat to stretch my tightened hamstrings.

Mr. Carter pulls the emergency stop on his machine, hops off before I have the chance to walk off. Tells me, "I am Mr. Carter, but not the one you're thinking about. I'm Brandon. Andrew's your daughter's teacher." He looks at me with a half-smile and raised shoulders. "Bad time for jokes, huh?"

"You're twins?"

"Identical."

I slap him with my towel. "Funny. You had me about to call the school board on you."

"Please don't do that. My brother would kill me."

"As well he should. You're ruining his reputation."

We share a smile. No harm, no foul.

He says, "People get us confused all the time. Even at our age, we still like to have a little fun with it."

"I'm sure it never gets old." I leave Brandon by the cardio machines and plop down on the mats. Not running in awhile only to push myself as hard as I did was not a good idea. Not a good idea at all. My quads and calves join my hamstrings in screaming for relief.

The moment I open my legs for a butterfly stretch, over walks Mr. Funny Man. I see his eyes focus in on the wet spot in my crotch area. Immediately, I become self-conscious about my sweating issue and close my legs.

"How far did you run?" he wants to know.

"Not as far as I'd like."

"And that is?"

"You sure are quite the joker *and* talker, I see," I say, my voice laced with bite.

"And I see all of my joking *and* talking has you a little wet between the legs."

My face burns with embarrassment. I want to explain I've been this way my whole life, how I would sweat so much in my sleep as a child, my mother swore she was going to invent diapers for eight-year-olds. Telling him that would only make me more embarrassed, so I hold my tongue. I pull my legs in and slide my shirt over my knees. Plan to sit here and rock in silence until Mr. Funny Man finds someone else to torture.

Brandon senses my discomfort. "That was inappropriate of me. Sometimes my tongue gets the best of me."

*Wet between the legs. Tongue gets the best of me.* All of a sudden a weird feeling passes through me. Maybe not weird, but definitely inappropriate. Why has my mind taken his words to a sexual level? What if he meant it that way? Do I dare sit around and find out? "Let me get out of here before the kids make my husband run away from home."

He reaches down to help me up from the mat.

"Thanks."

He nods and walks to the free weights.

As I grab my keys and other items from the storage rack, I catch a glimpse of Brandon through the mirror in the middle of a bench press. Don't know why, but my eyes scan his left hand. A silver band halts my curiosity.

Yep, he's married.

Then I have to remind myself: So are you.

Rene beats me home for the third night in a row this week. Ever since the night she left me hanging in the bedroom, things have been a little different around here. Still tense, but different. She's sitting in the dining room. A plate of roast, potatoes, and asparagus is in front of her. Glass of red wine in her hand.

Maybe there is hope after all. Maybe Andrew *was* right. Despite it all, my wife can still bring a smile to my face. I walk over, plant a kiss to her forehead. "Smells good in here."

"Your plate's in the oven. I'll wait for you."

I grab my gym bag off the floor, march upstairs to wash away my funk.

Sydney Holmes.

Rene is downstairs finally being the wife I've been longing for and I'm up here thinking about another man's wife. The ring on her left hand floats through my mind. Yep, I checked. Shame on me.

I pour a small amount of Rene's shampoo in my hands, rub it across my scalp. Try to lather up my inappropriate thoughts and rinse them down the drain. If only it were that easy. My towel falls to the floor when I push open the shower door. I grab it, dry off. Spray on a little chocolate seduction body spray. Maybe my wife will be willing to make me feel like a husband after dinner.

Rene is pulling my plate out the oven as I make it back downstairs. She places it on the table. Refills her wineglass, fills mine next.

I bless the meal.

After a few bites in silence, my wife cuts her eyes up at me, says, "You seem happy."

Her comment makes my heart pound with beats of guilt. Has one conversation from another woman caused me to come home feeling like a different man? No, can't be. My wife has surprised me with a great meal. That's what I'm happy about, right? I swallow another bite of food. "Everything's delicious."

One of Rene's eyebrows is slightly higher than the other as she peers at me over a raised wineglass. "The gym seems to be working out," comes out as a statement more than an inquiry.

There's nothing in her tone to let me know one way or the other whether I should be offended or not. Has my weight been the cause for her change in attitude all this time? My fork hits the plate. "So I was right, huh?"

She sips her wine ever so calmly. "I was simply giving you a compliment."

"Well, why does it feel more like an I-told-you-so?"

"If that's the way you took it…"

I'm hungry. Hungry like I just smoked a pound of marijuana. But I've lost my appetite. Lost my desire for food and for my wife. I grab the plate in front of me, scrape its contents into the trash. Tell Rene, "Thanks for *every*thing." Do my best to let my sarcasm spoil her appetite.

I'm dumbfounded. All I can do is shake my head. The longer we live in the space of complexity, the longer we will continue to have miscommunication and misunderstand each other.

"What do you want from me, Brandon?"

I look at the woman I've loved for more years than I have fingers. I no longer understand who she's turned into. "I'm starting to wonder the same thing."

She gets up from the table, blows out the candles, takes her wineglass, and heads toward the bedroom we once shared. Halfway up the stairs, she stops, turns around. She comes back into the dining room. Without making eye contact with me, she grabs the bottle of wine off the table and heads back up the stairs. The room door shuts a few seconds later.

I can't continue living like this.

Better yet, I *won't* continue living like this.

*I* finish putting together an offer for a lease-to-purchase one of my clients is interested in. They knew as soon as they finished walking through the house that they were going to submit an offer. They're newlyweds expecting their first child. Love is written all over their faces. I found myself temporarily envious. Don't know if I've ever looked a man in the eyes the way she looked at her husband. Can't say I've seen a man look at me that way either. Not even my own husband.

Soon as I fax the offer to the seller's realtor, a text comes across my phone. Eric won't be able to pick the kids up from school. A new recruit got shot and killed his third day on the job.

"Are you okay?" I ask my husband once he answers his cell.

"Little shaken up. We all are. But it's part of the job."

I understand the part-of-the-job mumbo jumbo. But somebody dies and he sends a text. I tell him to hold on while I grab my keys and head out to the car. This is a conversation to have with no one else in earshot. "No, really. Are you okay?"

"I'll survive."

He doesn't get it. "Eric, you don't text me about somebody getting shot and killed on the job doing the same thing you do. Do you know how that made me feel to read that?"

"At least it wasn't me."

"Yeah, not this time."

"I don't have time for this," he says, ready to end the call.

"Wait. Hear me out for a second." I swallow, add moisture back to my throat. "My heart dropped when I got your text. You're right, it's not you I have to bury, but somebody *is* making funeral arrangements right now. I just wish you'd take a little more consideration when you do certain things." I take a deep breath, calm my nerves. He just lost a fellow officer. No need in me adding any more stress. "I'll get the kids. Will you be home for dinner?"

"Yes."

We both hold the phone in silence long enough for it to feel uncomfortable.

I say, "Be careful out there."

He makes no promises. "Okay," is all he can give me.

I didn't mean to jump all down Eric's throat. I've been on edge ever since coming home with thoughts of another woman's husband. I know Brandon and I barely talked, but he made me laugh in a way I haven't laughed in a long time. And it was genuine at that. Not phony laughter to fill enough space to keep things from feeling awkward. Made my stomach feel like I'd done a hundred crunches in twenty seconds.

I've got to get control of my thoughts. Quick.

My husband puts his life on the line every time he puts on his uniform. It's imperative I keep that at the forefront of my thoughts, because I don't know what I'd do without him and I can't fathom how I'd be able to tell our kids that they no longer have a father. I have no time to be thinking about another man. A laugh isn't a good enough reason to even think about risking my family, especially when it wasn't *that* funny.

It was a good laugh, though.

"Is that it?"

I look in the U-Haul, see what pieces of my life I'm bringing on this part of my journey. Tell my brother, "Yeah, I got what I need for now."

Andrew trails behind me as we drive a few miles up the road to my new apartment. We decided it best for him to drive his car to avoid running into Rene coming back here.

Last night was about all I could take from my wife. When I agreed to love her for better or for worse, I had no idea it would get to this part of worse. At the altar, everything looks and sounds good. You don't think about "for poorer" or "in sickness" or "in bad times." All you see is what stands before you at that moment and what's going to go down during the honeymoon. A week later, things start looking real different.

Silence is not what I stood before God for and it definitely isn't what I agreed to.

The first thing I did when I made it in to work this morning was hop on a few apartment websites to scout out a place to live. The place I've called home no longer fits the bill. Instead of eating during lunch, I went and put in an application to a place around the corner from the gym. Before I made it back to work, I had been approved. Went to sign the lease and was handed over a new set of keys once I got off. A moving truck was already on reserve the moment I found out I had been approved. It was halfway packed by the time Andrew was able to help with the heavier stuff.

Twenty minutes later, we pull into the apartment community.

Once inside, my brother says, "I can't believe you actually left."

I look around at the empty space. Nothing is familiar. Reality sets in. "Man, I can't either."

Conversation is to a minimum as we unload what's left of my life into unfamiliar territory. In nine years, I've gone from a single man to husband to father to a man alone. This is what my life has become.

It takes us about half an hour to get everything out of the truck and placed in the apartment in no strategic fashion.

"All right, man, let's get this truck back," I say.

I stop at the gas station. Fill the tank back to where it was when I signed the truck out. "Want anything?" I ask Andrew before running inside to pay.

"Naw, I'm good."

I pick up a pack of watermelon Bubblicious gum and a bag of cool ranch Doritos.

My twin trails me back to U-Haul where my car is parked. After checking the vehicle back in with no extra costs, I see if Andrew wants to get a bite to eat and grab a couple of beers.

He puts his cell down against his thigh, shakes his head. "Not tonight, man. Melissa's already got plans for us." The despair in his eyes tells me her plans are no longer the same as his.

"Good luck. Hopefully, we won't be roommates anytime soon."

He chuckles, shakes his head again. "Yeah, I hope not."

We slap hands. I tell him, "'Preciate your help."

"I know it's not easy. The least I could do is be here for you."

"I hear you, man. I'd do the same for you."

He puts the phone back up to his ear, rolls up his window, and drives off to a woman whose biological clock is ticking.

On the way back to my apartment, I drive by the gym. Curiosity makes me do that.

The lights are on. I can see her on the treadmill. From the sweat building between her thighs, I can tell she's been in there for a while.

I park my truck, but don't get out. Instead I sit here watching, thinking. Wondering if I should go in or take my behind home. If I go in, I'd probably tease her about her sweating. She'd probably joke with me about not being able to take a joke. We'd probably laugh, maybe both loosen up some.

Or I could go home to an empty apartment.

My hands betray common sense by shutting off the ignition. My legs betray my better judgment by pulling me out the truck and leading me toward the gym's entrance.

I mess around with a few weights to give her time to finish her workout. Before long, I feel myself breaking a sweat. I finish the rep, clean the machine off, sip water from the fountain.

"Okay, which one are you?" Sydney asks.

"What, you mean you can't tell?"

That gets a laugh.

I was right. This could be fun.

"Taking it easy tonight," she says more than asks.

I rub the back of my head. "Actually, I had no plans to work out."

"So, why are you here? To make jokes again?"

My eyes connect with hers and I say, "To see you."

Sydney blushes. "You are relentless. Are you like this all the time?"

"Depends." I pick up two twenty-pound dumbbells to do a few curls. "How many miles you run?"

She wipes her forehead with a towel. "A lot more than last time."

"I can tell."

"How so?"

She follows my eyes to her lower torso.

"Are we back to that again?"

I shrug, put the weights down.

"Look, I've always been a sweater. Even sweat in my sleep."

"I'm sure that has to be tough on the hubby."

She holds up her index finger. "I am not, I repeat, not about to have this conversation with you."

Light chuckles as we walk over to the mats.

Sydney plops down, bends one leg inward, stretches the other leg outward. She lifts her head in my direction. "Why do you always want to know how far I've run?" she inquires.

"To be honest, runners intrigue me."

"Oh, so it's just my running?"

"What else would it be?" I stand back a little, rest my arm on the wooden arm rail. "Are you flirting with me, Mrs. Holmes?"

Again, she blushes.

Maybe I'm the one flirting. I back off. "No, seriously. Runners have this confidence about them. It's like all they have to do is put on a pair of sneakers and nothing else in the world matters."

Sydney nods, bends the other leg inward. Sole to sole, she stretches her inner thighs. "Well, speaking for myself, nothing does matter when I run. It's the perfect stress-reliever."

"What's got you stressed now?"

Two people walk into the gym. Breaks up our moment.

Instead of answering, she gets up, walks over to the water fountain and takes a few sips; licks her lips. Then slips into the restroom.

Not sure what's gotten into me tonight. It's been a while since I've had a real conversation with another woman in years. Guess the stress with Rene and not being able to communicate with her has me jumping at conversation with anybody. Maybe it was out of line to get personal with my questions, but, I have to admit, the conversation flows easily with Sydney.

She walks right past me when she comes out of the restroom, goes over to the storage rack to grab her stuff.

I walk over. "Did I offend you?"

"Look, Brandon. I doubt I would've said anything to you if I hadn't mistaken you for someone else. The conversation has already gone on longer than it should have."

"Understandable. Sorry if I've overstepped my boundaries."

"Well, I'm sure I'll see you again since we both work out here. Hopefully, it won't be too awkward."

"Can I ask you something?"

She nods.

"I'm thinking about running my first half-marathon in November and I was wondering if you would help me train for it. You know, give me some pointers and such."

Without answering, she walks out the door.

When I get in from the gym, Eric and the kids are sitting on the couch with a bowl of popcorn watching *Happy Feet 2*.

"Mommy," EJ yells, "come watch *Happy Feet* with us," and pats the space on the sofa next to him.

"Mommy stinks from the gym. Let me shower and I'll be down in a few."

"Aircorn." Eric throws a piece of popcorn up in the air to distract EJ while I run up the stairs.

As soon as my bare feet hit the tile in the shower, tears overtake me. I slide down the wall and cry into bent knees.

Downstairs is a good man. A good man who loves me and our kids. Eric's never cheated on me, never called me outside my name. Never raised his hands toward me in anger. He's worked the same job since we met. Pays the majority of the bills. Picks the kids up from school, helps me with the chores. I can't think of anything he's done wrong, yet I'm up here flirting with the twin brother of our daughter's teacher. What kind of woman am I? Many women would kill for a husband like mine.

A tap on the door jars me from my madness. I stand up, stick my whole head under the water. Do my best to keep my emotions in check. "Yes?"

My husband walks in, cracks open the shower door. "You okay in here? Been in here for a while."

I lather my hair with shampoo. "Yeah. Running all this week has my hair in need of a good wash."

He rubs his thumbs across my eyes. "Must've gotten some shampoo in your eyes; they're red."

"Must have."

He stands there for a second, just looking at me.

"Hey, babe, can you shut the door. Letting the steam out."

"You sure you're okay?" he asks again.

"I'm fine, babe. My woman-time is about to come on and has my emotions out of whack. You know how that goes," I say in between sniffles.

"I'll put the kids to bed and when you get out, I'll give you a nice rub down."

My lips part into a half-smile.

Eric nods, closes the door, and heads out of the bathroom. Twenty minutes later, he's back with a cup of hot tea and a warm bottle of massage oil.

This is exactly why I have to stay as far away from Brandon as possible.

No one leaves a good man.

*I*t's a quarter after eight and still no sign of Sydney at the gym. It was the same story last night. She hasn't been back since I let my mouth run the wrong course. Seems like miscommunication with women, or the lack of communication, is becoming the story of my life. I'm either saying the wrong thing or the right thing at the wrong time.

I grab my cell to dial my brother's number. Four rings later, his voicemail alerts me he's unavailable at the moment. I click the phone off before hearing the beep to leave a message.

Two nights in a row I've wasted waiting on another man's wife. Doesn't make any sense.

Wife. Speaking of which, I left mine a week ago and have yet to hear from her. I thought she would've at least called to make sure I was okay, that nothing had happened to me, that I wasn't run off the road by a drunk driver or something. She's definitely not the same woman I fell in love with almost a decade ago.

Instead of heading to my apartment, I find myself driving a path I rarely drive. Haven't been here since my son passed away. My wheels turn into DelCosta Funeral Home. I pull into the back of the building and use my key to unlock the service door.

I see Rene, but she doesn't see me. She has on a long white coat, black gloves, a mask covering her nose and mouth, goggles over her eyes. I watch as two men enter through another door, wheeling a table with a white bag on it. They grab the bag from each end and place it on the table in front of Rene. The two men wheel the now empty table out of the room, leaving Rene to herself again. She unzips the bag, stares at the man's body for about five minutes. Walks around him, views him from different angles. She takes one of his stiff hands in hers, closes her eyes, says a sincere prayer before rinsing his body with hot water and bleach, sprays him with more water and a soapy solution, and again with water.

I nearly gag as the smell of death begins to invade my nostrils. I cover my nose and mouth with my shirt, try to quickly fill my nostrils with the scent of life.

Rene slides the bag from under the man, rinses and places it in a bin with other bags to be sanitized for later use. She then covers the man with a white sheet.

I watch through a storage room window as she tosses her mask and soiled gloves in the trash. She removes her goggles, sprays them with a clear solution before placing on the shelf for another day's use. Her lab coat comes off next. It's placed on a rack and sprayed with a can of Lysol. She turns off the classical music and lights. Her footsteps stop in front of the door I'm behind. We're so close I can hear her hesitated breathing.

My heart pounds heavily against my chest.

"Rene," one of the male voices calls out.

"I'm coming," she says.

Finally, I'm able to breathe again as I hear her footsteps fade in the dark. A few minutes go by before I step out of hiding and into the hallway.

I find myself creeping up the stairs to the owner's office. A shallow light reflects off the hardwood floor underneath the door. I turn the knob slowly, see my wife nursing a half-filled glass of clear liquid.

We make eye contact.

"What took you so long to come up?" she questions.

"How'd you know I was here?" I do a poor job hiding my voyeuristic shame.

"I smelled you."

The fact that she could pick up my scent in a place saturated with death surprises me. Then again, her nose is trained for the aroma of death. Anything smelling different would put one on alert.

My eyes stare in her direction. Her face holds much more softness than Sydney's, but her eyes look as vacant as a midnight sky with no stars.

The window behind her desk is open. I can see the moon's reflection ripple on top of the lake. A burning candle is on the windowsill. Another one's on her desk. A third one is on the table, burning next to her drink. One tranquil, one citrus, another earthy. A mixture of moods floating in one room.

Rene's eyes are on mine when I notice an open cabinet next to the door. Inside are about twenty or so different bottles of hard liquor. I guess this is how she decompresses at the end of a day filled with death. And all this time I thought that's what the baths and red wine were for.

"Those are for nights like tonight," she answers my silent inquisition.

I sit on the sofa next to her. "I saw you downstairs with the body. Saw you hold his hand."

"Wesley Washington."

"Sounds like you knew him."

She nods. "He was a cop who worked for us every weekend on traffic patrol for the last four years. I could always depend on Wes. He was a good worker." The glass of clear liquid comes up to her lips. She swallows slowly. "A good friend."

The way she says that pinches at my ego. A husband's supposed to be a good friend, not another man. "How'd he die?"

She holds the drink in her hand, but doesn't drink. Just holds it and stares. "Cancer." The drink that temporarily rinses all pain away nears Rene's lips. She takes the rest in one hard swallow.

I want to reach my arm over her shoulder and pull her close, do for her what she depends on the drink to do. She gets up before I have the chance to do anything.

She stands by the window gazing out at the man-made lake. "Why'd you move out?"

I knew the question would come sooner than later. I was hoping for later. "I think you already know the answer."

Her voice cracks. "What's happening to me?"

My heart stops beating as my feet move in her direction. I wrap my arms around her, try to hold her together before she completely breaks. I do that while fighting back my own emotions.

The woman I've loved for so long is still inside. She's fighting with the woman she's become. Maybe if I hold her tight enough, I can pull the real her out, like Logan did Jean Grey in *X-Men: The Last Stand*. If only for a moment, long enough for her to love me back.

Rene pulls away. Her eyes darken. "Why are you here?" Her Phoenix side is stronger. "Just leave."

I have to become Wolverine. "I already left."

And with that, I walk out. Again.

I drive into the parking lot of Pick Your Fit.

This is the same time I've run into Brandon here twice. I'm not here to work out this time. I'm here with an option.

An SUV swerves into an empty parking spot, almost swiping off my side mirror. A crazed-looking man who looks like he hasn't shaved since Jesus walked the earth jumps out, slams his door shut, does the same to the trunk after he grabs a bag out of it. He flings the bag over his shoulder and chirps the alarm to his truck on.

I slink down in the driver's seat, hoping he doesn't see me. He doesn't.

Everything in me tells me to leave the madman to his madness and drive home to a man of calmness. Why am I here?

I honk my horn, roll down my window. "Tough day?" I ask, throwing all sensibility out the window.

He slows his stampede, turns around with furrowed brows and flared nostrils. He sees me, smoothes out the anger in his face.

"Let me guess, every barber within a forty-mile radius was booked today and your wife used the last razor to shave her—"

Brandon just stands there and stares at me.

I put my attempt to be funny on pause. "I never was good at telling jokes," I say.

Brandon walks back toward my car. "Wasn't expecting to see you anytime soon."

"Yeah, well, I wasn't expecting to see myself around here either."

"Ahh."

"C'mon. Where's the jokey-joke guy I met a few days ago?"

He shrugs broad shoulders. "Guess he doesn't want to come out and play today."

"Wanna talk about it?" I want to slap myself for asking that.

No response.

"Ohhhhkay." I turn my eyes away from him for a moment to break the stare. I restart the engine, tell him, "I came by to see if you're serious about running. If so, meet me tomorrow. Six a.m. Riverpoint Park. Google it if you don't know where it is. Show up a minute late and you'll just have to find someone else to help you train." I roll the window back up and put the car in reverse.

Once the kids are tucked in for the night, Eric and I retreat to our room. He goes in the bathroom, comes back out with string wrapped around his fingers, uses it to saw between his teeth. The popping sound makes me cringe.

"Babe, can you do that in the bathroom, please?"

He stops for a moment, sucking air through his teeth. "You check Kennedy's homework?"

"I looked over it a little after dinner."

"I think we have a little mathematician on our hands, don't you think?"

I go in the bathroom and pull out a string of floss. "Yeah, she's getting good. She's doing good in all her subjects."

Eric rinses his mouth out in the sink. "Hope we can get the same teacher for EJ when he gets to first grade."

The mention of teacher makes me think of Mr. Carter, and

thinking of him makes me think of his twin. Brandon. Can't seem to forget about him even when I try. I avoid eye contact with my husband when I say, "Yeah, that would be nice."

I grab a handful of curls and plop them on top of my head with an elastic band. Wash the day's makeup from my face. I do idle things in the bathroom, trying to figure out how to tell my husband I need him to drop the kids off in the morning so I can go for a run. A run with another man, but he doesn't need to know all the details.

He's pulling back the covers when I saunter back into the room. "I'm thinking about running in the mornings before heading into the office. My legs feel trapped on the treadmill. I need to get back to what I'm used to."

"Sounds like a good idea. You always did say you prefer the outdoors versus running inside four walls."

"Exactly. Plus, these thighs act like they're finally ready to lose their winter weight. I need to take them to the next level."

Eric lightly slaps my thighs. "I've noticed and I like." He leans over, gives me a peck on the cheek.

Though I appreciate the compliment, I wish he would've said something before I made mention of it. It's like I have to point things out in order to get him to take notice. I scoop out some Vaseline from the jar in my nightstand, massage it into my feet, in between each toe. Put my socks on to seal in the moisture while I sleep. "I was actually thinking about going in the morning. You could drop EJ off at daycare and I should be back in time to get Kennedy to school."

His lips turn down, head shakes. "I'm all for fitness, but tomorrow's a no-go."

"Why not?"

"Officer Bragg's memorial service. Thought I told you last night."

"Babe, it totally slipped my mind. I thought you said it was Saturday."

"Nope, tomorrow. I was hoping you'd make it."

Last night, my mind was so preoccupied with training Brandon that I hadn't heard a word Eric said. I have no way of getting in touch with him to let him know plans—or in this case, demands— have changed.

I tell my husband, "I'll be there."

Andrew picks me up a few minutes after nine.

"Can't believe Melissa's letting you out for the night."

"Man, I can't either. She's been keeping me hostage in the bedroom."

"That's not a bad problem to have, Bro."

He shakes his head. "It is when you feel like your sperm is more important than your love."

Nothing I can say to that. "Want a drink?"

"Naw, I'll grab something once we get to the spot."

I tell him, "Let me change my shirt first. We're too old for this twin-dressing-alike foolishness."

He laughs. "Mom had us doing that nonsense all the way through high school."

"She would've had us doing it in college too, if we went to the same school."

"You ain't never lied."

We both chuckle at the memory.

After changing my black shirt to a white button down, I grab my keys. "I'll drive."

"You won't get an argument out of me." He subconsciously rubs the scar under his chin.

My brother hasn't been much of a driving fan since his near-fatal accident over fifteen years ago after trying to make an eight-hour drive home for Thanksgiving with no sleep. NoDoz failed him not even two hours into the drive.

I called him up a couple of nights ago to see if he wanted to check out a new over-thirty dance club and restaurant on the east side of town. Figured we both needed to get out for some male bonding.

"It's pretty crowded out here," Andrew says once we pull up.

"Sure is. One of my coworkers said it's the best new thing in town for the grown and sexy."

I follow the cars going toward the side of the building until I find an empty spot. No sign of a ticket attendant gives my wallet a sigh of relief. Since I don't have to cough up parking money, I go ahead and pay a twenty-dollar cover charge for both of us to enter.

Soon as we walk in, Carl Thomas circa 2000 pumps through the speakers. I can dig it. This isn't the atmosphere for a beer. I order up Hennessy and Coke for the bro, a glass straight for me. I see he's found us a high-top table in the corner.

"It's thick in here," he says.

I'd been gone at least fifteen minutes. I slide his drink over to his waiting hands. "That it is."

*"You've got that Southern thang I like,"* blasts through the speakers. A sly grin flashes across Andrew's face.

I nod my head for an explanation.

"Sometimes I can't believe I met my wife up in a club. Told her she'd be the mother of my kids before I even asked for her name." His smile quickly fades at the memory. Eleven years later and his declaration has yet to come to fruition.

"Let's not go there tonight, Bro. Tonight's supposed to take our minds off of the wives."

Andrew swallows his drink in one gulp, takes it straight to the head. "Yeah, you're right."

I raise a brow and squint an eye in his direction. Got to keep an eye on the half of this duo who can't hold liquor too well. We both cut the conversation to a minimum as we allow the drinks, music, and sights of beautiful women to take over.

The DJ changes the mood of music from soul music to a rapper known as the King of the South. The crowd goes from grooving to throwing arms in the air. Not a track I was expecting, but it seems to be working for the crowd.

My twin taps his watch to the three o'clock position.

I turn my attention to the right, toward the entrance. Nearly bite the inside of my mouth when a woman with bronzed, shoulder-length hair and signature high cheekbones walks through the door with two other women. She spots me immediately. The look on her face is stuck between fear and I-need-you-in-the-worst-way.

I acknowledge her presence with a shaky nod.

"That was intense," Andrew declares. "How do you know her?"

I give him the skinny on Sydney.

He slaps the back of my head. "Can't believe you were in the gym acting like me, 'bout to get me fired with your foolishness."

"Hey, she put the bait on the hook. I snagged with honor."

"She is nice on the eyes for sure," he says. "Had me second-guessing my vows when she walked into my classroom the week before school started."

My eyes are still on her as I tell my brother, "Probably not worth the trouble for either of us." Though Sydney is very easy on the eyes—getting double glances from just about every guy up in here—I still feel my wife looks three times as nice.

"Sho' you right. Mom and Dad didn't raise us to be rolling stones. We married the women we wanted to marry."

I neither disagree or agree.

"Another drink?" Andrew offers.

"Yes, sir."

The slightly shorter, identical version of me leaves the table as Somebody Else's Mrs. slides into his place before he even reaches the bar. "I see you found a razor."

I smirk. "Yeah, and I wish you had seen your clock this morning and been where you threatened me to be."

"Please, please, please accept my apology about this morning."

"I don't think you should give up your day job to tell jokes or do James Brown impersonations, ma'am."

That makes her laugh. "I'm serious. I had a prior commitment."

I say, "That is what marriage is, right?"

She lets those words marinate for a moment.

The women she walked in with walk over to our table with my brother, drinks in all of their hands. Andrew introduces one of them as his former student's mother, Katrina.

Sydney says, "This is Rachel, my best friend. Also, her husband works with mine."

I catch the hint. Either this town is getting too small or the world is shrinking. I shake their hands. "Nice to meet you both."

The tallest woman of the bunch says, "I would hate to have been your mother. Wouldn't be able to tell you two apart if I stood before God and spending eternity in heaven was on the line."

I say, "You'd be able to if you changed our diapers."

Laughter blends in with the music. Everyone's humored, but curiosity lies in Sydney's eyes.

Folks on the dance floor are sweating like they just finished two marathons. The DJ senses the need for a slow down. A song about a dude referencing his manhood to a lollipop brings a friskier crowd to the hardwood. Women are grinding dudes' laps like they're trying to start forest fires.

One of the mothers at our table puts her drink down, grabs Andrew's hand and drags him to the floor. Don't know why, but her actions catch me off-guard. My brother's inverted eyebrows tells me he's caught off guard as well. I guess neither one of us were expecting the mother of his previous student to be so aggressive. He doesn't hesitate being her sandpaper, though.

"Katrina's so mannish," Rachel says to Sydney as they watch their friend grind the life out of the identical version of me.

"To be single again," Sydney confesses.

I add my two cents. "Who says you have to be single to have a good time?" Feel her eyes on me when I say that.

"Nobody says you have to be single to have fun, but what that girl is out there doing, men might start throwing dollars her way. And with her son's teacher at that." Rachel says, shaking her head.

I interject, "Well, she's single. She can do that."

Rachel sucks her teeth. "You're right, so let me mind my married-self's business."

All the women in the club go wild when an ex-Floetry member starts chanting, *"I hope she cheats on you with a basketball player,"* through the speakers.

"You play basketball?" That's Sydney, a little too close to my ear.

Answer I do not. Fall into that trap I will not.

Reggae is the next circuit of music on the DJ's turntables.

"Aw, what the hell?" the let-me-mind-my-married-business woman says while pulling me toward the dance floor.

*"Murder she wrote. Nah nah nah nah, murder sheeee wrote."*

I swear this woman is trying to ruin any chance of me ever having another child as she murders my pelvis with hers. She gyrates like she's trying to make her single friend know that her married-self can get down too. Whatever *get down* is. Something tells me the two took the same dance class.

Sydney's laughing her butt off at the table. Must be a sight we're creating.

My eyes beg for her to stop laughing and rescue me, to resuscitate what's left of my baby-maker. She's too busy laughing. Looks like she needs resuscitation herself from laughing too hard. If I wasn't in so much pain, I'd laugh myself.

Three songs later, I'm numb. If I don't get off this dance floor right now, I'll never see my penis get hard again.

On cue, rescue comes. "Mr. Carter got us another round of drinks," Sydney tells Rachel.

The woman reaches for the non-sipped on glass in her hand.

Sydney pulls her hand away. "Yours is on the table." She hands the glass to me.

I blink twice for "thank you" while grabbing the glass and heading toward the table myself.

Her hand is in mine, holds me back. "Not so fast."

I tell her, "As much as I want to dance with you, I need to ice down my groin."

She cracks up laughing, guffaws louder than the music. The situation tickles her so much I can't hold back my laughter any longer.

"Damn, so it actually hurt worse than it looked?"

"You knew what I was up against. Saw you laughing before we even got on the floor."

She slaps a hand against my shoulder. "You weren't supposed to see that."

"Oh, you owe me. First, for standing me up this morning and now this. You owe me big."

"Don't tell her I told you. Some years ago, before she got married, she put it on a guy so bad he had to be rushed out in an ambulance."

My eyes almost pop out of my head. "Again. You. Owe. Me."

The crowd pushes us together. A little too close for both of our comfort zones.

She looks at me the way a woman looks at her husband on their wedding night.

All of a sudden, I feel life returning to areas I thought were long gone. Every time I try to put some distance between us, another dancer seals us back together.

"What are we doing?" she asks with too much depth in her voice.

"Right now, dancing."

She lightly tosses her hand against my shoulder. "Don't play. I'm being serious."

"I am too."

"I feel like I barely know you, but lately you're all I think about."

"Somebody's getting deep in the middle of the dance floor."

She moves away. "Forget I said that."

"I'm flattered, actually."

Again, we're pushed back together by bumpers and grinders.

I say in her ear, "Look, let's go somewhere else and talk."

Her head shakes. "Can't. Came with my girls and Rachel's husband works with mine. Can't risk anything suspect getting back home."

"Yeah, you said that."

"Let's go back to the table and I'll think of something."

Back at the table, my brother says, "Mel's been texting me like crazy. You look like you're having a good time, so I texted her the address to come get me."

"Man, I could've taken you home."

"Not a problem, but," he leans in closer, "be careful with Mrs.

Holmes. Her husband's a cop, and you know how they have eyes all over the place. Wouldn't want the wrong thing to get back home."

I nod.

We hug and he says his goodbyes to the ladies.

Rachel says, "Wait up, I'll walk out with you. I need to get back home to my husband."

Both Sydney and Katrina roll their eyes at each other.

"Don't hate," Rachel says, flinging her blonde hair over her shoulders. "Toodles."

It's just me, the single lady, and the lady who wants to be single. "And then there were three."

"It's about to be two," Katrina says. "I think I see somebody I want to go home with tonight."

Sydney grabs her friend. "Umm, too much Patrón for you tonight, my dear."

"I'm perfectly sober, thank you very much. I'm the single one of this bunch, remember?" she says and looks us both in the eyes.

"It's not what you think," Sydney insists.

Katrina grabs her friend, hugs her, whispers something in her ear, and dances her way to a man waiting for her on the dance floor.

I ask, "What did she say?"

Her eyes are downcast when her lips part. "I know the smell of infidelity."

All of a sudden, an unfamiliar stench tap dances across my nose.

I'm in Brandon's car.

Neither of us are talking. Think we're both trying to Febreze the funk we've created in our lives.

Yes, I'm an unhappy wife, but I never imagined I'd be here, in a car, with another woman's husband. What if he has kids? Oh gosh, EJ and Kennedy. What would this do to them? I grew up without a father in the home because my dad didn't know how to keep his pants up when he wasn't around my mom. What if Eric leaves me? What if he takes the kids with him?

Brandon summons me from my thoughts. "Maybe we should bow out before things go too far."

I think about all I have to lose. "But we haven't done anything, right?"

He shakes his head. "If we keep this up, might be a different story."

I sigh.

"You have more at stake than I do," Brandon says. "Let me get you to your car."

My head hits the headrest. "How did we get here?" The question is more for me than him.

"You're easy to talk to. The moment I walked in the gym, you were all in my ear like a Chihuahua."

I don't let him see my smile. "I thought you were someone else."

He bites down on his lip. Finger taps the steering wheel. Actions of a man with serious thoughts.

My hand reaches for the door. It's not worth it, not worth it, not worth it. Is it?

"Things that bad at home?" Brandon summons me from crazy thoughts.

"What makes you say that?"

"A happily married woman wouldn't be in the car with a happily married man."

"You're giving me a ride."

"So that story's working for you, huh?"

I look out the window. Try to put my life in perspective without staring in the face of a man who's brought me so much joy in such a short time. I mean, literally. All it took was a five-minute case of mistaken identity and I drive home with a newfound crush. I'm too old for a crush. I catch a glimpse of Katrina getting in a car with a man who looks like he's out for one thing. What's sad is I know she's going to give it to him. She's been running around with all kinds of subpar men since her husband left. Am I staring in the mirror of what my life would be like if I keep entertaining my unhappiness with an illusion of happiness?

"Was he wearing satin pajamas?" Brandon asks.

"She has a type," I say. "You'd think after being dogged by every man she's ever dated, including her ex-husband, that she'd wisen up and try a different approach."

"Can't be good for her kid to see."

"Luckily, he doesn't see much. She puts her hoeish ways on pause during the week and his dad keeps him on the weekends."

They say if you hang around people long enough, you begin to take on some of their tendencies. Yep, I've been hanging around Katrina a little too long.

I turn to Brandon. "Do you have any kids?"

He shakes his head and watches the car Katrina got into drift away into the night.

My clutch purse vibrates in my lap. An incoming text from Eric.

Again, Brandon says, "Let me get you to your car."

I give him directions to Katrina's place, since we carpooled to the lounge. He parks behind my car and waits for me to get in and start the ignition. I roll down my window. "Meet me at the park Monday morning."

"Six a.m. sharp."

And with that, he drives off.

"Every time you go out lately, you stay out later and later," Eric says as soon as I push open the bedroom door. He's sitting up in the bed with the lamp on his nightstand on, a turned down book in his lap.

"Now, now, I haven't said anything about all those extra shifts you've been pulling lately."

He tosses the book on his nightstand. "That's because it's putting extra money in our pockets, ma'am."

I walk into the closet, put my shoes back in their box. Yell out, "Well, sir, according to your buddies at work, what I'm doing is putting money in our pockets as well."

"Not funny," I hear him say.

I snicker to myself, then peep my head out of the closet. "Aw, babe. Look, I had to make sure Katrina got home okay. She had quite a bit to drink." At least half of it is true.

"Don't make me have to put an APB out on you."

I roll my eyes as I slide out of my dress, hang it up and walk back in the room in bra and panties. Give him a longer than usual kiss on the lips. "Now why would you have to do a thing like that?"

He nibbles on my bottom lip. "Y'all have a good time?"

"Yeah, it was good, all three of us hanging out together again. It's only been Katrina and me for a while. Rachel's still acting like a newlywed."

"Everyone in the unit always has jokes about the leftovers he brings in for lunch. One of the guys tries to get to it when Michael's not looking, so he can read the note Rachel left to the rest of us. Or toss around his gold-wrapped chocolate treats."

"Leave the man alone. I'm sure y'all would love a woman to do that for you."

Eric sticks his finger down the back of my panties and pulls me back to him and nuzzles me down to the bed. "You used to do that way back when."

I lightly bite at his nose. "We both used to do a lot way back when."

He releases his hold on me. "What's that supposed to mean?"

"Aw, nothing, babe." I push him back against the pillow, spread my legs across his lap. "Come shower with me?"

He firmly grips my backside. "Thought you'd never ask."

My back is thrust against cold tile. Legs shake as Eric pumps his girth in and out of me like a jealous lover.

I claw at his back. "What has gotten into you tonight?" I pant in his ear.

He flicks his tongue against my neck, sucks hard enough to draw blood.

I moan. Yell out his name loud enough for the neighbors to have wet dreams about Eric Thomas Holmes, Sr.

There's so much steam in the shower, it now feels like my back is up against the sun.

Hands are on my breasts, lips on my nipples.

I suck on his earlobe, stick my tongue deep in his ear. He loves when I do that. My hands glide down his back, round the firmness of his rear end, usher him deeper inside me.

Staying out past my curfew seems to have worked in my favor. Brings out the lover in this husband of mine.

Eric raises my hips, slides out of me. "Turn around," he says.

Tonight, I'm at his will.

He slips back inside me from behind. Puts one palm up on the wall, the other one guiding my hips into him.

I'm no longer in this shower. I'm somewhere far away from here. A place where this feeling is everlasting, where I don't have to do something to set my husband's hormones off the Richter Scale. I'm somewhere feeling deadened places in me come back to life. I'm in an open field chasing butterflies, laughing.

I'm in a place where, when my husband calls out my name in ecstasy, I almost call out for someone else.

A white sedan pulls up next to my ride. I hit end on my cell phone without leaving a message. Toss it in the back seat.

Sydney doesn't greet me. She wraps a timer around her neck, says, "How long can you run without stopping?" while lacing up her sneakers.

I shrug my shoulders. "I don't know, maybe ten minutes or so."

"We'll run for five minutes at my pace, then intervals for thirty."

"Cool." I take a swig of my blue-colored drink. "Wait, what's your pace?"

"You're worried about the wrong thing," she says and starts jogging off.

I set my drink in the cup holder, set the alarm, and do my best to catch up.

As my feet hit the pavement, my mind drifts to the phone call I just made. I've been calling my wife for weeks now, and not once has she picked up or responded to any of the voicemails I've left. Same thing when I call the job. The receptionist takes a message, but I never get a call back. Thought things between us would've changed after my visit to her business, but she's left me hanging since. I should be used to it by now.

"Your head's bobbing. Steady your pace, Brandon."

Don't even know why I keep trying. Moved out, but I'm still

trying. And here I am with a woman who's allowed me to be me again, a woman who's allowed me to not feel so guarded and off balance. Yet and still, my mind is on my wife.

"Use your arms. You're working your legs too hard."

Sydney's voice breaks my trance. I do as she says and start pumping my arms.

I hadn't realized I had lost control of my run, but now that I'm pumping my arms, I feel like I'm in control. Wish I could get control of my marriage as easy as changing a simple movement. Then again, I've changed quite a few things, and at the same time, nothing's changed. I don't know what's happened to my wife. Seems like the more I try, the farther away she moves.

"You're. Going. Too. Fast," a voice yells out in slow motion.

I let thoughts of Rene drift with the wind. Look up and look for Sydney. Don't see her. Look behind me and realize not only have I caught up with Sydney, I've left her in the wind as well. She's not running behind me. She's chasing me.

All of a sudden, I'm aware of my heart, feel it racing faster than Usain Bolt breaking another world record. My lungs struggle to expand to their full potential. Can't catch my breath, feel myself falling.

"Don't stop moving," Sydney says once she's caught up to me. Her huffing and puffing is hard from the unexpected sprint. "Give me your hands."

I reach my hands out to her. She walks backward pulling me in her direction.

"You've got to keep moving. Your heart's probably on the verge of a nervous breakdown."

My legs feel like Jell-O. I want to sit, want to lie in the grass and close my eyes until the next lifetime.

"No. Keep your eyes open." Sydney continues walking backward. "Don't hold your head down, keep it up. Look at me."

I do as told, wait for the dizziness to wane.

Everything fades to black.


She holds my wrist with three fingers. Counts as blood pulsates through my veins. "What were you trying to pull?" she asks once she's assured I'm going to live. "You men and your egos."

"This has nothing to do with ego."

"So, you mean to tell me you had no problem with a woman outrunning you, that you found some sprint you didn't even know you had?"

My attention is drawn to the lake. Swear the water is rising above the banks and inching its way to me. Even nature is tired of my situation and is ready to drown me, put me out of my misery.

Sydney sits in the grass next to me, touches me on my shoulder. "Hey, you okay?" When I look across from me and see the concern in Sydney's face, I see the lake's tide still in my eyes. I blink and feel water roll down my cheek.

"Let's get you to the hospital."

I shake my head. Tell her, "I'm divorcing my wife."

She flicks a piece of grass from her shin. Does that to break eye contact. "Are we really about to have this conversation?"

For a while, the only sounds heard come from rubber striking concrete as other runners trail the lake. Walkers come and go with idle chitchat floating through the trees. Birds serenade us with high-pitched melodies.

I break our silence. "Look, this is my reality. It's what my marriage has come to."

"I envy you."

"Jealousy is dangerous, don't you think?"

"I wish I had the guts to leave my husband." She folds her legs up like a pretzel, brings them into her. "Wish I had realized my mistake like Kim Kardashian and called it quits after seventy-two days."

"Your husband that bad of a guy?"

Sydney shakes her head. "And neither was Kris Humphries. Just the right people in the wrong marriage. I feel like I'm the bad one for feeling like this. I take it out on him, punish him, blame him all because I'm the one who feels this way."

"And what way is that?"

Again she says, "Are we really having this conversation?"

I nod.

She sighs. "I'm not sure that I love him. Not sure I ever did."

Her confession takes me aback. Makes me wonder if Rene feels the same about me. Wonder if at some point during our marriage she had to be honest with herself and her feelings, and if pushing me away was her resolution.

"Don't get me wrong, Brandon. I do care about him, but there's always been this hole in the pit of my soul that he's never been able to fill."

I say, "Voids can lead you to places you might not be able to return from. My wife left me with a void, and now I'm here." I reach my hand across the way to hers. Intertwine my fingers with hers.

Sydney looks at our hands together, quickly releases mine like I have the cooties. Unfolds her legs and stands up. Says, "I need to get my daughter to school."

We walk back to our cars in silence.

Too much has been said as it is.

*I*'m running late for the office, so I head over to a possible new client's house instead to see if it's something we can list with our firm. I stayed out a lot longer than I anticipated, fooling around with another woman's husband.

Now is not the time to think about that. I've got to focus on the job.

Gated entry. I give the gate attendant my name. "I'm going to 3158 Oakwood Drive."

He gives me a piece of paper with writing on it. "Keep this on your dash."

I nod, tell him, "Thanks."

Nice brick fronts. Good spacing between homes. Yards are well taken care of. No cars parked on the street. I've already got a buyer in mind who would love this kind of neighborhood. If the inside meets my buyer's requirements, he may hop on a flight to come take a look at it tomorrow and put in an offer before noon.

The house's garage is on the side. Another check on my client's wish list. From the curb, I put the car in park, grab my camera from my bag and snap a couple of pictures. Back in the car, I turn into the driveway, walk up the curved staircase, ring the bell.

A woman with short, baby-fine hair answers the door. Her hair is so fine I can see through to her scalp. Big, beautiful bright eyes.

I nearly blush at how they draw me in. I reach my hand to meet hers and try to put my professional hat back on. "Ms. Ortiz?"

She takes my hand as she notices my name on the badge pinned to my blazer. "Yes, come in."

What I can see of the house just from the entryway tells me she's very meticulous, keeps a clean house. I won't have a hard time selling this house at all. "You have a lovely house," I tell her. "What year was it built?"

"2002."

A little over eleven years old. "You've taken good care of the place. Barely looks a day over five."

She glances at her watch. "There are four bedrooms and two full bathrooms upstairs, a bedroom and bathroom on this floor next to the living room, and a finished basement. Please take a look around. I have a few things to take care of before work. Press the red button on the intercom panel if you have any questions."

"Sure will, thanks." I flip open the portfolio in my hand and make notations as I go along.

The house is huge, too big for one person. One of the rooms is set up for a child. No sign of a husband when I look in the master closet, so I assume it's just her and a kid. On a dresser in the master bedroom is a worn black-and-white photo of a couple with a baby in the woman's lap. As I get closer, I'd be willing to gamble it's Ms. Ortiz as a baby with her parents. She definitely favors both adults.

One thing I enjoy about being a realtor is experiencing the lives of others. Something about going through their homes allows me to forget about my own life and, in a way, act as if their home is actually mine. Several times, though, some of the stuff I've seen made me want to click my heels three times, hard.

I snap pictures of every room and bathroom, one of the walk-in closet in the master. Before meeting Ms. Ortiz in the kitchen, I take a picture of the foyer entrance, den, and living room. When I walk into the kitchen, I catch her hurling last night's dinner into the sink. I quickly toss my camera back in my bag as my motherly instincts kick in. I toss my things on the counter and find myself going through her cabinets for a glass. I fill it with water from the fountain on the outside of the refrigerator. "Here, drink this."

She wipes her mouth, dabs at her forehead with a towel that was already wet lying next to her. That tells me she was expecting to throw up. I wonder if this is a normal occurrence for her. "Thanks," she says before taking a couple of sips of water.

I ask, "Morning sickness?"

No response.

A man comes through the door that leads to the laundry room. He's carrying a basket of freshly cleaned and folded linen. "I'll—" He pauses, looks at me. "I didn't know you had company."

She reminds him, "She's the realtor I was telling you I'm going to list the house with," then introduces us. "William, this is Mrs. Holmes."

He puts the basket down on the counter, shakes my hand. "Nice meeting you."

"Likewise," I say.

"I'll let you two get back to business." He pauses, looks at her. "Threw up again?"

She nods.

Though I try not to make assumptions, I'm thinking he's her boyfriend and that maybe they're wanting to downsize to something smaller. Not sure why, when it seems their family is expanding.

"Do you have any questions?" she wants to know.

I go over the list of questions I had written down. We go over the listing contract, discuss all pertinent information.

"I want to sell this house as soon as possible."

To make sure we're clear, I ask, "If I have a buyer, you have no problem closing within thirty days or less?"

"If you brought a buyer right now, I'd turn over the keys without thinking twice."

"That's all I need to know."

She coughs a few times, sounds like she's about to lose what remnants may be left in her stomach. Sipping on a little more water settles her for the time being.

"I hope you feel better," I tell her as I make my way to the front door.

Soon as I make it inside my car, I dial up my client. "I found your house," I say when he answers. I go over all the particulars, make sure to hit all his targets. "I'll email you a few photos once I get back to the office."

As I expected, he's ecstatic about the house. He and his wife want to move down and get the kids situated in school before the school year ends. They'll fly in in a couple of days. I end the call, sit the phone in the cup holder, and pull out my personal cell. A missed call from Eric and a new voicemail. He's pulling an extra shift and needs me to get the kids. This is the second time this week.

Here we go again.

A spitting image of me pops up on my smartphone. "Drew, what's good, brother?" I put my ride in park, shut the engine off.

"Same thing, different day. About to look over some homework while Mel gets dinner ready."

"Gotcha." I twist off the cap to a sports drink, take a few gulps before telling my brother, "Love to shoot the breeze with you, Bro, but I'm about to hit the gym. Let me call you back in a few."

"Hold up, Brandon. There's something I want to run by you."

I lean up against the truck. "Okay."

The familiar white sedan pulls up beside me. A smile spreads across my face when she hops out. Sydney grabs a towel and a bottle of water from the backseat. Mouths to me she's heading inside.

I put my hand over the phone, tell her, "I'll be in in a second."

She taps on her watchless wrist.

I wink.

She blushes and walks inside Pick Your Fit.

"I don't think it's right. That's all I'm saying," I hear my twin say through the other side of the phone.

I straighten my posture, realize I've missed the main reason for his call. "What exactly are you saying?"

"See, I knew you'd get defensive," he says.

"Hold on, Drew. Why would I be defensive?"

"Mom and Dad didn't raise us to be that way," he goes on.

My hand moves back and forth across my bald head, wipe the perspiration off on my gym shorts. "Man, you've caught me off-guard and I'm not so sure I like where this conversation is going."

"Am I wrong?"

"If you're talking about what I think you are, yes, you're wrong."

"All right, my bad. Things just looked real heated on the dance floor that night. And I haven't heard much from you since. I didn't know what to think."

"Damn, man. You didn't have to think the worst of me."

"My bad," Andrew says again. "Mel has me tense around here."

I want to tell him that's no excuse to accuse me of adultery, but say, "Look, my wife fell out of love with me. The last thing I want to do is fall for another man's wife."

As I walk in the gym and see Sydney running on the treadmill, I realize it's a lot harder to lie to myself than it was my brother.


After thirty minutes of speed intervals on the treadmill and twenty-five minutes—which felt like twenty-five hours—of strength training, Sydney and I find our way to my apartment.

I point her in the direction of the bathroom. She walks into my bedroom, stops, sees the bed, turns back and looks at me.

"Don't even think about it," I tell her.

She smiles, proceeds to the bathroom.

My brother's words come back to remembrance. *We were raised better than that.* I'm not doing anything my parents would be ashamed of. Not yet, at least.

I shake those thoughts off. Head to the kitchen, cut up a banana, toss it into the blender. Scoop out a couple of globs of peanut butter, two scoops of vanilla protein powder. Add it to the blender with eight ounces of milk, a few slivers of ice. Mix it all together and spoon into two Styrofoam cups, stick a straw in each. Hand one to Sydney when she comes back into the living room.

"Thanks." She takes a sip while looking around the place. Her cheeks pull in like she's trying to suck cement through the straw.

"Sorry about that. Got a little heavy-handed with the peanut butter."

"I can see my obituary now: Sydney Holmes went home to be with the Lord after suffering a brain aneurysm caused by a protein smoothie gone wrong."

"C'mon. It's not that bad."

"And that's exactly why yours is empty," her voice reeks with sarcasm.

I pick my cup off the floor. Two hard sucks later, my mouth is still dry. "Sucked so hard my head hurts," I say.

"My point exactly." She lifts her cup in the air. "An elephant would pass out trying pull this through its tusk."

I take the cup from her hand. Toss it in the trash right along with mine. Grab two bottles of cold water from the fridge. "I'm sure you won't have anything to crack jokes about now."

"Did you even put any milk in it? It was like nothing but a cup of peanut butter and cotton." She shakes her head. "Wasn't nothing smooth about that."

"Wow. I see you're not going to let up."

She chuckles. "All jokes aside, you have some Advil?" Her hand rubs her temple.

"Okay, I feel real bad right now."

"As well you should."

The smile on her face lets me know she's joking, but wetness between her eyelids says something else.

I get up from the floor, kneel down in front of her, place my hands on her face. My lips touch her temple. I kiss one side and place a kiss on the other. "Hope that helps," I say, then leave her to grab a dose of orange-coated pills.

"Why'd you have to do that?" she asks when I put the pills in her hand.

I shrug, not sure why I did it.

"Can I ask you something?"

I nod.

"What happened to your marriage?"

Saliva in my mouth grows thick, almost as thick as the protein smoothie. "I'd be able to answer if I *knew* the answer."

"How long have you been married?"

"Nine years a couple of months ago."

She sucks air through her teeth. "Going on seven for me. Don't know if I'll live to see nine."

"That bad?"

She leans back against the sofa. "He's the best husband and father any woman could ask for, but I'm bored with him. I feel like it should be a lot more, a lot better than it is. That's what makes it bad, what makes me the bad guy."

"You're willing to leave your marriage due to boredom?" I want to make sure I'm understanding her correctly.

"I'm not fulfilled, feel like I'm suffocating. Every anniversary is like someone is smothering my face with a hundred pillows."

I fold my arms across my chest, press my back hard against the base of the sofa. "Have you told him how you feel?"

She shakes her head. "I've tried a time or two. Never comes out right. He ends up taking it to mean we need to go on vacation or something."

"Well, how do you want him to respond?"

Sydney sits in the middle of my living room floor with her bottle of water in hand. She sits and screws and unscrews the cap, keeps doing that. "I want him to keep pursuing me like he did in the beginning. He's gotten settled in our relationship and our marriage. It's not always about a new place to go or a new food to try. I don't think he gets it, don't think he gets me."

I get up from the floor and march to the bathroom. Like the Southwest commercial suggests, I need to get away, even if it is just another square foot away. Need to be alone with my thoughts.

Listening to Sydney spill her reasons for being in an unhappy marriage makes me think of Rene. Makes me think about how despondent she's become over the years. Wonder if she felt like she was suffocating being married to me. Was I boring her to death so much that she felt leaving me would revive her back to life? Did she ever try to communicate to me in a way I didn't understand her, take her thoughts to mean something totally different? Did I stop pursuing her?

Back in the living room, Sydney's still in the middle of the floor, knees pulled into her chest, arms folded around them. She rocks back and forth, lost in her thoughts.

I sit back in my spot against the couch. Ask, "If he were to start loving you the way you feel you need to be loved, you think you'd stay for life?"

She twirls a few strands of hair around her finger, ponders the question. "I really don't know the answer to that."

"Sounds like you're not too clear on what you want then."

Her hair falls from her fingers. She kicks her legs out in front of her, crosses her ankles. "Let me ask you, how'd you end up here?" She spreads her arms outward.

I follow her eyes around my empty apartment. "Got to a point where nothing I did made a difference. Got fed up."

"Do you have kids?"

I shake my head. That's a place I'm not ready to invite her to. Didn't have an answer for her the first time she asked in my car a couple of weekends ago. Don't have an answer for her now.

"Well, you're fortunate. Kids make walking away a lot harder. At least for the woman it does."

My posture stiffens. "Walking away is walking away, whether you have kids or not. If the love between man and woman changes, kids won't make it any easier or harder. It's just a sacrifice someone has to be willing to make."

"Oh, it's different. Trust me."

Maybe she's right. I've thought about it before. Had our son been here, I would've fought a lot harder. Would've shown Rene I meant what I said when we stood before God, that death would be the only thing to separate us. But that's not how our story went.

"I just think kids complicate a lot."

"You almost say that like you regret having them."

She throws her head in her hands, rubs her hands down her face. "Jeez, I don't mean to sound like that. I just…I don't know."

"We had a son," I hear myself say.

"Had? What happened?"

"He went to sleep one night and never woke back up."

"I'm so sorry." She can barely look at me.

I fiddle around with the carpet. Rub my hands back and forth across it. Do whatever I can to keep her from seeing the sadness in my eyes.

"How old was he?"

Had. Was. Hate referring to my flesh and blood in past tense. "Five."

All she can do is shake her head back and forth. Don't know if she does it to shake away thoughts about being without her own kids or to keep herself from crying.

My throat suddenly becomes dry. When I swallow, it feels like my throat is being stuffed with dryer sheets. I get up to grab another bottle of water from the kitchen. "Can I get you something else to drink?"

She declines.

When I walk back out, Sydney's standing by the front door. "Didn't realize it was so late. Gotta figure out how I'm going to get out of this."

I say, "Talk it out."

"I wasn't talking about the marriage." Before walking out the door, she turns back to look at me. She looks down at her shoes, says, "The first time Eric and I met, I knew he wasn't the one for me, but I kept dating him. I kept trying to convince myself that I was falling in love with him, and for a moment, I thought I had." She fidgets with the keys in her hand, still avoiding eye contact. "When he proposed, my soul said no, but my lips betrayed me. Here I am, almost seven years and two kids later, and I still feel the same, like he's not the one for me."

For a moment, I feel like I'm her husband. Feel like I've been denied access into the heart of the woman I married. An innocent bystander in the demise of my own marriage.

I'm in a daze.

Been this way since getting back from Brandon's place. Don't remember picking the kids up from my mother's house. Don't remember cooking dinner or running EJ's bathwater. I'm so used to this life that I don't have to think about what I do day in and day out. It's who I am, who I've become.

Splashes from the hall bathroom reminds me my son is still in the tub. I push the door open, see him flipping around in the water like he's a dolphin auditioning to be a new member at SeaWorld. I pull the door back, leave it halfway cracked. Contemplate if I'd be a bad mother if I let him stay in there all night.

Eric Sr. walks up the stairs with a giggling Kennedy on his back. He drops her off at the top of the stairs, pats her lightly on the backside. Tells her, "Time to get ready for bed."

"Are you gonna read to me?" she asks.

I walk downstairs, let them have their moment.

Forrester is in his usual spot by the fireplace. I bend over, pick him up. Nearly break my back. "We've got to put you on a diet, buddy." He yawns in my face. His breath has the smell of a ten-day-old dead fish baking in an Arizona sun. I quickly put him back down.

My running shoes are tossed over by the front door. They stare back at me. I wanna put them on, lace them up and run away from here. The more time I spend with Brandon, the more it's evident I shouldn't be in this marriage. I'm not me, not the me I used to be. Not the me I want to be.

I feel lips on my cheek. Didn't realize I was no longer alone.

"How was your workout?" asks my husband.

I straighten a family picture on the mantle. "It was fine. Ran intervals, lifted a few weights. You know, the usual," I say, avoiding eye contact.

"I'm all for the fitness, babe, but maybe you should cut back some."

"Why would you say that?"

"Just seems like you're either at the gym every evening or getting up at the crack of dawn to run at the park."

I turn around to look at my husband. "I could say the same about you with all these extra hours you've been putting in at work lately."

"It's not the same."

"And why not? Time away from home is time away from home. Doesn't matter the reason."

"I'm just saying, Syd."

Forrester meows for my attention. I rub him a couple of times on the top of his head. He purrs his contentment as he walks off to his food dish. It only takes a few rubs across his fur for him to not feel neglected. Wish it were the same for my husband.

"Mom," Kennedy yells from the top of the stairs, "I gotta pee and EJ won't let me in the bathroom."

"Those two." I head toward the stairs.

Eric reaches out and grabs my hand, pulls me into him. My mouth barely opens as his tongue penetrates my lips and tiptoes across mine.

"Mom, EJ locked me out."

My husband's kiss leaves me breathless, leaves me wanting more.

He leaves me panting for air as he runs up the stairs to see what all the ruckus between the kids is all about.

I fall into the sofa.

A couple of hours ago, I was almost certain I was ready to walk out of this marriage. It made so much sense. The longer I stay here, the unhappier I become. The more I resent myself. And in return, the more I resent my husband and kids. They don't deserve this. I don't deserve them.

Is boredom really a reason to leave this home I've made?

I'm beginning to feel like that reason's not good enough, and that scares me.

The first thing I do after pulling into an open parking space at the job is grab my cell and call my good friend Katrina. "You were right," I say when she answers.

"About?"

"I'm falling for him."

"I knew it."

"How could you know? It wasn't even like that when we were at the lounge."

She sucks air through her teeth, then huffs. "Do you really believe that lie?"

My reflection grabs my attention in the rearview mirror. Crinkled brows, a pout in my lips. Hurt written all over my face. "Hey, Kat, where's all of this coming from? I'm calling you as my friend, and right now, you're not making me feel friendly."

"He's married, Sydney. And so are you."

"And so is his brother, but that didn't stop you from thrusting your butt into his man parts on the dance floor."

"Unlike you, I left it *on* the dance floor."

"Wow. I can't believe you said that." Obviously calling her was the wrong thing to do. I don't know what I was thinking. She would be the last one to remotely understand what I'm going through. Still wasn't expecting her to throw daggers my way.

"What do you want me to say? Aw, how cute. You two would be great together. Is that what you want me to say?" Her voice is full of contempt.

"Well, no. Not exactly."

"Good, because I'm not. And I'm not going to sit up here and act like I agree with what you're doing either. It's wrong. Point. Blank."

I can see her pointing her index finger in the air accentuating the point and the blank. "Can you cut me some slack? I've never done anything like this before," I say, feeling more angered than hurt.

She takes another labored breath before responding. "No one gave me any breaks when Elton came home smelling like another woman. No one cut me any slack when I was giving birth and my child's father came to the hospital with fresh hickeys on his neck that I didn't put there."

"And you married him anyway."

"Screw you. Oh wait, that's what you're doing to your marriage."

"Hold on, hold on, hold on. That was so uncalled for."

"And so was your comment." She shuffles around on the other end of the phone. "Look, we marry who we love, whether that love is right or wrong, it is what it is. If I had to do it all over again, I'd find a good man, strap him to the bed, and never let him loose. You have a good man at home. I suggest you forget about what's-his-name and do the same before it goes any further."

I sigh loud enough for the dead to hear.

After a long day crunching numbers at the job, all I want to do is kick my feet up at home with a beer in hand. But tonight, something more pressing leads me in another direction.

Sydney left a lot on my mind when she left my place the other night.

Life is funny.

Since the beginning of time, we are born to die. Everything that happens in between is up to chance and opportunity.

I often wonder what happened to my son's chance and opportunity. He was taken at a time when the only decisions he could make was between what cartoon he wanted to watch and which new toys he would add to his Christmas wish list. A parent should never have to mourn their child, no matter their age.

In a few weeks, Reggie would've been turning nine. Nine. Halfway to being a legal man. It hurts knowing I won't be able to show him how to shave, to tell him about women. Will never know if he'd be into sports or more into academics like my brother and me. The unknown kills a piece of me every day. His death tore Rene up. She wouldn't have any talk about having more children. Said it wouldn't be fair to his memory. I didn't push it. Sometimes, I wonder if we'd be separated if he were still living or would we have still grown apart. Questions that will never be answered.

Thinking about my son not only makes me miss him, it makes me miss the love that filled my heart. Love for my son and my wife, my love for life. In a way, Sydney's starting to bring a little of that feeling back. She's starting to help me feel good about life again, even if it's just to listen to me harp about my marriage coming to an end. Still feels good to be heard and given the opportunity to listen to her problems. Though she left me feeling a little unsettled with her reasons for wanting to leave her unhappy marriage, I still felt her pain. Still feel connected to her in some way.

I look over at the passenger seat, see the business envelope staring back at me. Never thought this moment would come, never wanted it to come. Being put in a vulnerable place will make you do some of the most unforeseen things.

The security guard signals for me to stop before going through the gate when I pull into the subdivision of darker times. I roll my window down. "Everything all right?"

"Congrats on the offer on your house! This economy has everybody making changes, but I see it ain't stopping somebody from buying your house."

I shake my head. "You must be talking about another house. Mine isn't for sale."

The severely gray-haired man looks me straight in the eyes. "I guess the Missus is making changes without you. Figures, since I ain't seen you 'round here in a while."

"Good night, sir," I say through a halfway rolled-up window. That old man is always meddling in other folks' business.

I drive toward the back of the subdivision, make a right onto a street that's become unfamiliar to me. My foot's barely on the gas. Speed limit's thirty-five, I'm driving five miles per hour. I slam on my brakes, create friction between rubber and concrete loud enough to scare the man on the moon.

As blinding as a fluorescent yellow jumpsuit in the middle of July, I see a "for sale" sign in the front yard of the house Rene and I shared for five years. Under contract. What the hell is going on here? Rene can't sell our house without my permission. My attention's so caught up in the words above the "for sale" sign, I almost shatter my teeth when I notice a familiar face plastered on the sign staring back at me with a huge grin on her face.

The whole town's laughing at me.

Been in the car fuming for the past two hours with nothing to do but sit and wait, wait and sit. I get out the car, pace the street back and forth to let off some steam without trying to look like a crazed man in this quiet neighborhood. Pacing makes me all the more heated in this too-hot-to-be-spring weather. I hop back in the car and put the air on blast.

I grab my cell, dial the number on the sign. No answer. End the call and dial it again. Every time Sydney's overly happy voice thanks me for inquiring about my own house I end the call. Not sure what I'd say if she answered anyway.

A blue hatchback pulls up to the curb. Figure they're interested in the house even if it is under contract. I get out the car to walk over and yell out, "This house is off the market," just to make sure they know it's not for sale no matter what the sign says. I take the under contract from off the top of the "for sale" sign, put it in my trunk. Would've taken the whole sign out the yard if it wasn't hammered six feet below.

"What are you doing here?" a voice I hadn't heard in a while demands.

I turn around, don't see her. A man with blond hair and a bag on his shoulder stands next to a dehydrated-looking woman with barely any hair. I stare into her face, blink three times as if my vision has suddenly disappeared. "Rene?"

"You shouldn't be here."

The guy comes over to my wife and touches her elbow softly. "Let's go inside."

"And who are you?" I try hard to keep my composure because nothing feels right about this moment, and everything seems to be wrong with my wife.

She looks up at him and gestures toward the house. "Can you give us a minute?"

I don't wait for him to be out of earshot before I say, "You're taking things too far, Rene."

She leans on the car, braces for a conversation she wasn't prepared to have tonight.

"What's going on here? How can you sell our house?"

"You don't live here anymore. Why shouldn't I?"

"You can't sell the house without my signature."

"It's in my name. And I can do whatever I want with it."

Now it's my turn to use the car to hold me up. She's right. She had the house transferred into her maiden name a few months before we got married after her parents died in a train crash. They were scared to fly because they didn't want to crash. Stayed on the ground and died the same way.

Rene is so strong. Endured losing both parents, then our son. Now the house. She only kept it because her parents put their hard-earned money into it and we had plans of filling it up with tons of kids. Maybe letting the house go is her way of finally letting her parents and our son go. All of our dreams. Now I'm wondering if it's her way of letting me go as well.

She's staring at me. I can feel it, so I turn to look at her. For a moment, we just stare into each other's eyes, eyes flooding in memories. She rubs her hand over her thinning hair. I want to ask what happened to all her curls, but now's not the time. With the same hand she used to rub over her hair, she reaches for my hand. Curves her pinkie finger around mine; something she started after the first time we made love. "I never stopped loving you," she reveals, words I've been dying inside to hear from her lips again.

I squeeze her pinkie tight. "Then what are we doing here? What's this all about?" I point to the sign posted in our front yard. "You know I love you, Rene. Whatever it is, we can work this out."

She shakes her head. "This is how it has to be. Let's just live with the memories of how it used to be, Brandon. The love we've shared, let that be enough. This is the best thing for us. I promise you."

We're not having another read-between-the-lines conversation tonight. "How is this the best thing for us? Obviously, it's tearing you up more than you want to admit." I let her finger go. "Are you even eating?"

"It's too complicated."

"I've got a degree in figuring problems out. Give me what you've got."

*Bored.*

I think about Sydney and her failing marriage. Ask Rene, "Am I boring to you?"

A light in one of the bedrooms comes on. Both of us look up at it. Neither of us say anything.

Both of us on opposite ends of the rope. I'm tugging to keep what we have, work on it, make it what it used to be. She's tugging her end to let it all go, hold on only to the memories. Start what used to be with someone new.

I ask, "Does he make you happy?"

Rene dabs at the corners of her eyes. "There used to be a lot of joy in there, a lot of life. We were so happy. I don't think we could ever get back to that place." Her eyes reveal tears on the verge of running a marathon down her face.

"Maybe not, but we can sure try." I leave her side to go back to my car. With the envelope in hand, I stand back by her side. I tell her, "These last few years haven't been easy, Rene. And I came to a point of calling it quits." I pull the contents out of the envelope. Let that truth stop time. "I'll tear these into a million pieces. All you have to do is say you want to give us another shot."

The new man in my wife's life walks out of our house, interrupts our moment. He beckons her attention, doesn't acknowledge me. She waves a hand in his direction. Then turns to me. "You're not the man you once were. I'll go to my grave knowing I'm responsible for that."

"What does that mean?"

She fumbles through her purse, pulls out a pen. Takes the papers from my hand, sets them on the hood of the car. Flips to the pages with a "sign here" arrow pointing to defendant. She scribbles her name, shoves the papers back at me. So much guilt rides her eyes when she looks up at me. "I have cancer. I'll probably be dead before the ink dries." She pushes herself off the car and runs as best she can toward the house.

*F*or two days, I've been in the same spot on my couch with signed divorce papers in my lap. Haven't gone to work. Haven't brushed my teeth or taken a shower. Don't know when I last ate. None of that matters now anyway.

*Boomboomboomboomboom.*

Cancer.

My wife's ending our marriage because she has cancer.

*Boomboomboomboomboom.*

My head throbs. Feels like whoever is knocking on my front door is in my head knocking my thoughts around like a game of cricket. I don't want to answer it. Not in the mood for company, but the knocker is relentless.

When I get up from the couch, I almost hit the ground. Weakness is in my knees. Head feels loaded and light at the same time. Maybe I *should* eat.

"Took you long enough," my brother says when I let him in.

"Your mouth is the last thing I need right now, Drew."

He sticks his nose in the air, takes rapid inhales. "What. Is. That. Smell?"

"Your gums." I plop back down on the couch. Spot so warm you'd think it was on fire.

"Funny." He lifts the lid to the pizza box sitting on the coffee table. "Man, this thing looks like it was made by Fred Flintstone."

The pizza went untouched. Sausage so dried and hard you'd think they were pebbles stuck in sheetrock. An unopened Budweiser sits next to it.

Andrew closes the pizza box and picks up my cell phone. "No wonder you've been missing calls."

I grab my phone from him, stuff it between the seat cushion. "You got me now. What's up?"

He looks at me for the first time since walking through the door. "I should be asking you. Everything all right?"

I nod.

He shakes his head. "Now you know I'm the last person you can lie to."

If only he knew. I slide the papers over to the edge of the table.

My brother picks them up, flips through the pages, sees Rene's signature. He sits on the couch with a hard thud, makes me bounce. "Wasn't expecting that."

I take them from his hand, rip the pages in half. "Wasn't expecting that either."

He looks at the ripped pages. "So, what are you going to do? Keep fighting? Is it even worth it anymore?"

I tell him what she told me. Tell him, "Man, don't know what I'm going to do at this point. Cancer changes everything."

Both of us lean back on the couch, press our heads into the cushion. Stare up at the ceiling.

First I lost my son, then I lost my wife. Now I'm really losing my wife. All this time, I've been walking around like I was the victim. Had my head held low because my wife wasn't giving me the attention a husband deserves. I've been selfish. My wife's been dying in front of me, but my ego blinded me from the truth. What kind of husband have I been?

The vibration from Andrew's pocket steals the silence away from this room.

"Negative."

"What's that?"

He stuffs the phone back in his pocket. "Mel's not pregnant."

"Sorry to hear that, man. I know how much you wanted to be a father by now."

"Yeah. But I'm beginning to think it's just not in the cards for us. I mean, it's been the same story every month now for ten, eleven years. It's draining."

"Literally," I add.

That gets us both to smile.

Twins. Born minutes apart, both of our marriages falling apart.

"That too, but emotionally, I can't take anymore. Don't know how she keeps wanting to try."

"How could she not want to? That's the first expectation you put on her."

He sighs. "And that's why I keep giving in. Feel like I'm responsible for making her obsessed with making me a daddy."

I dig my phone out from the cushion. Plug it up to the wall charger by the TV. It's so dead it won't even cut on after being attached to its life source. I'm in the room with my life source, but both of us are zapped of energy.

In the kitchen, I open all the cabinets in search of something edible. Come up short. Nothing but a jar of peanut butter. That makes me think of Sydney. I can see her cheeks all sunken in trying to sip on a smoothie thicker than the thickest contestant on *The Biggest Loser*'s thighs. I grab two cold bottles of beer from the fridge. Toss one to my brother back in the living room.

Andrew uses one of the napkins next to the pizza box to wrap around the bottle cap. Pops it, takes a long gulp. "If you could change anything about your life, what would it be?"

I pop the top on my beer, down a mouthful of carbs. "Probably would've pursued a career in photography."

He falls back into the couch. "Man, I thought you'd say something totally different. Why a career change, and photography at that?"

"And all these years I thought you knew me, Bro."

"Obviously, I don't know everything."

"You remember I took that photography class back in high school?"

He says, "Oh yeah, I forgot about that. We'd eat dinner late sometimes because Dad would have to go searching the neighborhood for you and that doggone camera. You'd be out there taking pictures all night if Mama and Daddy would've let you."

I toss the memory back and forth in my mind. That camera was the first time I felt needed and appreciated. It was like the camera needed me to fulfill its purpose. Without me, it was pretty useless. I'd take that thing with me everywhere, using it to capture anything the lens found interesting. The camera was my security until I discovered love. Until I discovered Rene. "I *was* serious about it," I say.

"That you were. I remember you went days without talking when Daddy hid your camera after the semester ended."

"Yep. He told me I needed to focus on math. Said pictures wouldn't make a woman happy."

"That's exactly what he'd say. '*Keeping food on the table makes a happy wife.*' He used to kill me with that," Andrew says.

"And look where that got us." I gulp back more beer. "What about you? What would you change?"

He rolls the bottle back and forth between his hands. Thinks about his answer to the question he asked of me. "Check this out. I'd actually change my career as well."

"No, not you."

My brother looks at me as if he's looking at himself in the mirror. "No lie. Being around kids forty hours a week is the main reason why I wanted to be a father. Kids make life worth living."

I raise my beer in the air. "Don't I know it."

"I know you do, brother. I know you do."

I ask him what he asked me a little while ago. "So, what are you going to do?"

"I put a lot of pressure on Mel up front. I pretty much made her a mother before I even took her out on our first date. That wasn't fair. Now she's putting pressure on me to fulfill my requirements of her. We've both grown lost in the midst of all of this. It's time for us to have a heart-to-heart about it. We'll see where it leads. One thing's for sure, it'll either make us or break us."

"That's life. Always something to make or break you."

And I've just about reached my breaking point.

What is it about men?

They put the bait on the hook, stick it in the water, wait for you to bite, reel you in only to take you off the line and toss you back in the water.

That's how Brandon's made me feel.

I've been to Pick Your Fit plus Riverpoint with no running partner in sight. He's the one who asked me to train him, and now he doesn't even want to show up. He's got me sacrificing sleep in the mornings and time with the kids in the evenings to be stood up. Not that I'm really complaining there, but still, it's inconsiderate. Ever since the day at his place, when he kissed my temples, things haven't been the same. Maybe my confession scared him away.

Eric was the same way when we first started dating. A mutual friend introduced us. Took a few phone calls, texts, and emails before we could get our schedules together. He had been on the police force for a few years and was in the process of trying to get in with a special unit's division. I was just getting started in real estate. Neither of us had much free time to play around with. He was charming in our communication. Had me interested. Told me he wasn't dating anyone else, he was a one-woman kind of guy. I was rather smitten before meeting him. It was one of those moments where you just fall for someone's words. When we met, though, the chemistry was lacking. I found myself more interested in him behind the scene than face to face. But I kept dating him. Really wanted to give him a shot since he was different from the men I was used to dating. I got used to him, overlooked his quirks. The moment I started to feel a little something, he told me he was interested in another woman and that he wanted to date us both.

I was taken aback by his honesty. I dodged his bait for months. When I finally decided to go for it, he reeled the hook in to cast back out in another direction. I should've stayed right where I was instead of swimming to the other end of the pond in search of another chance at what he had to offer. Every time I tried to get more involved with him, it was like his line was pulled more from another direction. I began to doubt myself, felt insecurity creeping in. Made me feel like I had to find ways to prove to him I was worth dating exclusively. I needed to make him know I was a good catch.

The clock on the dash reads six-thirty-three. Another morning left hanging by another woman's husband.

Men.

I secure the laces to my sneakers, press "Go" on the running app on my smartphone. Soon as the GPS finds my location I hit "Start." Clip the phone to my running belt, put one earphone in my ear, leave the other ear open so I can stay connected to nature at the same time. Need to make sure I'm always aware of my surroundings. Never know who's hiding in the bushes waiting to pounce on an unsuspecting soul.

Not a mile in, rain taps on the top of my head. I slow down momentarily to unclip the music player and place it in the waterproof pouch, then pick my pace up, hear my feet slap against wet concrete. Run like I'm trying to outrun the rain clouds. Legs feel good through the pressure I put on them to get me to the end of the path and back.

Seven miles and some change later, hands on hips, I make a steady stroll back to my car.

"Thought you were going to run until midnight."

Saw him the moment I stopped running. "How long you been out here?"

"Pulled up when you took your first step."

I check the running app on my phone. Sixty minutes and a few seconds. "You act like you've been out here for hours."

"Time moves slow when you're waiting."

With my shirt, I wipe sweat and rain from my face. Unlock my doors to grab a bottle of electrolytes and a protein bar. "Seeing as though you've left me hanging these past few days, how'd you know I'd be out here?"

Brandon rubs a hand across his scalp. He pulls out his phone, fidgets with it.

I step away, give him privacy. Bend over, fingertips to toes, stretch out tight hamstrings. Feel my stomach vibrate. I unzip the pouch, look at the caller ID on my phone. It's not Eric or my mom, so I don't answer. Then I realize I brought my work phone because I didn't want to be interrupted with anybody during my run and knew nobody would be calling about a house this early. They hang up before I can answer. As I put it back in the pouch, it vibrates again in my hand. I put my business voice on.

A finger taps me on my shoulder.

I turn around. The lips in front of me move to the voice on the other end of the phone.

"How'd you get my work number?" I ask through the phone.

The call disconnects. "The question is how do you know my wife?"

One of my knees buckles, makes me lose my balance. "I wasn't aware I knew your wife."

"You know her well enough to have your picture plastered in my front yard."

"Bear with me. I have three houses currently listed." I rack my brain trying to figure out which one he's referring to. One client is an elderly widow, another a married couple with two kids, and one on the way needing a larger home. "Are you talking about the property in Farrington Isle?"

"How do you know my wife?" he questions again.

A breeze passes through me. Clothes are wet from the rain and sweat. I fold my arms across my chest. "This is weird."

He just stands there, eyes on me. Waiting for answers.

If looks could kill, I'd be lying in an open grave with dirt being tossed on top of me like a Jane Doe. "Look, I had no idea she was your wife. She called about selling her house, I went out, a contract was signed. She didn't mention a husband. How was I supposed to know?"

Hardened eyes turn away from me as he walks back over to his ride.

I finish off my drink, toss it in the trash. Need every ounce of energy possible for this conversation.

He leans up against his truck. "It's in her maiden name. Rene Ortiz."

I know exactly who his wife is.

"Nothing makes sense to me anymore. Wish I could fast-forward to the good parts 'cause this right here…"

"I've felt that way before."

Out of nowhere, Brandon chuckles. Then doubles over in laughter. "Wanna hear a good joke?"

His laughter and wanting to tell a joke catches me off-guard, but is needed at the same time. "Our conversations *have* been pretty deep lately, huh?"

"Get this, my wife's dying. She's got cancer." He's laughing so hard tears stream from his eyes when he looks up. "Funny, huh?"

It takes the hand of God reaching down from heaven to keep my hand from slapping this insane individual across the face. "No. That's not funny at all, Brandon. I can't believe you."

He pulls air through his teeth so hard it sounds like his teeth shatter. "You're right, it ain't funny." He says that, turns around and sends his fist through his car's window.

Sydney's motherly instincts kicks in.

She whips her car through morning traffic. Does her best to get me to the hospital before all the blood in my body flows out my hand.

"It's not that bad, Syd. Not worth getting in an accident over."

She looks at me. Worry in her eyes, hint of a smile on her face. "That's the first time you've called me Syd. I like the way it rolls off your tongue."

I wink until the throb in my hand steals my attention.

"Keep the towel tight. We're almost there."

A car in front of us is going too slow for Sydney's taste. She swerves around it, makes her tires scream.

Again, I say, "A few cuts aren't worth dying over."

As she presses down harder on the accelerator, a siren blares behind us. I look out the side mirror, see an all-black vehicle with blue flashing lights on our tail.

"I'm not blind." Still she refuses to apply the brakes.

"Now wouldn't be the time to be Bonnie and I sure as hell ain't trying to be no Clyde."

"And now wouldn't be the time for your jokes."

I keep my mouth shut. Let her handle her.

Sydney puts her blinker on, moves two lanes over to the right. The cop follows. She slows, puts the car in park on the side of the road, flashers on. Beads of sweat mark her forehead as her vision's glued to the rearview. My bleeding hand no longer her concern.

I bounce my head on the headrest. No matter what I do, Rene continues to screw my life up, and now it's affecting other people.

Anxiety grows on Sydney's face as she watches the cop walk up to her window.

"Let me handle this," I tell her.

She positions her body in a way that blocks me from looking out her window. She runs her hands through her hair, but they get caught in tangles. The rain earlier did a number on her hair. Has her looking like Raggedy Ann's twin sister.

The officer drops his arm on the top of the car, leans his head down. "Well, well, well."

"Michael, now I know you saw how slow that car was going."

"If you weren't going so fast, I might've."

"Can you cut me some slack this morning? I've got somewhere I need to be."

"I let you slide the last time. Don't want you getting into the habit of thinking just because you're married to a cop and best friends with my wife that you can get away with breaking the law." He reaches his hand in the car. "You know the drill."

I should've stayed my butt at home, stuck to the couch, starved and pissed at the world. I may have been miserable then, but it sure beats being in this car with my DNA dripping in my lap.

Sydney huffs, reaches across me while still trying to block me from view. Pulls her wallet and registration out the glove box.

"Is that blood on your shirt?" the officer questions.

I take that as my cue to speak up. I raise my hand with the soiled towel on it. "Yes, officer. It's mine. This kind lady was just trying to get me to the hospital."

He takes a look at my hand, then says to the driver, "Goodness, Sydney, why didn't you just say something?"

"Well, you came to the car with a chip on your shoulder and you needed somebody to take it out on."

The officer reaches his head in the car. "Sir, I'm sorry you have to be witness to this." He smirks at Sydney, then looks back at me. "Let's get you to the hospital."

"Thank you," she and I both say. One with more of a sarcastic tone than the other.

He hands her back her identification, pausing as if he has something else to say.

"Come on, Michael."

"Just a minute." He looks back at me. Tells Sydney, "Step out of the car," in a way that makes me feel like there's a warrant out for my arrest.

"What for, Michael? You see the man needs medical attention."

"Why didn't you call him an ambulance?"

I don't know the history of these two and I couldn't care less. Either he gives her a ticket or he doesn't. At this point I'm willing to walk the rest of the way to the hospital, even if I pass out along the way.

Again, I raise my hand toward the officer. "Sir."

He no longer looks at me with concern, but now his eyes reveal a distaste that even I can taste.

"Just get out the car, Sydney," I tell her.

She flings the door open, nearly pushing him into traffic.

My hand no longer throbs. Think it's numb. Kind of like my consciousness. Rene has me jacked up in the worst way. Got me busting my fist through windows, got me falling apart all because I fell in love with her all those years ago. A wife should never make her husband feel like this. And a husband should never have his wife feeling like Sydney.

She jumps back in the car, eyes refusing to blink or look in my direction.

"What was that all about?"

Sydney slowly moves the car back into the flow of traffic. Voice barely above a whisper. "He recognized your face from the park. Saw us holding hands."

All of a sudden, my brother's warning of cops having eyes everywhere comes to mind.

This world just got a little smaller.

# 25
## SYDNEY

I haven't been happy with Eric for years. The first time in my life I do something about it, the whole world finds out.

Michael and a few other officers from Eric's unit went running at Riverpoint Park the same morning I decided to start training Brandon. Said he saw everything. Saw him pass out and watched us sitting in the grass having an intimate conversation. Saw his hand slide in mine. Saw me practically run back to my car. I thought I was being smart about not meeting with Brandon close to home. Driving thirty minutes outside of town for a running lesson seemed like a good idea. Had no idea I'd run into Eric's badge-buddies, and one who's my close friend's husband at that.

The only reason Michael didn't tell Eric is because it was right after one of the new recruits got killed in the line of duty and things were tense. He forgot. Seeing Brandon in my car brought it all back to memory. Before I could even get to the hospital, he'd called his wife and told her everything. Rachel turned around and called Katrina. My phone's been blowing up ever since. No calls from Eric, though.

The doctor in the ER put a few stitches in Brandon's hand, bandaged him up, gave him a few painkillers and sent us on our way. I drove him back to his car in silence.

No one's home when I finally make it in. Kennedy's in school,

EJ's at daycare. I'm sure Eric's at work getting an earful from Michael.

My legs move up the stairs slower than a snail sliding across the moon. Once I make it to the bathroom, I fill the tub with water so hot steam rises. Sitting in a cold hospital in wet clothes wasn't a good idea. Being sick is the last thing I need.

I don't soak long. Got two showings before noon and I'm already behind. I hop out the tub with a little more pep in my step. What will be will be.

On my way out the room I almost trip, have to hold onto the wall to keep from falling over. Inhale. Exhale. Do that three times. Calm my nerves. Life has taken an unexpected turn, nothing to lose my composure over. It's not like I'm sleeping with the man.

I look down to see I wasn't tripping over this morning's events, but a pair of shoes I haven't seen or worn in years. I pick them and just as I'm about to toss them in the closet, my attention is pulled to something lying on the bed. The shoes fall out my hand and I pick the envelope up. It's addressed to Eric scribbled in my handwriting.

It's the letter I wrote him the night before our wedding.


Work was torture.

Every second was spent thinking about what was going through Eric's head. From the moment I laced my sneakers and put one foot in front of the other, things have been like hell. I should've known today would be crazy after getting caught in the rain. Usually I find running in the rain to be liberating. But something about the calm drizzle should've been a sign that today would be unexpected.

Never did I imagine what life would be like if Eric found out the truth about my feelings for him. It's funny how you want something so bad and when it finally happens, you want to take off like a dog trying to chase down a fly.

I was watching an episode of *Army Wives* a few weeks back. One of the wives on the show said something that comes to mind. *"More tears are shed over answered prayers."* That statement resonated so deeply, and at this moment, it's so close to the truth it's unsettling. For years now I've wanted a way out of my marriage, a way to go back to a life of just me. Now that that opportunity may have come, I'm finding myself not so sure.

I've been avoiding going home since I left earlier this morning. Lollygagged in the grocery store after picking the kids up. They were antsy and so was I. Trying to create a last-minute meal was futile. I'd take them out to eat instead. Figured the longer we stayed out, the more time Eric would have to simmer down. My phone rang not once from him. No text message, email, nothing. There's no telling what Michael's beefed his head up with, and the letter... Oh, that darn letter. Why have I still been hanging on to it?

One can never avoid the inevitable.

I'll just have to deal with that after dinner.


I watch as a mother looks at her child with vacant eyes. She looks at her as if she doesn't exist. Her son is normal. Her daughter is not.

She watches her four-year-old child terrorize their section in Olive Garden with such a numbing emotion I feel for the child more than the mother. The kid kicks at her chair, screams as four crayons fall to the floor. No one at the table moves to pick up the crayons, no one even moves to calm her from her tantrum.

A mom and her unwanted child. The father digs into his ravioli and sausage like this is an everyday occurrence. The mother's food is untouched. She continues looking at her child as she runs circles around the table with her napkin folded around her head. For a second, our eyes connect. When I look deep into her blue eyes, I see she desperately has regrets. Wishes that night she had just told her husband she had a headache. Deciding not to forgo her hormones and oblige her lover, she ended up pregnant. Had she known she'd end up with a child whose energy was never-ending, she would've ran to the kitchen and stuck a turkey baster inside her womb and sucked out every abnormal sperm before it contaminated her normal egg.

"Mommy." EJ pats at my leg.

I'm so caught up in this woman and her life that I forget I have my own kids and life to worry about. "Yes, EJ?"

"I gotta pee."

Grateful for the break from Terror at Olive Garden, I take my son's hand and lead him to the restroom. My reflection in the mirror catches me off-guard as EJ does his thing in the stall. A look of regret stains my irises. Other than a few minor issues with the kids, they haven't been a burden on me. So why am I regretting their existence? Why do I feel as hopeless as that woman in the dining room looked?

The toilet flushes, brings me back to reality. "Did you shake?"

He nods as he comes out of the stall pulling on his shirt instead of stuffing it back in his jeans.

"Stop wiping your hands on your shirt and wash your hands," I tell him and hand him a paper towel to cut the faucet off with, then dry his hands on another one.

Back at the table, I'm relieved to see the family is gone. From the faces of the surrounding patrons, they're glad to be able to enjoy their unlimited salad and breadsticks in peace and quiet. Kennedy tells me she's ready to go home. For once we're on the same page. I flag the waiter to bring a to-go box for my barely-touched lasagna.

Apparently, the kids caught a little of the rambunctious child's spirit, because as soon as we get in the car, they start bickering over mint-flavored chocolate.

At the red light, I turn around, tell the two, "Knock it off." The car behind me lays on his horn. By the time I turn my attention back to the traffic, the light is yellow. Mr. Anxious skids around me while still laying on his horn and gives me a look that says I made him miss the last call for alcohol. "Get a life," I mumble in his direction. All of my energy for foolishness has been zapped.

My mind drifts back to the regretful mother at the restaurant. The way her husband just sat there void of words reminded me of Eric. No, he wouldn't have let the kids cut up like that little girl, but when it comes to dinnertime or any time conversation is expected, he usually just sits there and has a one-on-one conversation with his food. It's those moments when I wish I had cut things short after our first date, and definitely wish I had given him the letter when it was fresh in my hand. Wish I had listened to my instinct to keep it moving where he was concerned.

Not listening to my gut has me here.

*I* dropped the kids off at my mom's house before heading home. It's been at least eight hours since I've heard from or laid eyes on my husband. This would not be a battle the kids need to be a part of. It's a battle I'm sure I don't want to be a part of.

*"But all is changed with time, the future none can see. The road you leave behind, ahead lies mystery."*

The words of Stevie Wonder slap me in the face when I walk through the door to my home. Volume is on one hundred. There's no denying I'm being sent a message.

It's dark in the house. My sight's diminished, other senses heightened. I smell a madman on the loose. A movie scene pops in my head and all I can see is Wesley Snipes taking a hammer to anything within reach in Sanaa Lathan's brownstone in *Disappearing Acts.* I knew I wasn't ready for war, but this takes it to a different level.

No fear, Sydney. No. Fear.

A flicker of light leads me to the living room. I can see a bundle of fur nestled by the unlit fireplace. Forrester. Can always depend on him to be where he's supposed to be. That makes me smile in the midst of all of the above.

A large shadow moves on the wall. I look over by the speaker, see Eric standing by the stereo. The lit candle on the mantle helps me see everything clearly.

I walk over, cut the music down. "Can we talk?"

"Should've done that years ago." He cuts the music back up.

I hit the power button. "Let's be adult about this, Eric."

*"Be adult about this?"* My husband turns around, his face contorted like I've disrespected him in the worst way. "Let me get this straight. You wrote me a damn letter to call off our wedding less than twelve hours away because you couldn't face me like a woman and you want to be adult about this now?"

Instead of defending my actions, I turn around and bolt out of the living room and up the stairs.

Eric is standing in the room against the dresser when I walk out of the bathroom. I ran up here to take a shower. Needed the water to help soothe my thoughts. Needed to give him time to cool down from his.

I toss my robe on the bed, grab a T-shirt from my dresser and put it on without a bra. Can feel my husband's eyes pouring over my body with every move I make. I pull up a pair of boxer shorts before this conversation goes in another direction.

"Why did you marry me?"

"I don't know," I say too fast.

Eric tosses a seven-year-old letter in my direction.

I pick it up, flip it, remove the papers from the envelope with anxiousness as if I don't know what it says.

"You knew a lot when you wrote that," he says, pain etched in his voice.

I stuff the letter back in the envelope, wishing I could stuff the words back into Neverland just as easily. "It felt like the right thing to do at the time."

"*The right thing to do?*" My husband glares at me, yet his voice holds more intensity than his eyes. "For who? 'Cause the way I see it right now, you've messed up life for four people."

I think about EJ and Kennedy and how their lives will never be the same.

"You had a lot to say in that letter, but you're not saying much of nothing now."

It's obvious to me that the time I took in the shower did nothing to calm his anger. He's just as mad now as he was when Stevie Wonder was instigating our situation. "What do you want me to say, Eric?"

"Something. Anything. But don't sit there and act like a mute."

The letter's still in my hand. I rip it in half without giving it any thought. Get off the bed and toss my feelings in the trash. Should've done that years ago. "I'm sorry," falls from my lips.

"Sorry won't give me back the ten years you wasted."

"*Wasted?* Wow."

"What else would you call it?"

"Well, if you hadn't spent so much time 'getting to know' me, it wouldn't be ten years I wasted."

"Obviously, I didn't get to know you at all."

"I'm not going to do this, Eric."

He's leaning on the dresser with his arms folded across his chest. A scowl on his face that would cause the Bloods and Crips to call truce. "You know, I would've been able to take being rejected on our first date, but this is beyond comprehension. I would've rather you cheated."

"Be careful what you wish for."

He unfolds his arms, pushes off the dresser. Comes closer to me. "What was that?"

I step back, go around him. Walk out of our bedroom.

Adamant footsteps follow me down the hall and down the stairs. "Why. Did. You. Marry. Me?"

I stop at the bottom of the stairs, turn around and look into his eyes the same way I did as I repeated my vows on our wedding day. "Tell me something. How could you not know I wasn't happy?"

He brushes past me, leaves me hanging like a person at the end of a bungee cord.

I dangle in this emptiness for a moment, not long enough for it to take over, though, and join him in the living room. Fall victim to the sofa's cushion right along with him.

Eric moves over to the fireplace, stands in front of a picture we took on our first wedding anniversary. Kennedy was only a month old. "You've wasted almost ten years of my life."

This time it doesn't sting as much as it did the first time he said it. "I'm sorry," is all I can say.

"That's not something you can apologize for."

"Well, what do you want me to do, Eric? I can't give you those years back." Lord knows if I could, I would, because I've wasted the same amount of time.

"I'm not asking you to." He turns to face me with such fury I feel like I'm in the room with Bruce Lee. "Every day, I put my life on the line for this family. I risk not coming home and leaving my kids without a father, and you without a husband. I put that uniform on knowing I'm making a major sacrifice to keep this family afloat. All this time, I thought it was a mutual effort. Now I see things so differently."

We're here, at this place of no return. I've held my tongue long enough, spared everyone's feelings but my own. "Eric, do you think going to work is enough to keep a home together?"

"Obviously not. According to your words I'm boring, lack drive, and let's not forget bad in bed."

I open my mouth too quickly, feel my jaw pop. "I didn't say it like that."

"Doesn't matter *how* you said it. You said it."

He's right. The truth is the truth, no matter how it's said. "It's not like I hadn't told you those things before, Eric."

"Maybe you did, Sydney, but things are a lot different when they're staring you in the face." He scratches his hairless face as if visualizing my words makes him itch. "What were you thinking when you wrote the letter?"

As I rewind time in my head, I sit down on the sofa. Feel like I've been on my feet all day. My legs thank me immediately. "You really want to know?"

"I asked."

Now's my chance to finally tell him how I've felt all these years. For some reason, it doesn't feel right. I twist my wedding ring around my finger several times before my lips move. "I was thinking about how much I wanted out. My feelings were never stable in our relationship. One minute, you'd have me smiling from here to Kansas, the next, I wondered if you even knew me or wanted to be with me. I questioned if I even knew me or knew what I wanted. You made me feel invalid, made me feel confused. Felt like I didn't have a mind of my own."

"Invalid? Wow." He sits down slowly in the chair by the computer desk like he's having a bad episode with hemorrhoids. "You never said anything."

I let out an exasperated sigh. "I've lost count of how many times I've told you that. You never listen, Eric. It's about how you feel and if you feel like everything's okay in your world, everything's okay in the rest of the world. But you're not in this world alone."

"That's not true. I don't know how you can say that."

"You asked me how I felt. There you have it."

Confusion intoxicated with anger stains his face like a cup of cherry Kool-Aid spilled on a white carpet. "I don't get you."

"Bingo." I clap my hands. "That's the problem. You stopped getting me after you felt you knew me, but I've grown since we first started dating. Hell, I've grown since we've been married."

"I'm not going to let you sit up here and say I don't listen. I've lost count of how many times I set the DVR for your favorite shows, or how I spend time with the kids because I can hear the tiredness in your voice. And let's not forget the times I rub your feet after you've had a long day just by the way you toss your keys on the counter. I do listen, Sydney. Even when you haven't said anything."

He's right. Damn it, he's right.

"I just don't know what you want from me."

I get up from the sofa and stand next to the chair he's sitting in. I wrap my fingers around his jaw, raise his face up toward mine. Need him to face me, need to see if his irises and tongue speak the same language when I ask the question he diverted earlier. "Did you really think I was happy?"

He stares at me so long I swear he was born without the need to blink. "No."

My hand falls from his face. I lick my lips, then cough. Struggle with what to say. "Does that mean you've been unhappy as well?"

"Yes."

I walk back over to the sofa and drop. His one word replies have me feeling like I've jumped out of an airplane with no parachute.

We're staring at the final moments of our marriage.

We can't go back to before this moment. Can't go back to the end of our first date and rewrite our relationship. All we can do from here is face the truth and make changes accordingly.

I'm not happy.

He's not happy.

Never did I think a confession would boil down to this. Never did I think my husband could possibly feel just as suffocated in this marriage as I have been. All these years, he's been putting on the same fake smile as me. Neither one of us acknowledging the other's misery. What kind of man is he? What kind of woman am I?

Eric sits down on the sofa next to me.

I ask, "If you've been unhappy, why are you trying to put all this all on me?"

His voice a whisper, "You knew I was just out of a long relationship. You knew I was in a vulnerable place. You could've stopped this instead of pulling me in."

"You're a grown man, Eric. You could've just as easily not have even agreed to go out with me until you were truly ready." I take a deep breath, try to keep myself from getting heated.

Something tickles the side of my leg. I reach down to scratch and feel Forrester rubbing against my leg. All of a sudden, I hear him purring, feel him vibrating the inside of my palm. Don't know how I missed the sound of his motor; purrs louder than a machine gun in the middle of a war.

War.

Something Eric and I are in right now.

The battle of who's right and who's wrong.

The battle no one ever wins.

Eric breaks my thoughts. "My parents have been married forty-two years. I wanted that. Wanted to be with someone I could grow old with." It's his turn to cough and struggle with what to say next.

I look down at the diamond on my ring finger. "So I was convenient timing?"

He nods.

Ouch.

"When we first got together, I still had feelings for my ex. We were still communicating, still flirting. Still sleeping together when she came to town. Still wanted to be with each other, but pride stood in the way on both of our parts. You came along and I just transferred those emotions to you."

Before he can finish, I jump across the sofa with the back of my hand making hard contact with the side of his face.

He doesn't react. Just sits there, blindly staring in the dark.

I look down, see my hands nestled in my lap. I never slapped him, just wish I had. My jaws clench, feel like my teeth will fall out if I open my mouth. I open it anyway. "That's messed up. Really, really messed up."

"Why?" He turns in my direction. "Just like I knew you weren't happy, you knew I still loved another woman, but you had to invite me over to your place at night, had to cook me dinner and offer me dessert in bed. You knew where my head was."

"Yeah, well, it would've been nice for you to share those thoughts with me instead of using your other head to tell me a different story."

"You knew I was seeing other people, too. You made that decision."

"But I didn't make it alone."

He breathes hard into darkness. "Why did you marry me, Sydney?"

The candle on the mantle casts a glow on our wedding picture above the fireplace. I gaze at the picture. For the first time, I have to come to terms with what I see. The truth is all in my husband's eyes. He didn't want to be there just as much as I didn't. His eyes held just as much uncertainty as mine. Both of us denying ourselves the last opportunity to be honest about our insecurities before saying those two words that would commit us for life.

A smile tells a thousand lies, but the eyes never deny the truth.

I turn my gaze back to Eric. "I should be asking you the same thing."

# 28

## BRANDON

The sky is dark, nearly pitch black. Not because it's night, but because a storm is brewing.

Thunder roars. Sounds like God's clearing His throat, giving me some kind of warning that lightning's about to strike.

It's a quarter to ten in the morning, looks like it's a quarter after midnight.

*April 2, 2004 – November 21, 2009.*

Days before Thanksgiving, and I was robbed of all reasons to be thankful.

Today, my son would have turned nine. Nine. Halfway to being a legalized man. An age where he could stand and stare me in the eye and tell me he was ready to make his own decisions. An age where no matter how tall he was or how deep his voice got, he was still growing. An age I'll never see him reach.

Today is the first time I've been to Reginald Brandon Carter's gravesite since his death. I never wanted to come back here, never wanted the memory of that week to replay before my eyes. But, no matter how long I try to avoid it, my mind will never be able to fully hit delete. Holding your child's lifeless body is something a father should never have to do. "Why didn't I come check on you that night?"

My heart threatens to stop beating as light raindrops mix with my heavy tears. I don't understand why God didn't send me a message to let me know my son had stopped breathing. I was the head of the household and didn't know what was going on in my own home. "What kind of man am I?" Now my wife tells me she's been sick and I couldn't tell. Instead of getting to the heart of what was troubling her, I start getting close to another man's wife.

I squat at his grave. Run my fingers across his name.

Footsteps draw me out of an emotional beatdown. I wipe tears and rain from my face.

A shaky hand touches my shoulder. I turn around and see Rene standing above me. "What are you doing here?" I question as if she has no right.

"I come every year on his birthday," she answers in a condemning tone. She knows I don't come here at all.

In the distance, I see the blue hatchback again. Ask her, "Did he have to come with you?"

She doesn't have to turn around to see who I'm talking about. "He's my nurse."

"Nurse? Are you *that* sick?"

Her eyes tell me yes, but her lips tell me nothing. In her hand is a small bucket with soapy water inside. She sits it in the grass. Takes a few moments to pull overgrown grass from around the tombstone, tosses the excess to the side. Wipes leftover fragments on her jeans, then pulls out a brush from the bucket of water. Begins scrubbing away at dingy marble engraved with our son's date of birth and date of death.

All of a sudden, rage takes over. I snatch the brush from her hand, toss it as far away from her reach as possible. Grab the bucket, turn it over until every drop of suds slide from the plastic container.

"What'd you do that for?"

"Do you think any of that matters to him?"

She's still on her knees, picking away at nothing in particular. "It shouldn't look like this."

"Like what, Rene? No matter how hard you scrub it with bleach, it's still going to get dingy. It's part of the ground."

"He shouldn't be part of the ground," she says, her voice barely above a whisper.

I make sure my voice is heard. "Told you we should've had him cremated."

Quickly, she rises to her feet, shoves me in the chest with more strength than I thought she had. "You're so damn insensitive."

My anger goes up a level. "I'm insensitive? You've been walking around with cancer, and instead of talking to me about it, you lead me to believe I had done something wrong. Made me self-conscious and insecure. Had me pack up and move out of a house I've been making payments on. Left me vulnerable and open like a mother-fucker, and I'm insensitive?"

With folded arms and solid posture she stares me down. "Who is she?"

"What? Who is who?"

"You said I left you vulnerable and open. That could only mean one thing."

I nod my head at the car not too far in the distance. "I could say the same."

"He's. My. Nurse."

"That's what you say."

Just like that she turns and walks away. Goes in search of the brush I tossed.

Thunder roars, sending another warning to take cover.

I look up to the sky, find the darkest clouds looking down on me. Any minute, they're going to unleash a multitude of broken dreams and desperation.

I go after Rene. "We need to get out of here."

She makes no rush to move. "It's all my fault," she reveals with her back turned toward me. "I pushed you away. I wanted you to find someone else to love because I knew I would no longer be in the picture."

All fears of downpour forgotten. "I don't understand. Why would I want to love someone else when you're the only woman I've loved?"

"Because I'm dying, Brandon." She says that as if I was supposed to know. "There's no hope for me, no hope for us."

"Who says this has to be your death sentence? We could go to that cancer treatment facility in Oklahoma. I've seen the commercials on TV a million times. People are living years after being diagnosed."

Her eyes survey the many tombstones surrounding us. Takes it all in with shallow breaths. "I've lost count of how many funerals I've done out here. One day, I see someone in the grocery store, the next I'm draining blood from their body and replacing it with formaldehyde. The last twelve months have been the hardest. More passed away from cancer this year than in the eight years I've been in business." She starts walking slowly in the direction of where the rain has started falling.

My footsteps are right behind hers.

We stop in front of a gravestone with the words *Served His Community With Pride* etched above his name.

Rene rubs her index finger across the words of remembrance. "I was the first person Wes confided in when he got his diagnosis. It was a Saturday morning. We were getting ready to head out for a service. He pulled me aside, told me in a couple of months I'd be preparing for his service. He found out in his final stage. Had no idea how to tell his wife and four kids."

"I guess you two *did* have a lot in common."

She turns to face me. "I'm dealing with this the best I can."

"But that's what I'm here for, Rene. I'm your husband. We should be dealing with this together." I take a second to wipe rain from my eyes, try to give myself a minute to calm down. Doesn't work. "I stood at the altar and vowed to love you in sickness and in health. And you took away my rights as your husband when you decided I couldn't handle your sickness." I turn to walk away. Though it would've been hard, I could've handled the cancer. What she did to me makes me feel like less than a man. And because of that I walk away.

"Brandon," she calls after me.

I stop momentarily, turn to look at her.

She rubs her hand across her forehead, moves tiny curls from her face. The rain makes her hair look matted, looks like a bad toupee. Her lips quiver.

It's a struggle to look at her struggle with whatever it is she has to say.

My wife stands so close to me she's almost standing on my feet. "I'm scared."

I let her fall into my open arms. With as much assurance as I can muster up, I say, "We'll beat this."

*I*t's been days since Eric and I last spoke. After our talk, I packed some clothes and went to stay at my mom's with the kids. Figured a weekend apart would give us a little time to be able to sort through our thoughts, make a little sense of the marriage we created.

"So what are you going to do?" Katrina asks.

I look across the table, see Rachel's eyes on my mouth waiting for an answer. Her stare is so intense I'm sure she can tell how many times I've been to the dentist in my lifetime. "Honestly, it would make sense to go ahead and cut my losses, but…" I sigh. "I don't know."

The woman I've been friends with the shortest says, "I'm surprised he didn't have your bags packed when you got home."

I told them about the letter, but I kept the fact my husband didn't want to marry me either to myself. Some things your friends just don't need to know, and I've told them a lot as is. "Katrina, it's not that easy." She and I have barely talked to each other since she went off on me during our last call. Her attitude toward me seems to be the same as it was then.

"Well, what do you want? Do you even know anymore? I mean, you're around town gallivanting with another man like you're a single woman. Now, you might have the opportunity to be that and are scared to make a decision. Elton didn't hesitate spreading his seeds all across town, but the second I told him he was a free man, he wanted to get his act together. I swear, cheaters never know what you want."

"I'm not a cheater."

"Michael said you two looked real comfortable together." Rachel adds her nickel to the conversation. "I told him it was the same way at the club."

I push my plate away from me, appetite no longer existent.

"You may not have crossed that line with him, but you've been spending private time with him. What were you thinking holding his hand in the wide open?"

"Michael was overanalyzing what he saw."

"Say he was, Sydney. What were you doing with him one-on-one?"

I defend myself. "Helping him train for a race."

"Oh, come on," Katrina starts. "Anybody can see you two are attracted to each other, and put in the wrong environment, that can be dangerous. Running was just a copout for you two to put curiosity to the test."

My head flings back, mouth wide open. Laughter spilling out in a long stream. "This is ridiculous." Nothing's funny. I'm frustrated and laughing is the only way to keep me sane.

I excuse myself from the table. Step outside for a dose of fresh air. Minutes later, Rachel joins me.

"Katrina had to get back to work." She hands me my food in a to-go box.

I set the box on the ledge. "Don't know why I thought she'd be more understanding. Yeah, I get she was cheated on, but she knows what it was like to be in an unfulfilling marriage."

"Maybe so, but all she sees is betrayal. All she feels is the pain.

Whether she was unhappy or not, she felt devalued for not being able to fulfill her husband enough to keep him at home. You're making her relive that."

"Did she tell you that?"

Rachel nods.

"How do you feel?"

"Walk me to my car."

I grab my food, follow her back through the restaurant and out the front door.

"You want to know why Michael and I are so happy? I cheated on him in the beginning of our relationship. He was a workaholic, spending more time on the job than coming home to me. Neglect and loneliness are an awful combination. One afternoon, Michael wanted to surprise me by taking a half day off work, came home, and saw *who* I had for lunch."

My mind takes a trip without her having to say much else. "Are you serious?"

"He was livid. I packed my bags, told him I'd be out within the hour. Not even three days passed before he was calling my phone, begging for another chance. Said I was the best thing to happen to him and he'd rather lose his job than lose me."

"That's deep."

"You knew how much I liked him. I didn't want to lose him either, but I refused to be a mistress to his nine-to-five."

"Why didn't you tell me this before?"

"Never had a reason to."

"Why now?"

"I slept with that guy to get Michael's attention. It was a random fling. What you're doing is building a relationship with Brandon. That's dangerous territory. That's a lot harder to walk away from."

"Mr. Carter?" I turn my attention to the doctor tending to Rene. "Your wife has developed pneumonia. Her immune system is weak and being out in the rain wasn't the best idea in her condition."

"Exactly how bad is her condition?"

He looks over the chart in his hands, closes it shut. "She's pretty sick. She's more prone to catching infections, and when she gets them, it hits hard. We'll move her to ICU, pump her with fluids, keep her warm. Treat the infection as best we can. We'll keep an eye on her, but there's not much else we can do at this stage of her cancer."

"At this stage?"

He shifts in his stance, raises an eyebrow. Questions my questions as if I should know the answers. "I'm sure her oncologist can explain further." He quickly walks away before I can demand any more answers.

Wednesday, Rene and I were fighting in a rainstorm over the death of our son and our marriage. Here it is Friday, and she's fighting for her life. It's frustrating because there's nothing I can do. Still so much I don't even understand. Still so much she won't tell me.

My hand throbs from thinking about how much life has changed within the past couple of weeks. Reminds me how I sent it crashing through a window because life got very complicated. Nothing in life is promised. What's the point of marriage, saying vows that no one remembers after the ceremony? Just words spoken for the sake of being spoken. I swear, at the rate we're going, the world will soon have more people getting divorced than there are death certificates being issued.

Sydney crosses my mind. Feels inappropriate to think about her at a time like this. I wonder what's going on in her home since we last saw each other. I'm sure her husband knows about us now. Another set of vows gone down in flames to add to statistics.

While the nurses prepare to move Rene to an area reserved for those teetering the lines of life and death, I step outside for fresh air. The moon is so bright I almost forget it's close to midnight. Such a clear sky. With all the stars out, you'd think the Universe was happy. I want to take a gun and shoot all the stars out of the sky like a game of Duck Hunt.

I pull the card out of my pocket the ER doctor gave me. Hospice. He wants me to call a place where people give up hope for miracles. My son died without a choice. No way I'm going to choose to give my wife to the afterlife.

I rip the card into a hundred pieces, tossing it into the trash on my way back inside to stand by my wife's side.

"Take me home," Rene whispers when I make it back to her bed.

I hold her hand, rub my warm thumb back and forth against her cold skin.

"I don't think that's a good idea."

She looks up at me with water framing her bulging eyes. "Please, Brandon. I don't want to be here."

*"There's nothing else we can do at this stage of her cancer."* The doctor's words come back to mind. I look at Rene's frail body lying under

a pound of blankets. She didn't want to come here in the first place. My ego made me send her nurse home. Thought I could love her back to health. She didn't need another man for that. Then her dry coughs became bloody. That's when things got scary. Fear left me no other option than to bring her here. I wasn't prepared for that, nor am I prepared for this.

"Get my phone," Rene instructs. "Look for William's number. Tell him I said to meet us at the house."

My voice cracks when he answers.


The house is empty. Everything that made this house a home is gone. "I can't believe somebody else will be living in here in less than a week," I say to no one in particular.

Rene slowly climbs the stairs, holding onto the rail with one hand and her nurse, William, with the other. They don't need me. Rene doesn't need me.

When William comes back down the stairs, I say, "Hey man, I—"

He interrupts my apology speech with a nod. "It's all part of the job," he says, letting bygones be bygones. "She wants you upstairs."

I push open the door to our bedroom. No furniture, no Rene. Same thing in the guestrooms. The only other room on this floor is the room our son had—which we never went in after he passed. I open the door to find my wife lying in his twin-sized bed. "Rene?"

She lifts the cover, invites me under his sheets with her.

I slide my shoes off and join her. Instead of lying in front of her, I slip in behind and wrap my arms around her, holding her with all my might.

"Can you feel him?" she asks.

I can. His presence is so overwhelming I can't even form my lips to tell her so.

"Every night, long after you'd gone to sleep, I'd come in here and just lay."

I don't know how to take that, so I say nothing. I just let her talk.

"For the longest, I could still smell him." A light chuckle makes her thin body shake against mine. "Remember how he loved to puff out half the container of baby powder and smear it on his chest?"

I smile in the darkness. "I remember."

"You started it when he was just a baby. It always got a giggle out of him."

"I wonder if he'd still do it now."

For a while, neither of us can muster up any more words. We lay and hold each other in the memory of our son in his bed.

A tender knock at the door breaks our silence. William walks in, asks Rene, "How are you feeling?"

"I'm still breathing."

"Not for long if you don't keep this in." He lifts a tube from the pillow, placing it around her head and up her nostrils. He checks her temp and pulse. Holds a cup of water with a straw in it up to her mouth. "Take these. They'll help you sleep better."

Before heading out of the room, he asks if I need anything.

I want to ask if he has something to help me sleep better. "I'm good," I say instead.

My wife rubs her hand back and forth against mine. "I'm glad you're here."

I take my hand from hers, turn her face toward mine. It's hard to look at her frailness so close, but I tell her what my heart has been feeling since the day we met. "There's no place I'd rather be."

A tear rolls from her eye and saturates her hairline. Then another. And another.

I kiss her tears. Kiss her eyes. Kiss her lips. I love this woman.

In between kisses and tears, I feel her voice. "I never should've pushed you away."

"Why did you?" I whisper back.

"Because I didn't want this."

I didn't want this either.

Rene says, "You remember a few years back, when I had a little meltdown after we made love?"

How could I forget? That was the night everything changed between us. "Yeah."

"I had found out that day about the cancer."

It all makes sense now.

"After Reggie left us, life didn't make sense anymore. Didn't seem like anything would last. Had watched my grandmother struggle with her cancer; my aunt, too. Then burying Mama and Daddy. I lost hope."

I kiss her shoulder. "Wish you had talked to me about it, told me something. Shutting down confused me."

"I know," she says, then lays her head on my chest, buries herself in my embrace.

I hold her and pray time stands still.

A cool draft pulls me out of the warmth of my dreams. My chest feels light. "Rene?"

No response.

I call out again.

It takes my eyes a little longer than normal to adjust to the darkness. Once they do, I see my wife balled up in the corner of our son's closet, trembling. I pull the covers off the bed, wrap them around her. "What are you doing in there?"

In her eyes is so much fear, so much regret. "I killed him. I killed Reggie."

"What did William give you?" I reach for the door to call the nurse up here.

Rene grabs my hand, stops me. "I fed him bad milk." She touches her chest. "From here."

Nothing's making sense. I want to pick her up from the floor and shake sense into her lips.

She stands up, holds my hands in hers. "I'm not crazy." She leads me over to the bed. We sit together. She picks up Reggie's favorite bear from the floor. Its nose is worn from years of Eskimo kisses. She rubs her finger across the spot where the nose should be before rubbing her own nose back and forth against it.

I touch her hand, touch the bear. Feel memories travel through my fingertips.

"About a week after we brought him home from the hospital, I couldn't get him to stop crying. I gave him a bottle, rocked him, walked him all through the house. Nothing would calm him down. My breasts began tingling, so I thought maybe I should try to breastfeed him. He latched on immediately. It hurt me at first, but since it calmed him down, I let him continue sucking. The same thing happened the next night. The more he did it, the more we both seemed to look forward to it. It seemed to be what both of us needed. We bonded." Her cheeks spread and she gives Bear another nose kiss.

"When he was around six months, we were having another bonding session. He had his hand on my breast. I put my hand on top of his, then gave him a kiss on his forehead. That made him stop sucking to give me a quick smile, then he went back to business. I held his hand in mine for a minute, rubbing his soft skin with the pad of my thumb. I put his hand back on my breast and watched him drift to sleep. That was when I felt it. The lump. I slowly slid my nipple from his mouth and patted him over my shoulder until I heard a burp. I lay him in his crib and practically ran to the hall bathroom. I touched my breast again to see if I had really felt a lump. It was still there. The next night, I fed him from my breast again. What kind of mother does that?"

"Rene, look at me. You didn't kill him, if that's what you're trying to say."

"But I had a lump in my breast and every night I fed my child from it like it was normal. I didn't even get it checked out."

A mixture of emotions flood through my veins. Anger being the main one. "How could you not go to the doctor, Rene?"

"I was scared."

"Well, why didn't you tell me?"

"I was scared."

Her fear didn't change the outcome, didn't change the lump in her breast. I tell her just that. "And we're still here."

"You're right, we still are."

The truth is Eric broke my heart a long time ago. Long before I had even thought about walking away from our marriage. It was months after we began dating seriously. We'd already had sex. Had already met both sides of the family. We were moving in the direction where a future together is undeniable. The first time I'd said those infamous three words, we had just finished a late night run. Adrenaline was pumping, pheromones were riding the night's sky. In the middle of stretching, the words slipped out. I'd actually felt good saying them. It felt right. He didn't say anything back. He was bent over in a deep hamstring stretch. When he looked up and our eyes connected, I searched his face for any indication that he heard me. He blinked, asked if I was ready to head home. Outside of the radio, the car was in complete silence. He didn't say anything about me putting my feelings out there. Didn't say he felt the same way back. I knew he heard me.

Almost a year later, he finally said those three words back. It was well past the other side of midnight when a call from him woke me out of a crazy dream. Though pissed at the late call, I was relieved to be back to reality. His voice was just as breathy as mine, sounded desperate. I quickly gave him my full attention. He needed me to come to the hospital. He'd been shot. Twice. His shoulder blade and gun hand. He was on his way home after pulling a double shift when he was almost hit by a car speeding through a red light. It was late at night with barely any traffic, made it obvious a maniac was on the road. Eric flipped his patrol car around and hightailed after Speedracer. The car pulled over almost immediately after seeing flashing blue lights in his rearview. Eric didn't call it in, didn't run the plates. Just got out his car and marched up to a tinted-out window. When the driver refused to roll down his window, Eric gripped his gun a little tighter. The driver swung open his door, fired at Eric's hand on his gun and ran to the front of the car, fired another shot before running off into the night. He didn't want to kill Eric, he just didn't want Eric to kill him. The shooter was a bipolar ex-cop off his meds. Was having a manic episode. Thought the Force was after him and needed to protect his sanity, not realizing he'd already crossed the line of insanity. He'd made a bad decision, thinking he could handle his mental illness on his own.

Being shot made Eric realize that when it all boiled down to it, I was the only one he knew would be there. He'd called me in the midnight hour to be by his side before going into surgery. He needed me. He wanted me there. It took close to two years and two bullets for him to utter the words, "I love you." He changed my life in a moment of desperation. Another moment when my presence in his life was convenient for him. He couldn't say it back when I said it, couldn't say it at any other time. Had to clear his conscience before going into surgery, after his life flashed before his eyes.

It's times like that that force you to make an honest confession to yourself. I had spent the bulk of my relationship with Eric trying to prove to him that I was worthy of his attention, his love, his future.

I was competing with myself, the me I would be if he decided someone else was worth his time instead of me. I was competing with his options by making sure I was his only option, the only one he'd want to be with. I wanted him to forget about the woman before me. If giving him what was between my legs was the key, I was going to give him the best sex he'd ever had. I cooked him some of his best meals. I bought him the best gifts. Whenever he wanted me around, I was there. I tried to sell myself to his family, knowing good and well I'd never win over his mother. But I tried. Sometimes it felt like his heart was just as cold toward me as his mother's. Still, I decided I was going to put my best offer on the table, hoping one day he'd sign on the dotted line. I, too, acted out of desperation when I looked in the mirror and saw the possibility of my life resembling the same lonely life as my mother's.

In the end, we all do what we need to do to make our life be what we want it to be. We put our hopes and dreams on the line for the sake of making someone else happy, for making it convenient for the next person. We make the wrong decisions, hoping one day they'll turn out right. And when they don't, well, we just keep on making wrong decisions.

Whether Rachel is right about what I'm doing with Brandon—building something—I know what I feel and it feels far from wrong.

Six miles later, my legs feel like they've been dipped in hell.

I should've given him the letter. Should've just given him the damn letter and moved on a long time ago. I wouldn't have had to explain my feelings because I'd be long gone, in some faraway place, building a new life with someone else.

No matter how fast or how much harder I run, I can't seem to outrun the thoughts chasing down my sanity. This is not the time to lose it, Syd.

I pick my pace up to an eight-minute and one-second speed, shave thirty-one seconds off my normal pace. Pound the pavement hard enough to leave my size eight-and-a-half ASICS' impression in the concrete. Been running for a little over an hour. My smartphone's running app tells me that. Tells me I've put over eight miles on these thighs. I come to a halt, bend over a patch of grass. I dry heave for a few seconds too long to count. Nothing but air. Then it all comes out. The bile from my failing marriage, from being the woman that my friends look down on, the woman who's gone half crazy trying to put it all together while falling apart, all of that comes up from my pit and gushes from my lips like a fire hydrant being released for maintenance. My high levels of frustration, anger, regret, consideration of adultery and then some have built up to the point my soul can't tolerate another drop. I hurl some more, soil the earth with my pain and tears.

"Are you okay?"

I wipe residue from my mouth with my shirt, turn around and see a car pulled over to the side. A female's head hanging out the passenger window.

"You need me to call nine-one-one?"

I wave my hand. "No, I'm—" Another wave of bile flows from my mouth, feels like a barrel of cayenne pepper's lodged in my throat; burns my esophagus.

Now there are three cars pulled over. Someone runs up behind me. "Drink this."

I look at the half-empty bottle of Gatorade sideways. "No, thank you. I'm really okay," I tell the guy.

"You're dehydrated. You need something."

I give the stranger a once-over. He's in spandex and a soaked T-shirt. Looks like he just finished a workout himself. He needs to replenish his electrolytes, yet he's concerned about mine. I grab the extended bottle from his hand and say a quick silent prayer over the lemon-flavored drink. Down it in one long gulp. "Thanks."

"I've been there before. Ran my first marathon a few years ago and almost died from dehydration."

Lacking energy, all I can do is nod.

"Are you running alone?"

I nod again, mouth "thank you" to the other drivers as they slowly pull away.

"Do you live near here? I can drop you off."

None of the houses around me look familiar. I ask, "What street is this?"

"Putney Road. Not too far from Hillside Boulevard."

It dawns on me where I am. I spent the night at Mom's after Eric came home hours after his regular time, smelling like he'd drunk a gallon of tequila. The kids had already been at her house. I brought them over a few days ago to give Eric and me a little space to try to figure things out without them getting in the way. What good that did. I tell the guy, "Thanks for all your help, but I'll be fine."

He gives me a look that lets me know he's not buying it.

Again, I thank him and begin a slow jog in the opposite direction. I jog far enough to ensure the man is long gone, then I turn back around and walk toward my mom's house. I may have been crazy enough to drink from a drank-on bottle from a stranger, but I'm not crazy enough to lead him to my mother's house, especially not in such a weakened state. I'm too weak to fight off a ladybug at this point, let alone another person.

I walk past my emotions stenching up the ground. Almost makes me hurl again. It looks like I let go of a week's worth of food and years' worth of misunderstandings and lies. I feel much better letting all of that go. Physically and emotionally.

My stomach does a few tumbles. I swear Gabrielle Douglas is in there flipping around for another gold medal. It amazes me how much we allow ourselves to hold on to for the sake of looking like we've got our lives together.

No more of that.

A door has been opened and misery is finally taking a step out.

*B*ack at my apartment, I get things situated for Rene's arrival. She didn't want to stay at my place originally, but I told her she had no choice.

A knock at the door disrupts my flow.

I look through the peephole, see Sydney standing by the stairway. I open the door.

She comes in, takes a seat on the couch. "How's your hand?"

I look at my hand, rub my fingers across it. "Almost all of the stitches have fallen off. Still feels a little stiff, but better."

I move a pile of clothes from the couch to give her more room. Toss them on my bed in the room. Tell her, "Rene's going to be staying here once she hands over the keys to the house."

"That'll be in a few days."

"Don't remind me."

Sydney asks, "How's she feeling?"

I shrug. "She's had better days. We plan to get her into one of those cancer treatment facilities."

"Oh good. That'll be great."

"Yeah." I sit next to her on the edge of the couch, sit with my elbows pressed into my knees. "Look, I've been wanting to talk to you."

"I've been wanting to talk to you too."

I say, "My wife changed. I thought it was me. Then you came. Things aren't the way I thought." I flick at a peeling bandage on my hand. "I think it's best we stop here."

"You're right." She bobs her head up and down. "I totally agree."

"Seeing my wife all broken made me realize it was never about me. Maybe talking to your husband, you'll see things differently too."

Sydney asks to use the restroom.

"You know the way."

Something about her being here throws me off. Before she came over, I was sure about my stance about us. There could never be an us. I still have a chance to love the only woman I've ever loved, whether it's short-lived or for another decade. I'm not letting her go or risking this opportunity for anyone.

"Hey, Brandon." Sydney stands in front of me. "You're really a good guy. Wish I had met you sooner, maybe then I wouldn't be so confused about my life right now. It's obvious you truly love your wife. I don't want to be the one to jeopardize that in any way. I hope she gets better."

As much hope as I have in my wife getting better, the reality is she's dying. There's nothing that can be done, no treatment facility for her to go to. No magic eraser to wipe her disease away. Lying to myself and everyone else makes me feel a little better, gives me a taste of hope. But this is it. No lie can change that. "I can't lose my wife."

Sydney wraps her arms around me. "You won't. Everything's going to be okay."

I've been trying to hold it together since Rene first told me about the cancer. Been beating myself up like I was the one holding secrets, like I'm the one who put the lump in her breast. All I did was love a woman, marry her, was fruitful and multiplied. What was so wrong in that?

My good hand slides down Sydney's waist, lands on her hip. Stays there a little too long, long enough to feel her hip curve against my hand.

She stands in between my legs and looks down at me. There's no regret in her eyes for the way she feels toward me. If this was another lifetime, we'd be sharing space as husband and wife. Not Eric and her. Not Rene and me. She reaches for my hand, pulls me up.

I kiss her.

She doesn't pull back. She looks at me as our lips touch, welcoming all my hurt, pain and moment of weakness into her mouth.

We kiss long, slow, deep.

I welcome her frustration, confusion, and moment of weakness into my mouth. My tongue loses itself in the unfamiliarity of her kiss. Try to lose myself in the unfamiliarity of her touch.

I rake my fingers through her hair, pull her face deeper into mine. Her kiss is soothing yet gritty at the same time, holds a yearning that demands my attention.

She tugs at my jeans.

I tug at her shorts. Tell her, "You'll go home another woman."

"Is that a promise?"

My response is putting my lips back on hers. Finding my tongue doing the salsa with hers.

She raises my shirt up over my head, tosses it to the side. Traces her fingers up and down my spine, tries to become familiar with my unfamiliarity. I do the same with the fingertips of my good hand to the lips between her thighs. Her wetness warming up the coolness of my touch. My finger finds its way into her hunger as our tongues continue making love to each other. My stirs in her womanly place makes her bite down on my tongue.

"Sorry," she says, barely able to catch her breath.

Though my tongue throbs, I don't stop making her throb down below. She wraps her leg around my waist, letting my finger go deeper. Her hand has a firm grip on the back of my neck, the other rubbing my thickening manhood. Her lips graze my ear. "I wanna go home a different woman."

I get so lost I can't think of nothing else. I want to be so far inside her my wife and her husband are no longer a concern of ours.

She sits down on the floor, lifts her shirt up over her head. Legs wide open.

My knees hit the floor, in between her legs my hips go. Her bra comes off next. Hardened nipples dance against my chest.

I continue playing in her wet spot with my fingers, she rubs her hands on her breasts, tickles her nipples. Takes her pleasure to another level. Eyes roll to the back of her head as she reaches back down to help escort me into her heat. Needs me to help extinguish the fire growing in her soul. She teeters between consciousness and ecstasy, but her high quickly comes down when she sees my fire's gone out. Her leg slides down from my waist, feet touch the floor. Her eyes full of questions and a hint of insecurity.

"I'm sorry. I can't do this."

"What's wrong?" she pants.

I pick her shirt up off the floor, hand it to her. "You need to go."

"*H*ormones are crazy like that," I tell my brother over a couple of beers. "They distort your conscience and make you unconcerned with reality."

Andrew lifts his beer in the air. "I'll drink to that."

I take a swig myself. "I almost slept with another man's wife while my wife is barely hanging on to life. I mean, man, what if he's tipping out on her too? He could've brought home a disease, and there I was about to lie with her with no protection. Had Sydney not taken off her bra and had her breasts all in my face, you and I would be having a different conversation."

"Damn."

"I never wanted to, or even thought about, cheating on Rene. She was enough for me. And the one moment when she needs my loyalty the most, I do some mess like this."

He shakes his head. "Can't believe you went there."

"Me either."

My reflection in the bar's mirror makes me choke on my beer. I don't recognize the man staring back at me. Don't recognize who I've become. "I'm losing it, Drew."

My twin throws a few dollars down on the counter. "Let's go outside."

We stand against the passenger side of his car. Man to man, brother to brother.

"I know you think what I did was wrong."

"And you don't?"

"Of course I do, but it's more to it than that. My feelings toward Rene changed a long time ago. She was being an absent wife, treating our marriage like it was something I dreamt up. After a while, I got tired of trying. I started pulling away. I met Sydney. Then found out Rene's truth. She never fell out of love with me. She just didn't know how to love me and live with her diagnosis." I take a deep breath. "Man, I love Rene something serious, and what happened earlier with Sydney made me realize that I'm going to have to move on from the only love I've ever known."

"I wish you would've come to me before running to the next man's wife."

I scowl at my brother. "Is there something you need to say?"

"I said it. I don't feel like you're making the right decisions."

"You lose your child *and* your wife and tell me what kind of decisions you'd make. Oh wait, you and your wife can't even have a child."

"That was low, real low." He shakes his head and starts walking down the street.

"Hold up." I run up behind him. "You're right, Drew. That was a low blow."

He's still shaking his head. "I swear, sometimes, you were conceived in another womb."

"Cut me some slack, damn. I'm losing my wife and right now I feel like I'm losing me." I throw my fists at the wind.

"Last time you went tossing your fists around, you ended up with stitches."

I feel like I'm in the ring against my will. Feel like someone's got my feet and hands tied to a string, trying to get me to take down a man who looks just like me. Got me taking hits at his emotions, principles, his will and determination. They're trying to get me to break myself down in the worst way and succeeding.

We walk back to the car in silence. Before we get in, I say, "Is it possible to hate and love someone at the same time?"

He plops his arms on the roof of his car, ponders the question a little longer than I expected. "Nope. Can't say it's possible. You can't have love if you have hate."

I get in the car, give myself a second to my thoughts. So many things going through my head it's hard to keep up or sort things out on my own.

Andrew gets in, revs up the V6. "Where'd that come from?"

Since Rene told me about her finding the lump while Reggie was just an infant, I've kinda had some different thoughts toward her. No, I don't think she's the reason he passed away, but I do blame her for her present condition. Had she gone to the doctor back then, terminal cancer might not have been her diagnosis. I tell my brother, "I feel like Rene brought this on herself, and all the while making me feel like less of a husband, less of a man in the process."

"Wow. That's a lot to hold inside, Brandon."

"And there's nothing I can do about it now."

When Andrew comes to a stop at a red light, he looks over at me. "Do you know how much time she has left?"

Luckily the light turns green and he can't see the despair in my eyes when I say, "Any day now."

I pull up to the front gate to the subdivision I called home with my wife for the past seven years. Recognizing my truck, the meddlesome security guard comes out of the hut and waves my way. I keep my window up this time, wave behind the glass and keep it moving. Won't let him add any salt to my growing wound. I drive around winding streets until I'm parked in the familiar driveway. Sydney's smiling face still sitting in the front yard with the word *Sold* plastered on top.

There was a time when I'd open the garage and see Rene's car with a carseat in the back. It would fill my heart to know my wife and son were in the house, filling it with laughter and love. Tonight, when I open the garage with the opener I never got rid of, Rene's car is nowhere to be found and the carseat went missing a long time ago. So many changes in just a short amount of time.

I enter the house to a deadening silence. In a couple of days, it will be filled with new owners. New voices, new problems to invade this house and make it a home. Walking through the coldness of a home I left months ago, you'd never know it was once filled with warmth. It's so cold in here I feel like I'm in a morgue. I guess I am. Three people died in here.

Reggie's room is the first place I go in once I make it upstairs. A few nights ago, his bed, his clothes, all his toys, even his spirit was still in here. Don't know how his mother was able to come in here every night long after I'd gone to sleep. Being in here for one minute was hard enough for me. Every minute after that, staying in here dug deeper into my core. He was my son. He was part of me. Now all of that is gone. As I stand in the memory of the short life we shared together, I swear I feel his arms wrap around my waist. "I miss you, Reg."

The next room I enter is the one I shared with my wife. It's the room our beloved son was created in many moons ago. It's the room we held each other in as tears consumed us as that same son was no longer a part of our lives. It's the same room my wife lost herself in and killed our marriage in.

There's nothing in here but memories. The heaviness of all that was lost weighs me down, causes me to lose my balance. My knees hit the floor so hard it sounds like the space shuttle soaring back into the earth's atmosphere. Major parts of my life, major people in my life will one day become fading memories in my life. Reggie and Rene will soon reside in the recesses of my mind.

Being surrounded by the emptiness of this place, the loneliness carves a hole in my heart, and makes me wonder, *How am I going to move on from this?*

*H*ow do you look into the eyes of a dying woman when you know less than twenty-four hours ago you tried to save *your* life by sleeping with *her* husband?

My nerves do their best at keeping my attention. As I reach for a copy of the HUD-1 statement to look at while the lawyer goes over the facts, my hand taps a glass of water and makes a puddle in the middle of the table. I grab the papers before anything can get wet. "I'm so sorry about that."

Rene's eyes peer up at me, I see them in my peripheral vision as my eyes are on the man sitting next to her. He reaches for the roll of paper towels in the middle of the table. He unrolls several sheets, dabs at the mess I've made.

"Thank you."

"Good thing it wasn't coffee," the lawyer says.

I give him a half-smile. I wasn't expecting to see Brandon this morning. I knew there was a possibility of him showing up, but with his name being nowhere on any of the documents, and with what went down yesterday on his living room floor, didn't think he'd want to put that tension in the air. Then again, maybe the only tension I feel is what's tugging at my heart.

Brandon stares at me, I can feel his eyes on me. Can feel him analyzing me, trying to see if I'm going to break under the guise of my attempt of having some control over the situation. A situation his wife has no inkling of. Or maybe she does, because I feel her eyes on me too.

"This is a statement swearing you have the right to sell your home." The lawyer tells her as he passes over the Certificate of Title to look over and sign.

I glance up at Brandon. I don't want to feel like this. I want to be mad at him for how he left me. Handed my shirt to me and told me I had to go. Left me wet and exposed. Why couldn't he tend to my need then as he did to the water that almost soaked the closing documents on the home he shared with his wife a moment ago? Had he just finished what I started, there wouldn't be this feeling of unfinished business stifling this business deal. I know he feels the same way, know he wishes he would have sealed the deal. He doesn't have to say it. It's in his eyes.

A hand lands on top of mine, a voice in my ear, "You okay?"

The pen in my hand tapping the table enough to annoy a woodpecker. Nerves taking over once again. I nod at the lawyer who's been in the room with me one too many times to know I'm not myself. I can't muster the words, so I nod and place the pen on the table. There's no need for me to have a pen anyway. I'm not here to sign anything. My purpose of being here is to support my client in the selling of their home. What support I'm actually giving Rene at this point is debatable.

Why can't I shake this? This is not me. Tapping the pen like someone who's downed five energy drinks in five seconds. Spilling water, nearly making a mess of official documents. Feels like the whole room is looking at me. Feels like they can see me falling apart in a seat I've sat in too many times to count.

My eyes close. I press my fingers to my temples, rub them in circular motions. Not that I have a headache. I'm trying to channel Princess Aura and send my Flash Gordon a telepathic message. *Why'd you have to ask me to help you run? Why'd you make me laugh, make me feel appreciated, desired? Why'd you let my vulnerability cross your threshold?* "Why'd you leave me this way?"

A throat clears.

I open my eyes, find that all eyes *are* on me. Something tells me my telepathic messages weren't so telepathic. The first person I look at is Brandon, the cause of my current dysfunction. He looks at his wife. His wife looks at him, her eyes penetrate him so deep I feel like they're dissecting my soul.

"I think you need to step out for a minute, get yourself together," the lawyer says to me as discreetly as possible. "Ms. Ortiz, if I can direct your attention to the bill of sale."

"I know the documents say Ortiz and I have to sign as such, but I'd prefer it if you called me Mrs. Carter."

I don't have to look back as I walk out the door to know her request is directed at me.

Rene is silent as we drive out of the parking lot to the law office.

I don't know what happened back there. Don't know how much she sensed from Sydney's breakdown. Not sure what sense I can make of it.

*"Why'd you leave me this way?"*

The crazy part is I'm not sure what sense to make of how I felt sitting in the same room with my wife and the woman who's given me more attention than my wife over the past few months. I wanted to reach across the table, grab Sydney's hand. Wanted to tell her I was sorry for kicking her out of my place, for rejecting what she had to offer. It was something we both wanted. Something we both needed. But I couldn't cross that line. As much as I felt I was ready to, it didn't feel right. I'm just trying to figure out why I feel bad for honoring my vows.

"Are you sure you want to do this?" I ask a few lights down from our next order of business for the day.

"You do what you have to do, right?"

Okay, that wasn't the best question to ask. I deserved her response. Yeah, we *do* do what we have to, even if sometimes it's not what we *want* to do. I drive around to the back of the building, a place I can count on one hand how many times I've been here.

Rene doesn't wait for me to come around to her side of the car and open the door for her. Though her movements are slow and it takes quite a bit of effort, this is something she wants to do on her own. She uses her key to unlock the door. I honor her need for independence. This is her business. She built it after her parents' deaths. It was her dedication to them and so many who'd gone before them whose images weren't honored properly.

The smell of death slaps me in the face with reality. I don't want to be here, don't want to go through this with her. In a matter of time, she will be here, lying on the table, having done to her what she's done to so many others who've gone on before her.

There's a body on the table. We're on the other side of the room, watching through a window, the same window I watched her through months ago, before I knew this was the reason our marriage was falling apart. Her assistant, Peter, sprays the body down, prepares them for the next step in their final moments on this side of life.

For a moment, Rene stands still, stands in her reality. She doesn't blink, doesn't talk. Doesn't breathe.

I watch my wife through blurred eyes. This is our reality. "You don't have to be here."

She jumps at the sound of my voice. Fear lies in her eyes. "I don't have a choice." She pushes with a newfound strength into the room with the man who will soon be hosing her down, preparing her for her final chapter.

Ever since finding out Rene has cancer, I've been concerned with how it's affected me. How it's made me feel not knowing all these years she was battling something on her own that she should've been able to turn to me to help her fight. Not once have I considered how she feels. She's the one who has cancer. She's the one who's got a disease eating its way through her body. She's the one leaving, the one who has to say goodbye. How could I have been so selfish?

Watching her put on her white coat, eye goggles, gloves, the same things she's put on so many times over the past few years, I know this time holds a different meaning. She's had to do this since learning her time on earth had been shortened, but as she grows more ill, as her diagnosis forces her to take notice, she knows this *is* her last time.

Rene places an incision in the body's neck. As blood drains out, another substance fills its place.

I turn away.

Can't watch this.

Peter wraps his arm around Rene's waist as he helps her up the stairs to her office. They don't see me sitting here in the dark, where I've been since emptying enough food into the toilet to feed the disciples at The Last Supper.

I brush my hands down my thighs as I give myself strength to stand. Today has been a day of more than I can handle. My emotions have done their job of overtaking the control I once thought I had. I go back into the restroom, fill my hands with cold water, toss it on my face. Do that a couple of times before patting myself dry with paper towels. I can't bear looking at my image in the mirror. Back in the hallway, I hold on to the rail as I climb the staircase to see what Rene and Peter are discussing. Sometimes, you do what you have to do, even if it's the very thing that'll break you.

Rene's handing Peter a picture when I walk into her office. "I want to look just like that."

He nods my way, acknowledges my presence. Says to her, "And you know you will look just like that," then gets up to give me a hug. "You hanging in there, Brandon?"

I hug him back. "Considering the circumstances."

"I know it's hard."

Rene gets up from behind her desk, walks over to the cabinet by the door. Opens it and pulls out a bottle of clear liquid. Pours a hefty serving in a glass. "Anybody else?" she asks, holding the bottle of vodka in the air.

Peter reaches for a glass and passes one my way without checking to see if I want a drink or not. What the hell, why not? I grab the glass.

Behind her desk, Rene looks to the man who's been by her side in this business since a year after it opened. "I hate that I'll have to turn over the keys to this place. It's the second baby I have to say goodbye to." She lets her eyes reminisce with mine when she says that. "There's no one more deserving, more passionate about this business, more fitting than you."

"What I hate is having to run this place without you." His voice breaks.

Rene reaches her hand across the desk for Peter's hand. He meets hers halfway. They squeeze each other's hand, give each other a strength and support that only the two of them can share. So many times they've had to watch others break down in front of them. Now it's their turn to shed tears over what they'll be losing. Business partners and a special friendship.

When my wife was made aware this day was unavoidable, she asked if I had any desire of taking over the business. I didn't have to think about it. There was no desire to do any such thing. It was her baby, her passion, her vision. I wanted to keep it just that. Plus, I didn't want to attach to anything I didn't need to attach to. I was glad to tell her I'd pass. I knew she only extended it as a courtesy. She had every intention of passing it on to her friend.

"I know I'm leaving DelCosta in great hands."

Peter nods. "Nothing will change."

Her eyes find me again, they peer over the glass in her hand as she takes a nice-sized sip of her drink.

I know Rene's not dumb. Her attitude hasn't been the same since leaving the closing of our home. A corpse could feel the tension in that room, could hear and see there was something going on between her realtor and me. She's treating me like she did before she received her death sentence. I did what I had to do, even though it wasn't what I wanted to do. All I ever wanted was to love my wife until the end of time. Just happens her time is ending a lot sooner than I was ready for.

"Brandon, will you give us a moment?"

I step out of the office to give them space. Whatever Rene thinks went down with me and her realtor is one thing, but I'm grateful she has enough compassion in her heart to spare me of having to hear the final details for her service.

I want to go back in there and ask her what Sydney asked me. *"Why'd you leave me this way?"*

"Do you love him?"

"We really don't know each other."

Mom throws the wet dishrag in the dishwater, turns to look at me. "I'm talking about your husband, Sydney Marie." So much disappointment in her voice.

Words fail me in my embarrassment. Thoughts of Brandon dominate thoughts of anything else at the moment. Can still feel his lips on mine, his hands on my skin. Can still feel the coldness I felt when he handed me my clothes and left me to sort through what we did and didn't do in the middle of his living room floor. All the shame and embarrassment I felt after leaving my job with my job undone won't leave me. Brandon saturates me. So much of that is unsatisfactory.

I tell my mom, "I'm not sure love is enough anymore." Just like with my friends, I avoid telling her my husband's love for me is just as unsure.

She rolls her eyes up to the ceiling, fights hard to keep tears from drowning her own pain from my father's infidelity. "Have you thought about how this will affect EJ and Kennedy?" Her head shakes as she answers her own question. "Obviously, you haven't. You don't do stupid stuff like that. You have it good, you don't just mess up a family like that."

I have no response. It is what it is.

Coming here was a mistake. I should've just gone home and faced my demons without involving anyone else, especially my mother. Her emotional connection to betrayal is too strong. I get up from my seat and stand behind her at the sink. Wrap my arms around her waist, whisper in her ear, "I'm sorry, Mama."

In some way, my apology is not only for me, but for the pain my father caused her as well.

Her posture stiffens. "I'm not the one you need to be apologizing to."

No one seems to accept my apologies anymore. Not my husband, not my mama.

She breaks away from my embrace, puts some distance between us. "How could you do it?"

"I can't answer that."

"Yes, you can. You just choose not to."

My mother stands and stares at me until her eyes penetrate my thoughts long enough for an answer to form.

I speak what I feel, tell her the same things I've been saying to Eric the past few weeks. "I mentally left our marriage a long time ago. Brandon's arrival in my life just proved how unhappy I've been and I've been denying that truth to myself all these years."

Mom puts her hand in the air. "Spare me the details."

"It's the truth."

A tear runs down her face making a loud splat on the hardwood floors. "You're just like your father. Both of you always run from your problems and run into someone else like that's going to solve everything."

"Oh no, no, no, no, no. Don't even compare me to him. This is not the same situation."

She sits down in the chair I had been sitting in. "Do you know why your father cheated on me?"

I shake my head, pull out another chair from under the table.

"I was his mistress."

It's hard for me to not let the shock on my face come across as judgment.

"Yes, that's right. Your father cheated on his first wife with me. He wasn't happy with her. Said she was very insecure and would always accuse him of cheating, though at the time, he was just as faithful as a dog, ironically. She would call him on the job every five minutes, sometimes showing up because she didn't believe he was out of the office as much as his secretary claimed. One day, he had enough of being the opposite of what kind of man she thought he was. I ended up being his convenient escape. I worked at a diner he'd frequent for lunch. Soon, our conversations traveled beyond pleasantries and orders of pot roast. He was flirty, entertaining. Gave me lots of compliments. Said I was sweet and interesting. Both of us were to each other what our spouses were not. Before long, lunch turned into quickies in the back of his car."

I cut her off. "Whoa, so you're up here condemning me making out, while you ditched work for sex in the backseat of a car?" I swallow her bitter confession with a scrunched up facial expression to match.

"Go ahead, judge me all you want, Sydney. But eventually, I ended my relationship and he divorced his wife. We made it right. We got married. We had you."

"Please help me understand where you're going with this confession, because you're losing me fast."

She looks at me with crooked eyebrows, looks at me in a way that says she wishes I was still a child so she could take a belt to my backside for not minding my manners. "The point I'm trying to make is your father ran from the problems in his first marriage without resolving the real issues. I was everything for him. Cooked, cleaned, helped him with his construction business. Had bathwater ready for him when he got home, a hot meal on the table. He didn't want for anything."

My cell phone vibrates in my purse on the table. I grab it, make sure it's not the school or daycare. See Rachel's name displayed on the screen. Hit the red button to ignore.

"Like I was saying," Mom continues, "I was a convenient escape for him. Made life too easy, to the point I didn't realize he was slipping away from me and back into the arms of his ex-wife."

Convenience seems to be a familiar occurrence with men. Eric says I was the same thing for him. I say, "Well, they say how you get your man is how you lose your man."

She swallows the truth with a hard gulp. "And that's exactly what I'm trying to get you to understand. I never told you about why your father cheated because I knew I was in the wrong from the beginning. We get caught up in the moment and make lifetime mistakes. I don't want to see you end up like me."

There's so much pain coupled with regret in my mother's eyes when I look at her. "Why'd you stay as long as you did?"

My phone interrupts us again. Rachel again. And again I press the red button for ignore.

"You need to get that?" Mom asks.

I wave my hand in the air. "I'm listening to you right now."

"To answer your question, I never left. He started stepping out a few months after you were born. I hadn't worked since getting fired from my waitressing job at the diner. I had no money and had to worry about another mouth to feed. Just made sense to stay. In the end, he left me."

"Jeez, Mom." All these years I've had it all wrong. Always blamed my mom for leaving my dad and making me decide who I wanted to spend my summers and holidays with. Dad always made himself out to be the victim, acting like his love had always been for my mom. Several times, he used me to get back into her life and make us the family we should've been. Mom shut it all down.

"I never meant to mislead you, Sydney. I didn't know how to deal with the truth." She softly grabs my hand from my lap. "No matter what his wife is or isn't doing in their marriage, isn't up to you to fix. Same thing goes for him. He can't be who Eric isn't."

I tell my mom, "His wife has cancer. She's dying."

Her grip loosens from my hand. "Ohhh, Sydney. That makes it worse."

The first time I stood in front of my lover's wife—well, I don't know if I can even call him that—she was no different than any other person wanting to sell their home. Had I known she was Mrs. Carter, as she so sternly reminded me, I'm actually not so sure I would've done anything different. Quite possibly, I would've handed the contract to another realtor in our office. Would've done that before considering walking away from her husband, even if he did have higher morals than me, enough for him to decline my offer for a way out. Granted, she would still have cancer and her death would be imminent, and he would have to put the pieces back together, but at least my distraction would've given him another way to look at it. Another way to handle things. Who have I become?

I swallow the guilt. "I know."

She stands up, goes back in the kitchen, back to a sink full of dirty dishes.

I follow her.

She looks at me over her shoulder. "You really need to be honest with yourself, because a man should never be the source of your happiness. And another woman's husband definitely won't be able to do that for you. As for your marriage, you're either going to make it work or move on. Either way, you have a big decision to make; a decision I hope doesn't leave you as empty as my decisions left me."

There's nothing left to say. I grab my purse and head to my car.

Soon as I get inside, I dig out my phone. See Rachel left a message. I debate checking it, but end up tapping in five digits to retrieve the message anyway.

*"There's been an accident."*

*M*y heart's racing as I speed through traffic like I'm being pursued in a high-speed chase. Rachel didn't say much in her message. Just said our husbands had been in a car accident and that she was on her way to the hospital.

I'm doing my best not to panic as my thoughts race faster than the odometer. What were Michael and Eric doing together? He was supposed to be picking Kennedy up from school and EJ from daycare. They were to grab pizza and meet me back at the house. Rachel didn't mention anything about the kids.

Soon as I pull into a parking space, my feet hit the ground running for the Emergency Room. I hit the nurse's desk so hard feels like my kneecaps crumble. "I was told my husband was brought here."

The nurse barely makes eye contact when she asks for his name.

"Eric, Eric Holmes. Are my kids here? Kennedy and Eric Jr.?"

"Sydney." A hand grasps my shoulder.

I turn around, see my friend standing there with red-rimmed eyes and an even redder nose.

"The kids weren't with them."

"Where are they?"

"I don't know." A tear drops from her eye.

"Okay, okay." I pull her into me, give her a warm embrace. My kids' location isn't her concern, especially while her husband is lying up in a hospital bed. Though I have no idea where my kids are at this moment, I'm relieved to know they weren't involved in the accident. At least that much I do know. "Let's not worry about them right now. How are the guys?"

She dabs at the corners of her eyes with her fingertips. "Michael's in stable condition. They're bandaging him up now to be released."

I let out a sigh of relief. "That's good to know."

By the slight smile in her lips, I can tell she's relieved as well, but her eyes tell a different story. "Eric's, umm…"

"Eric's what?" My heart slows to a turtle's pace.

"He was, umm, he was unconscious when they got there. I don't know anything else."

"What do you mean unconscious? What the heck happened? I don't understand this."

She grabs my hand. "Let's go outside." I follow her eyes to the uniformed officers standing in the corner talking with a young lady, notepads and pens in hand.

Something's not adding up. I let her hand go, but follow her out the door.

"The accident is under investigation. Michael called me at the scene frantic when Eric wouldn't wake up. They were tailing some guy they thought was guilty of a crime. Michael said the driver slowed and was pulling over to the side of the highway when an eighteen-wheeler came out of nowhere. The truck jackknifed, clipping the backend of the suspect's car. Michael tried to avoid hitting the truck, but there was no way around it. They slammed sideways into the trailer."

I feel my knees buckle.

Tears flood from Rachel's eyes when her attention is drawn to something behind me. "Michael." She leaves me and tends to her bandaged-up husband.

I follow behind. Rub him on his shoulder. "You okay?"

He flinches his arm away from my touch. His eyes reek of disgust, matching the scowl on his lips. "You better pray to God Eric makes it through."

# 39
## BRANDON

It's been a week since Rene has been in my apartment. Seven days I've been living in hell.

A week ago, we packed up our son's things and donated all of it to a shelter for battered women and children. Every article of clothing, his linens, toys, every matchless sock. The only thing she wanted to keep was his noseless bear. We turned over the keys to the house, signed it over to a new family. Closed that chapter in our lives in more ways than one.

This week has been hard on her. Getting rid of the tangible things left from Reggie's life, handing over the keys to the house her parents purchased just before their unexpected death, signing over her funeral home business to her assistant. Loss after loss after loss, knowing the loss of your own life is on the line. It's enough to make anyone lose attachment from reality.

This week's been hard for me as well. Carrying around the guilt of what I did with Sydney. Though we didn't go all the way, it went far enough to go farther. I tried to tell Rene several times since. Every time I'd try, she'd grab the bear and turn away from me. It's like she knew, like she saw the confession in my eyes. The silent treatment on the way to the funeral home and the way she kept staring at me intently. I know she knows, but the selfish side of me can't let her leave this world without my truth because I wouldn't want to carry around the guilt for the rest of my life.

Guilt.

The reason we're here. Guilt resided in Rene's heart, made her think she was the reason our son met an early death. Guilt traveled from her heart and sat in her chest, built a home there. Sat there until it was no longer something that could be ignored. Had she just gone to the doctor when she first felt the lump, she could've gotten treatment and had a better chance for a long life. She let fear from watching her grandmother and aunt lose their breasts and eventually their lives render her the same demise. She let the guilt of our son's death lead her down the same path.

I love my wife. At the same time, she made major decisions without including me. I'm her husband and knew none of this. Knew none of her pain or the suffering she was experiencing. All I know is she made me feel less than a husband, father, and friend, and for that, there's no coming back. Even as she breathes her last breaths, I can't help this feeling of anger from staining my heart.

Rene shifts in the bed.

"You okay?"

She says nothing.

I rub her shoulder lightly. When there's no response, I rub a little harder. "Rene, are you in pain?"

"If you keep nudging me like that, I will be."

She hasn't been in the best of moods lately. One day, she's quiet, the next, she's biting my head off. Then there are days she just wants to be held. Today doesn't sound like it's going to be one of the latter days, but some things have been plaguing my mind since the night we shared in Reggie's room. Things that keep this angry side of me dominant. "I need answers."

She shuffles, turns away from me. "Can we talk about this to-morrow?"

I think about what she's asking. No matter how hard it is for me to say it, the words fall from my lips anyway. "You may not have tomorrow."

My wife's silence reminds me of how the last few years have been in our marriage. Unbearable.

My heart skips a beat, then skips two. All of a sudden, it feels like my heart's trying to pump blood for a village. "Rene?" I shake her.

"I'm still here," she says in a tone that lets me know I've struck a chord.

I wrap my arm around her waist, scoot her body closer to mine. Spoon her. "I didn't mean it like that, babe."

"But it's reality."

"Maybe so, but there's no need in me reminding you."

Her hand sweeps across mine a few times before resting on top.

My eyes close. Maybe now isn't the time for Q & A. Tomorrow may not come for her and I could wake up a widower. Right now is all that matters, and I want to make the best of it for both of us.

The sun peers through the blinds, tells me a new day is upon us. Slowly, my eyes open to embrace reality, see my wife's eyes staring back at me.

She blinks.

I smile. "Morning, beautiful."

"I'm sorry."

I thumb a tear running off course from her face. "For what?"

"For not letting you be my husband and for not being your wife."

Those words sit in the air like smoke in an unventilated room. I breathe them in, let them filter to my soul.

"What are you feeling?" she wants to know.

I don't answer right away. Need to make sure my words come from a place of love and understanding, not anger and blame.

She reaches under the covers, finds my hand, wraps her pinky around mine. A simple gesture with a lot of meaning.

"How did it get to this point?"

Her eyes stay focused on mine. "I beat it once. Thought I could beat it again."

My finger loosens its grip to hers. This is news to me. The way I feel right now, I want to knock out all the walls in this room with my fists. What would that solve, though? My wife's condition wouldn't change and the past would remain the same. Only difference is I'd probably be without my hands and that would just make me even madder.

"I should have told you," she says, jerking me from a place of anger.

"You think?"

"Brandon, I'm sorry."

Another apology to fill a void.

Her pinky hangs on to mine tighter, tries to bring life back to mine. "I was scared to go to the doctor at first. Didn't want to get the same results as my grandmother and aunt. I thought about my grandfather and my cousins; couldn't fathom leaving you and Reggie like that. He was getting older, starting to walk. He made life complete for us. I wanted to give you more babies, fill our house like we planned."

All I can do is watch my wife bare her truth as her eyes mirror the emotions flickering through mine.

"The lump was getting bigger. Didn't want to miss any more moments, so I went to the doctor. A mammogram was done and it confirmed my fears. A biopsy was done a few days later. When

I got the call, the first thing I did was call you at work. You'd gone to lunch and weren't answering your cell. By then, I had lost the courage to tell you."

I hate that she only tried to reach me twice before giving up and deciding to bear the pain alone. I don't tell her that. No need in making her feel any worse.

"My gynecologist told me breastfeeding can make cancer spread faster. I guess that's why the lump had grown from a pea to a grape in a couple of months."

She stops talking. Gets caught up in the unpleasant memories of the past three years of her life.

There's nothing I can say to alleviate her discomfort in this moment. I tighten my pinky around hers, hoping it helps in some way. It works.

"Reggie had just turned two when I began treatment. They removed the tumor, then I had radiation." She raises her nightgown and grabs my hand from under the covers. She takes my index finger and traces it across a long scar underneath her left breast curving upward.

My finger feels like it's being drawn across a freshly sharpened butcher knife. I quickly pull my finger back, look at it to make sure there's no blood. When I see Rene's brows turned inward, I realize I've made the wrong move.

She snatches her gown back down. "And you wonder why I've kept this to myself."

Seeing the anguish in her eyes, I want to take my actions back, but I can't. And neither can I find the words to apologize. "Where was I when these treatments were going on? Shouldn't I have been there to sign papers for your surgery?"

"Told them I was separated and told you I was going out of town for a conference for funeral directors and morticians. Checked myself into the hospital and did what I had to do. Two treatments a day for a week. I was making sure I'd be around for my boys." A tear balances on her eyelid before falling onto the pillow.

I toss the covers back, swing my legs to the side. Sit here fuming over the confession lingering in this room. How could I have missed all of this? What kind of husband have I been that my wife could get surgery and I not even know? I turn back around and ask her.

She sighs. "I went into work mode. Hid all of my emotions, even from myself. Just became numb to it all. It became my second job."

I look down at my finger, remember it rubbing across her scarred flesh. "How come I never saw the scar?"

"I get paid to make death look pretty. The scar was nothing a little makeup couldn't handle."

"But what about when we'd shower or make love? Wouldn't it sweat off?"

"Waterproof. Sweatproof. Idiotproof."

That last proof was meant for me. "Kick a man when he's down, why don't you."

"They make it for burn victims, people with severe acne scars to make them feel better about themselves. I used it to feel better about myself, to make me feel like I wasn't a victim. Wasn't meant to camouflage my truth from you."

"When did it come back?"

"Months after Reggie passed away. Came back in my lymph nodes. Felt something underneath my arm." She raises her arm, shows me another scar. "Had it removed, went under radiation again. Was okay for a while. Then it showed up in my lungs. I knew it was only a matter of time. By then, you'd moved out. Started chemo. Lost weight, lost my hair. I didn't have to hide it from you anymore. Could be sick in my own house and not have to answer to anyone."

I'm no longer in this room. Can't listen to her anymore. She reveals her secrets as if she's reading the beginning chapter to a novel. No emotion, no regret. I get up from the bed and physically remove myself from this room.

I grab a beer out of the fridge. Pop the top, take a long gulp, and lean up against the sink. This is the reality we live in. Always finding ways to appease our broken egos. If only we realized it only prolongs our pain, never eliminates it.

My eyes peer into the living room. Lying in the middle of the floor is Sydney, half naked with me in between her legs. Rene walks into the room, stands over us, then comes into the kitchen. I blink away from my moment of weakness and look at the phone my wife's handing me.

"It's Melissa."

Guilt washes over me as I grab the phone from Rene. "Hey, sis-in-law. What's up?"

Her weeps let me know this is a serious call. "Andrew's been in an accident."

Melissa collapses into my arms as soon as I make it through the ER's doors.

I escort us to nearby chairs. "Got here as fast as I could."

"He's in stable condition, but they won't let me see him yet."

Her shaky hand is in mine. "What happened?"

"He was ran down by a truck on eighteen wheels." The paramedics brought my twin to the hospital covered in blood. His car had to be sawed in half in order for them to get him out. He'd been scared to drive since his first accident years ago where he nearly died. Now this. It's crazy how your fears have a way of catching up to you.

"Damn."

"Oh, Brandon. I freaked out when the hospital called. I called you first, then your parents. Said they'll be on the next plane out."

I pat her hand. "He's stable, right?"

She bobs her head. "Well, you know how the first accident had him. This will make him paranoid to even look at a car."

"Let's not worry about that now." I repeat my question as to how my brother ended up in the hospital.

Her hand slides out of mine. "I've heard different stories and none of them make sense. There were witnesses at the school who saw two men approach Drew. One guy was agitated while the other stood off to the side, watching the crowd forming. They said something about him sneaking around with one of their wives. I know that's not true because Andrew is always at that school, with me, or with you. I can always account for his absence."

"Exactly. Andrew wouldn't do anything like that."

She looks at me with a hesitated expression before continuing. "Things got a little out of hand, Drew got in his car and they sped after him. But the cops told me the men involved in the accident were two off-duty police officers who happened to see him driving out of control, swerving lanes like a maniac. When these two cops tried to pull him over, a diesel got in the way and they all crashed. What I don't understand is these cops weren't in uniform and just happened to be together driving the same route as Drew, but they match the description of the men from the school."

Every single pore in my skin opens and floods me with anxiety. It. Can't. Be.

Andrew told me from the beginning not to get involved with another man's wife, let alone a cop's wife. I refused to listen because my heart was hurt, my pride shattered, ego blistered. I was in a bad way. Couldn't hear my brother's warnings. He knew I was headed for danger. We were split from the same egg. He had a responsibility to me, an accountability to my livelihood. But I failed to listen, failed to realize my danger would be his danger.

It's hard for me to look at my sister-in-law because I'm the reason her husband's lying in a hospital bed.

Mel sees the trepidation written on my face. "Did these men confuse my husband for you?"

Before I can offer up an explanation to the guilt she sees in my eyes, a man with a long white coat comes out and summons her. "You can come back and see him now."

We both get up to follow the doctor back.

He stops me, says, "Only Mrs. Carter can see him right now."

"This is Andrew's brother," says Mel.

He nods my clearance.

My brother looks how I feel. A broken, battered man whose life has been broken into a million pieces.

"It's not as bad as it looks," he manages to say without looking at me.

Mel stands by his side, her hand on top of his bandaged hand.

My hand throbs.

The doctor speaks, "His leg got pretty tangled. We'll get him prepped for surgery to make sure there's no extensive damage. Other than that, a few stitches here and there, but nowhere near what it could've been. He'll be ready to go home in a couple of days."

"I was so scared when I got the call," my sister-in-law shares with my brother.

"You're a lucky guy," the doctor tells Andrew on his way out.

I reach my hand out to shake his. "Thanks for all you've done, Doctor."

He nods and leaves us to sort out the details.

Mel looks over at me, then back at her husband. "Drew, there's a lot being said outside these doors. Please clear the air. Are you having an affair?"

Drew makes eye contact with mine this time. Stares me dead in the face like a deer staring into an approaching car's headlights. "No."

"Then why were those men confronting you at your job?"

"They thought I was him." His eyes still on me.

My sister-in-law nods. "Just wanted to hear you say it."

An identical version of me says, "I told you what you were doing was wrong. But just like when we were kids, you failed to think about what effect your actions would have on me."

I let my emotions get the best of me. Again. My emotions are what made me miss the real reason my wife was pushing me away, they're what led me to get involved with that cop's wife.

Our parents always said I was the more emotional one out the duo. Came out of the womb crying. Was the first to cry in the morning, the last to cry at night. I was told my mother was well into her sixth month when they found out one baby was two. Technology wasn't as advanced back then and they couldn't see me hiding behind my brother. We started out so in sync our heart-beats beat as one. Every time Mom's expanding belly got rubbed, they thought it was just one baby. My brother got six more months of loving than I did. Maybe that's why I turned out this way.

"Get out," Andrew tells me.

I look over at his wife for support. "He's right, you need to go."

*E*ric is barely recognizable. Gauze wrapped around his head down to his chin. His face is swollen, looks like he was beaten with a sock full of rocks. All kinds of machines hooked up to him, wires hanging from him like he's some kind of medical experiment.

"He's slipped into a coma," the doctor tells me. "The next twenty-four hours are critical."

Eric's head hit the passenger window so hard it shattered. Knocked him out cold. Not sure when he'll wake up. Meanwhile, Michael walked out of here with nothing more than a few bandages. Why does the passenger always end up worse off than the driver?

Michael.

The reason my husband has lost all consciousness of reality. He instigated this. I know he did, and he had the nerve to threaten me.

After the doctor walks out of the room, I flop in the chair positioned next to Eric's bed. Tears clog my throat, temporarily prevent me from being able to breathe. I want to scream, want to run, want to be anywhere but here. That always seems to be the case with me when it comes to my husband. And for that very reason, he's lying here in this bed, not able to say or do anything to make life any different for the either of us.

Rivers flow from my eyes, saturate the fabric of my shirt. Stains the fabric of my life.

"Sydney," a familiar voice beckons.

I turn to my left to see my mother standing by the door. She points behind her. I get up from the chair with urgency, run out of the room and pick EJ up, hold him tight. Use my other arm to pull Kennedy close to my hip. Hold both of them like I've never held them before. Had things gone another way, they would've been in the car and things would be a lot different.

My mom called in the midst of me trying to find out my husband's status. The school notified her when they weren't able to get a hold of me. Kennedy went to the principal's office crying after her dad left her on the curb. She had been abandoned by a man on a mission to find out what was happening to his family. Mom went to the rescue to console her grandchild and pick up her other one from daycare; brought them straight here.

"Why are you crying, Mommy?" EJ questions. He always seems to catch me at my breaking point.

I look to my mom, search her eyes to see if she's told them anything. She shakes her head. Mouths, "They don't know anything."

Kennedy draws away, stands against the wall with her arms folded. "It's Daddy, isn't it?"

I put EJ down, look to my daughter.

She points a shaky finger to the ICU entrance. "In there. He's in there, isn't he?"

I nod. If I say anything my tears will choke me to death. How do you tell a daddy's girl her Numero Uno is lingering somewhere between life and death?

"Good." She shocks me and runs down the hall in the opposite direction.

Life hasn't been normal in the Holmes' household for weeks now. Today's accident magnified things to another level.

It took hours to get my children to calm down enough to allow sleep to do its job. I can't blame them. Doubt I'll be able to get my nerves to settle this lifetime.

"Wanna talk about it?" Mom says when I drag myself into the kitchen.

I plop down hard in the cushionless chair. "What's there to talk about? I messed up."

She shakes her head. "We were just talking—"

"I can do without the I-told-you-so right now." I ditch the chair, walk to the fridge. Don't find what I'm looking for because I have no idea what I'm looking for. I slam the door shut, trot off to the living room. Can't sit still, feel antsy. Need to lace up my sneakers and run this off.

As if my thoughts have a voice, my mom comes into the room behind me and tells me, "You can't run from this."

"Watch me," I say, and out the door I go.

Hands on the steering wheel, foot on the accelerator, I give them control to take me where my will won't lead me. Twenty minutes later, I'm standing in the doorway to my husband's hospital room.

There's been no change. He's still unconscious to reality.

My legs carry me to the chair positioned next to his bed. Slowly I sit, my eyes focused on his bandaged face, ears focused on the beating of his damaged heart.

According to Katrina, from what she was told by Rachel, when Eric got off duty, he noticed he had a flat tire. He was pressed for time, needed to pick Kennedy up from school. Michael offered to give him a ride to get her, then they'd come back and switch to the spare. Michael recognized a familiar face standing next to Kennedy at the school. Seeing them together, he realized it was the man he had caught me with at the park and in my car with a bleeding hand. He had been putting off sharing this info with Eric, but when he saw the man with my child, he knew it was time to break the news. Eric wanted to talk; Kennedy's teacher didn't. Said he actually laughed at the accusation. That set things off.

The police report tells a different story. Said Michael was the aggressor, while Eric was the bystander. Said Michael attacked Mr. Carter. Eric tried to stop him, but Michael wouldn't let up. Mr. Carter ran off, ran to his car and sped off. Michael jumped back in his car with Eric hopping in the passenger seat; sped off after him.

Now we're here.

Rachel's not answering my calls, won't settle this feeling in my stomach that this had nothing to do with my infidelity, but more so Michael trying to score revenge on a man who had nothing to do with the one he caught his woman with years ago. His past came back to get under his skin at a time when it had nothing to do with him. Not only has his inability to control his emotions messed up life for my family and me, he's also screwed up an innocent man's life. Even if he had the right twin, he still had no right to get involved.

I can't think about that right now, though.

My husband isn't able to tell me his side of the story. Only God knows when he will, if he ever will.

The last words we shared were filled with regret. My heart feels like it's being sucked deep into the ocean on a sinking ship. I let my thoughts drift to our honeymoon.

That night, after we'd finished making love as husband and wife, I had locked myself in the suite's bathroom, climbed in the tub and cried. He was sleeping so peacefully in the bed, skin stained with sweat from making love to his wife. He was satisfied, knowing he made the right decision. His life was working out the way he'd planned in his mind. Meanwhile, I had died inside. I made the wrong decision. I sat in the tub and cried so hard it felt like blood was pouring from my eyes. I cried because there was no turning back. I was his wife. Neither divorce nor death would ever be able to erase the fact that I vowed to love him in good times and in bad, in sickness and in health. I made that choice. And I had to live with it. Never thought it would lead us here.

A loud, steady beep on one of the monitors grabs my attention. A nurse walks in, unhooks an empty bag, replaces it with a bag full of clear liquid.

"What's that?" I want to know.

"Just something to help with pain," she says before walking back out.

"He can feel pain in a coma?"

The nurse nods, says, "He can feel and hear, just can't do anything about it." A beep across the hall sends her on her way.

I look back at my bandaged husband. He's felt and heard a lot in this marriage, and just like now, he didn't do anything about it. Whether he could or not is up for debate on another day.

He last told me he didn't want to marry me just as much as I didn't want to marry him. Another woman broke his heart before I even had the chance to. He was already damaged. I was just a Band-Aid on his wounds. By the time he realized it, we were walking down an aisle with peach rose petals.

A warm tear rolls down my face, followed by several others.

Sleep betrays me.

I've been in bed tossing and turning for hours. Thoughts are on my husband, on our failed attempt at marriage. On the kids we created when our passion was fueled by ignorance, ignoring the reason for the existence of us. On the lives torn apart by the wrong decisions made in my need to feel fulfilled.

The indigo-blue numbers on my nightstand flash at me, tell me it's eleven minutes past three. It's an insane hour to run, but I find myself rummaging through the dresser for my sports bra, a tank top, and a pair of leggings. Stagger to the bathroom, empty a beyond full bladder. Rethink the half-bottle of wine I downed when I got in from the hospital a couple of hours ago. I toss off pajamas, throw on running gear. Slip anxious feet into ASICS. Out the door I go.

Pulling into the parking lot of Pick Your Fit, I realize this is not where I want or need to be. I want to run with a freedom the treadmill could never be able to allow. I need space, need air. Need to feel like I'm going somewhere other than here.

I drive to Riverfront. It's still dark out. Any woman with any sense wouldn't dare run or be out here alone. Any woman other than me, because I haven't done much to make sense in my life as far back as I can remember. I bend over, give my hamstrings a good stretch as I tie my sneakers. Say a quick prayer asking God to keep me safe. My prayer makes me chuckle. It's not like someone is holding a gun against my head making me run out here in the dark. I'm out here on my own accord.

I put my feet to the pavement and do what I need to do.

As one foot lands in front of the other with a force hard enough to shatter the concrete to ashes, I release a part of the guilt I've been holding on to. I couldn't marry a man who didn't agree to the vows as well. I couldn't have had Kennedy and EJ if there wasn't another willing participant. I wasn't the only one who kept feelings hidden in the vault of truth. I didn't tell Eric to get in the car with his crazy partner and run another man off the road. I'm not responsible for my husband's coma. Yet, I cry for him.

It is my fault for not being honest, for not telling the truth to a vulnerable man, for keeping the truth from myself. I accept my part in all of this, but I won't carry the burden alone.

Thinking about Brandon moves me at a faster pace. I think about how his life has unraveled at the hands of my decisions. I could've left things alone at the gym when I mistook him for my daughter's teacher. I didn't have to take his offer to train him in running. God knows I didn't have to dance with him, hop in his car and listen to the stories of his unhappy marriage. I had no right to console him, give him my ear. I was out of line showing up at his front door with an offer to what only my husband should be privy to. But again, I wasn't acting on my own. It wasn't all on me. He played just as much a part as I did. He could have as easily backed away as I could have. Two weak people have no business playing tug-of-war against Goliath.

I cry for Brandon. Had I not been operating out of a place of negligence and regret, I would have seen his pain wasn't something

I could heal. Instead of being his ear, I should've encouraged him to go home and talk to his wife. Talking to me wasn't going to make things better at home and it wasn't going to make him feel any better about what wasn't going on at home. His wife was dying, and there I was inviting him in between my legs. He didn't need me to make matters worse.

Yes, he was a man and was able to make his own choices, but a man will go as far as a woman will let him. I had no boundaries. He was walking in open territory.

We always have a choice.

Hindsight is everything. I heard my intuition tell me to just walk away, heard it from day one. Instead, I stayed and made it Eric's problem, blamed him for my unhappiness. I tried to make him do something he would never be capable of. Never took responsibility for myself. Something else I'll be paying for the rest of my life.

For every wrong decision, another decision has to be made. You keep making decisions until the right one is made. Either way, it's up to you. I don't know if I'll be able to right my wrongs, but I'm sure as heck going to give it all I've got.

Sweat pours from my pores, drips in my eyes, mixes with the tears running down my face. I raise my soaked tank to wipe my face. Tired of crying, tired of abusing my body to get rid of the stress my actions created. This has got to stop. Got to get control of me.

I pick the pace up even more. Swear I'm hitting qualifying speed for the Olympics. I run until I feel pounds shedding, feel misery dissipating. Run until I feel my sanity coming back as a fuchsia sun rises above the horizon, tainting a blue sky with shades of purple. I run until night becomes morning.

A family of ducks waddle a few feet in front of me, make their way to the lake for a morning bath. If only life were that simple for me. Then again, it could be. I'm the one who makes it hard. No more, no more, no more. From this point on, I will not let anyone else control my emotions, nor will I let anyone else define what my heart feels. I will love who I want and how I want. I am a wife and a mother, but most importantly, I am Sydney.

I run until my declaration becomes freeing. Frees me from the bondage I've kept myself in. My feet hit the ground in applause, they slap the pavement as if they've been set free as well.

Finally, I slow my pace to a light jog as I near the entrance to the park. I shake my hands, fling as much moisture from them as possible; wipe my eyes.

When my vision's clear, I look up and walk right into Brandon.

# 43
## BRANDON

*M*y eyes reek with disgust. Can tell by the way fear scatters across her face and make her run in the opposite direction. I move forward until her footsteps relent.

"How'd you know I'd be here?"

Sydney's question reminds me of the last time I stalked her here. "Followed you here from the gym."

"You've been here the whole time?"

"Pulled up next to you while you were tying your shoes."

"You've been here the whole time?" She repeats her question enunciating each syllable in disbelief.

I nod what she already knows to be true.

"Why?"

I ask myself the same thing. Don't know why I'm standing in front of the woman responsible for my twin no longer wanting to be in my presence. We shared the same womb for nine months, now he doesn't want to be in the same room together. "We need to talk about what happened."

She sighs. "I'm still trying to put those pieces together myself."

"That's not good enough. Your husband and his cohort lost their cool and have scarred my brother for life. Cops committing crimes; something's wrong with that."

"Well, my husband's not able to tell his side of the story, so until then, keep him out of it."

Sydney stands in my face and defends the man who bored her to death, the man who led her to my apartment. Led her to open her legs for me. "You brought him into this." For a second I lose my cool. "Don't try to subtract him from the equation now."

"He's in a coma, Brandon. Have some compassion."

How dare she ask for compassion. "Oh, like the compassion you reserved for my cancer-stricken wife when you came knocking at my door with open legs."

She charges at me like a lion in heat. Her hands land on my chest, shoves me and shoves me some more until I lose my balance.

"So both you and your husband respond to problems with violence, I see."

She comes at me again. This time I wrap my hands around her wrists, stop her before she has the chance to make any more impressions in my chest. My hands defy my judgment when they pull her into me. Her feet defy her when they move toward me.

I don't kiss her first, nor does she kiss me first. Our lips meet at the same time. Tongues dance to the same tune. Both of us trying to make sense of how we got here, while letting our frustrations dig this hole deeper.

Sydney slides her tongue from my mouth, but her lips stay on mine. "This is how we got here."

I know she's referring to the first time we were out here and unbeknownst to us, we had been caught at the beginning of an affair. I rub my fingers through her hair, feel the wetness of her scalp. Makes me think of the wetness between her legs from the last time we were in this position. I draw her face closer into mine.

She kisses me hard, kisses away the consciousness to our sin.

I kiss her hard, kiss away whatever consequences our sin will create.

Another man's wife comes out of the bathroom with a towel wrapped around freshly cleansed skin.

I'm sitting on the edge of a rented bed as naked as I was the day I was born.

She stands in front of another woman's husband, lets me remove the towel from her body. My hands linger across her skin, feel her shiver underneath my fingertips. She parts her legs, lets my fingers travel to her warmth. Wetness welcomes me into her cove, makes my nature rise. My finger stirs her deep, makes her moan loud enough to make doves cry. She straddles my thighs. I slip deeper, try to get lost inside.

"Promise me something," she whispers in my ears.

"Hmm?"

"Don't leave me hanging like last time."

I make no promises as my lips graze her neck, teeth leave impressions on her skin. I do say, "You know you'll go home a different woman, right?"

"And you'll go home a different man," she says back.

We kiss hard. Definitely no turning back from here.

This wasn't supposed to happen. I wasn't supposed to be here. I went to the gym because I knew she'd be there. I wanted to confront her, blaspheme her for speaking to me many moons ago on the treadmill. She interrupted my life with a common confusion. But the way she locked eyes with me, showed interest in trying to get me to know who she was…I've been stuck ever since.

Sydney leans against me, chest against chest. I lie back on the bed, she follows. Trails her tongue down my neck, comes back up, sucks my lips.

I'm still stirring her insides, her juices making a smacking noise as my finger slides in and out of her. She removes my finger from her, places it in her mouth. Watches me watch her. She winds her hips against mine, moves against me like she did on the dance floor. Her swollen lower lips glide up and down my manhood, giving me a hint of what it'd feel like to be inside.

That gets me.

I raise her up off me, lie her on the bed in my place, plant myself in between her thighs and let my nature rise inside of her.

We've officially entered the place of no return.

I'm lying in the bed next to another wrong decision.

My body aches from running it into the ground to clear my mind only to turn around and fill it back up with a hunger for a married man. A man whose wife is on the verge of her last exhale.

Regret fills the air like carbon monoxide in a closed garage with the car running. It's always the moments after when your actions hit you with the force of an avalanche.

"I didn't think it would be so easy to do this." Brandon breaks the silence and awakens my ears as if I'm hearing for the first time. He's lying on his back staring into darkness.

I swallow. "What?"

"This." He rolls over, places his lips on my bare shoulder still damp from our second session of exploring each other.

Unlike the last few times he's kissed me, this time I freeze under his touch. Feel a part of me tiptoe out of my body and out of this bed.

He pulls back causing a draft to blanket over me. His eyes gaze in my direction, penetrate my thoughts. "Wow."

This wasn't how I was expecting to feel. Ecstasy turned to regret in a matter of seconds. A few minutes ago, we brought each other to pleasure beyond words, filled the longing our souls longed for. Now all I want to do is run out of this room. Guess I was expecting him to feel the same way. "I'm sorry," is all I can find to say. At this moment, I truly am.

Brandon tosses the covers back, the comforter grazes my lip.

Again, I apologize.

He flicks the switch on the wall lamp, shines the light on our adultery. Stands above me in the buff, his manhood as lifeless as a man on insulin. "You're no better than Rene."

I fling the covers off me, stand up on the bed in front of him. Every hair on my body raises along with the octaves in my voice. "Did you just compare me to your wife?"

He shifts back a step, but doesn't back down. "I did. She turned cold toward me when she felt I couldn't do anything else for her. You've turned cold toward your husband, turned to me, got what you wanted. Now you don't even want me to kiss you anymore."

"That's not true, Brandon. You can't even compare your situation with your wife to this."

"Why did you come here with me?"

My eyes stay on his as his eyes stay on mine. "The same reason you wanted me to. Let's not kid ourselves, there's been chemistry brewing between us for months now. *This* was inevitable, no matter how much we told ourselves it wasn't going to happen. But that doesn't mean I have to be comfortable with the end result."

He bites on his top lip. "Do we end here?"

Feels like someone knees me in the back of my knees. My balance falters. He reaches to catch my fall, places my feet on the floor. I take that as my opportunity to look for my clothes; put some distance between us. Need space to gather my thoughts.

Brandon speaks up for me. "Take that as a yes."

I drop my clothes. "No, that's not what I said at all. I honestly can't say what I want right now. I've got to get to my kids, make sure they're doing all right. Need to go to the hospital and check on my husband. You need to see about your wife and your brother. Too much is going on right now for us to make any decisions."

"Tell me how you really feel," he says, his feelings spoiling the good sex we just had.

An aggravated sigh rumbles between my lips. I pick my sweaty clothes off the floor, take them with me into the bathroom.

I don't know how I was expecting to feel after having relations with another man other than my husband. Part of me hoped it would give me an excuse to be able to leave my marriage. Another part of me hoped it would cause me to realize what a good thing I have at home. Right now, I don't feel either way, but I do know an affair doesn't settle anything. It only creates more chaos and confusion.

When I walk out of the bathroom, Brandon is sitting on the edge of the bed, his clothes in a pile at his feet. He looks up at me, his eyes swimming in a pool of a fading memory. "Thanks for nothing."


Brandon was right; I have come home a different woman.

As I step in the shower I've stepped in every day for the last few years, all of a sudden it doesn't feel like I belong. Doesn't feel like I deserve to be here, though my money has helped pay for it. Everything in this house I have helped pay for. Feel like my money is worthless. Feel like I'm worthless.

I rinse the residue from another man away from my skin in a shower I've made love to my husband in. Watch as the suds of adultery bubble down the drain, watch as they travel down to a place I might be going soon.

I dry off regret, but it drips from my heart. As I walk into the room, my eyes focus in on the bed, see visions of me rolling around with another woman's husband. I was happy. I felt good. It felt right. Not necessarily being with him, but not being with my husband felt right to me. The moment that moment ended, reality came rushing in like waves in a tsunami. Came crashing in, drowning me in the decisions my heart led me to make.

I have become my father trying not to be like my mother. I've become an adulterer, all because I was afraid of becoming a lonely woman.

My fears brought me here, to this place of brokenness.

I shake my head too hard for comfort, feel an immediate throb in my head. I have got to get myself together. This pity party isn't going to help matters one bit. This is one of those moments I need to confess my sins to someone who can do more for me than a priest.

Before I can finish dressing, the phone is in my hand, speed-dialing my favorite spa in town. Soon as I can confirm, I'm in the car, wheeling my troubles to Conscious Kneads. Whoever canceled ten minutes before I called needs to have a national holiday recognized in their name. Talk about perfect timing.

"Jeez, girl," she says as soon as I walk through the door. "Say nothing. Room 3. Flick the light when you're ready."

I nod, because if I say anything, I might just choke on my tears.

She adds aromatherapy oils to the diffuser, puts on my favorite song and sets it on repeat. "La Jetée" by Isotope 217. Sounds like a marriage of mystery and the blues. The first time I heard it was during a customer appreciation mingle she had a few months ago, I asked her who the artist was and requested she give me a massage to it the next time I was on her table.

"Thanks for remembering," I tell her.

"It's my job," she says, then flicks the light to red.

The moment her trained fingertips smooth oil across my back, I swear I'm about to lose it.

"Breathe, Sydney. Just breathe."

I comply.

Inhale.

Exhale.

Inhale.

I hold my breath as long as I can as she slides her cupped hands up my back. On the downward pressing movement, I exhale. Feels like the last exhale my lungs will ever make.

An hour later, I'm standing up front, handing my massage therapist my Visa for the best therapy session known to man. "Fatima, you don't know how much I needed that."

"It was written all over your face when you walked in."

"I looked that bad, huh?"

"Stressed, not bad. Felt it in every fiber of your skin."

Another pained exhale. I want to confide in her, though I feel like she already knows. The way her eyes hold sympathy toward me is as if the knots in my body told her my secrets. I divert the conversation. "How's that baby of yours?"

"He's walking and talking like he was doing it in the womb." She grabs a picture from the desk and hands it to me. "Can't remember what life was like before him, and can't imagine my life without him." Her voice tells me that's nothing but the truth.

I've known Fatima since high school. We ran cross country together. Both of us running from unhappy lives. Both of us trying to recoup from lives being torn apart from our fathers' departures. Though mine was still around part time, I had to help repair the damage from the woman he left. That put more strain on me than a child should have to face.

I ask her, "How're things with you and your dad?"

"Much better." She walks around from behind the desk, walks with me over to the waiting area. "It took some time to digest it all. After having Bennet Amir and seeing how my father treated him, I finally came to a place of forgiveness. I spent all those years without him, didn't want to waste any more time not having him in my life. I'm sure things could be better, but each day is a new experience, you know."

I nod. Each day *is* a new experience. The past two days have proved just that. "I'm happy for you, Fatima." I truly am happy for her. In the years we've known each other, this is the happiest I've seen her. The way sadness is hidden behind her irises lets me know this is the worst she's seen me.

"How are your two?" she says.

I shake my head. "You don't even want to know."

She chuckles. "I can't imagine. I may soon find out, though." A smile creeps across her face.

I feel my eyes expand beyond what an ophthalmologist would consider normal. "You're kidding." I look at her belly, don't see signs of a baby growing inside.

Her left hand, with a serious sparkle to it, flies up to stop my suspicion. "No, no, no. Not yet, at least. But Cory wants us to have a brother or sister for Bennet."

I glance at her engagement ring. "Have you two set a date yet?"

Fatima moves her head left to right. "It'll definitely be before another baby comes along, that's for sure." She twists the ring on her finger. "Our situation is more complicated than most, so it's a lot for us to talk about."

"Yeah, I can understand that," I say, wishing I had thought long and hard when Eric suggested we have another child. Kennedy was a lot to deal with as it was because she made leaving him all the more harder. It's not easy to walk away from a marriage, but even harder when kids are involved. Another baby would make it that much harder. And it did. They're both here now, so no point in wishing life were different. Though, I wonder how he'd feel if I told him about the abortion.

It was three months before we got married.

I never believed in abortion. Never thought I'd be in a position where I would even consider getting one. Then again, never thought I'd end up pregnant out of wedlock. Eric and I had been so careful not to have any accidents like that. We always used protection. Except this one night in particular when hormones betrayed good sense.

I was more open about having unprotected sex with him than he was with me. He was a by-the-books kind of guy for most things, condoms being one of them. Engaged or not, he wasn't having it. Until I put my mouth on his manhood and gave him the best oral sex he had or would ever have in his life. I was horny and we were out of condoms, it seemed like the only option available. I wasn't about to get dressed for the store, neither was he. He knew what he was doing; said he'd pull out. A kiss filled with desire sealed the deal.

Unfortunately, that kiss wouldn't protect his one disobedient sperm from diving in my womb and swimming right into my disobedient egg.

When I first found out, I freaked out. Pulling out is not a smart form of birth control, this I knew, but damn if I didn't have hope it would work. Disappointed was one of the hundreds of emotions that ran through my veins when the second faint line on the home pregnancy test laughed in my face. I broke the test in half, tossed it in the trash. Pulled out another only for it to repeat the same bad joke as the first. All throughout high school, girls and boys bragged how pulling out worked for them. My girl Fatima was one of those girls. But just like her, an immature decision came back to make us pay in our you-should-have-your-shit-together-by-now years. She chose to have her baby. I didn't.

It took a few days for things to fully sink in. At first, I wondered if it'd be so bad to let Eric in on the result of what our hormones lead us to create, but threw that option out the window because I knew he wouldn't be able to handle the ridicule of being a father before being a husband. Then I thought about calling off the wedding and moving out of state to raise the baby on my own. That wouldn't be fair to the child or to Eric, so I crossed that option off the list. Abortion? I couldn't do that, that was the irresponsible way out. I had no right to take a life I helped create. My options quickly decreased.

Telling Eric and letting his response determine the future of our unborn child weighed heavy on my mind. His parents were devout Christians and did a good job of raising him with Biblical principles. But even with his church upbringing, I do believe he would've considered abortion if it came down to it. He'd be more worried about how it would look explaining to everyone that we messed up and got pregnant before we had a chance to say our vows. He wouldn't want his parents seeing how irresponsible he could be in the heat of the moment.

Luckily, we didn't live together so he never suspected a thing, never saw the fear in my eyes after hours. The only time he even raised a brow was when I told him we needed to put the sex on hold. To throw him off, I reassured him it was because I had something very special in store for our honeymoon night. That worked. Plus, rearranging his bachelor pad to accommodate his new wife in a few months was at the forefront of his thoughts. He didn't have the energy to be too concerned with not having sex for the time being.

As for me, I had a decision to make, one that would ultimately change the dynamics of our relationship if he were ever to find out.

At six weeks, I terminated the pregnancy. It was the only decision that made sense in the big picture. Was it the best decision? At times, I seriously doubt it. Telling him about the baby could've ended us, and for sure telling him about the abortion would've ended us. And I do feel had we ended things back then, both of us would be a lot happier now. He would've found a woman more suited for the love he had to offer and wouldn't be laid up in another state of consciousness in the hospital, wondering what the hell happened to his life. I would've found someone I could love without questioning my love for him every five minutes, and wouldn't be walking around with another man's scent dangling in my panties while carrying the guilt of my husband's well-being in my heart.

I chose to keep it all to myself.

And have paid the heavy price ever since.

*I*t's been hard for me to look at Rene since sleeping with Sydney. Guilt does that to me, clings to my conscience like a dryer sheet to Velcro.

I know she knows. Her breathing changed the moment I walked in the door. It quickened as if she could smell an unfamiliar scent tainting the scent she had become familiar with all these years, then it softened, a faint rise and fall of her chest. I betrayed her. Betrayed me. Betrayed all that we stood for.

Rene looks me dead in the eyes like she's trying to read the last twenty-four hours of my life. Tries to see where I've been and who I've been with. A tear rolls down her face like it did Janet Jackson in *For Colored Girls* when the truth was in the air but she refused to acknowledge it. Just like Jo, my wife says nothing.

I did it because she betrayed me when she chose not to let me do my part as her husband. The Bible says if your eye offends you to pluck it out. My wife offended me by keeping her life a secret, so I did the only thing that would break her heart. Maybe I'm taking the scripture out of context, and I'll probably burn in hell for it, but a man doesn't think about that when he feels he has no other choice.

But I did have a choice.

I could have walked away from what I was building with Sydney. It would not have been easy, not in the least. Her attention was a seed planted deep in my soul; and she kept watering it, giving it sunshine with her laughs, warming it with her longing for my attention. The seed grew into a desire that I liked feeling. Made it hard to walk away. Still, I could've walked away.

I lean against the opening to my bedroom door, watch as my wife does a weak job of engaging my mom in conversation. Rene turns her head in my direction, looks up at me with eyes asking *How could you?* I blink away the guilt, try to put a smile on my face. My lips shake as they try to spread. Standing in my lie makes me feel like crap. This is the woman I vowed to love forever, the woman I'd marry a million times over if I could. No matter what, I shouldn't have crossed that line.

As if she can hear my thoughts, Rene starts coughing. She coughs so hard bile drips from her lips. My mom gets up from the corner of the bed to clean up her daughter-in-law. I can't let my mom do my job. I go to my wife's side, remove the cloth from my mom's hand, do what I vowed to do.

My parents made it in late last night before visiting hours at the hospital were over. I took them straight to the hospital to see their good son. They came for him, to make sure he was okay. They shouldn't be here helping me. I'm the one who's caused the tides to turn for so many lives.

A tear falls from Rene's eye. Another one falls out the other eye. *"Life has a way of humbling you down."* Lyrics from an Anthony Hamilton song comes to mind. Life has done so much to my wife these past few months. Enough to make me wonder what she did in her past life to deserve all of this. I thumb her tears away, kiss her forehead.

My mom walks over with a fresh gown to put on Rene.

"I'll do that," I tell her.

She stands her ground. "Your father and I are here to help, son."

"You're here for Andrew."

"Andrew is going to be okay." She says that as if I'm not. "Why don't you let me clean up here, and you and your father go on up to the hospital."

I'm the last person my brother wants to see. And the way my wife's eyes glare up at me, I'm the last person she wants in her presence as well. Seems like I'm always doing the wrong thing to the people who matter most.

Before I can decline my mother's demand, she takes the gown back from my hands, leaves me with no other choice.


My father sits in the passenger seat in silence as I drive us to the hospital. I can hear him cursing me out in tongues in his silence. Hear him questioning himself on how he raised me, why I turned out so different than the son who was conceived from the same egg. His silence kills me a thousand times.

"I know you're disappointed in me." I hear my thoughts break the silence.

He taps his fingers against his thigh. "I just don't understand, son."

This lack of understanding goes beyond the past two days, beyond the accident. They reach back over the last three decades. I've been causing problems since I was in the womb. If I could do it all over again, I'd stay hidden in the womb until I ceased to exist. Making my presence known six months after the fact threw the course of my parents' plans off. Part of me feels I threw things off for Andrew back then as well. Maybe he wishes his existence could have kept me hidden, maybe he would've suffocated me by all the love and affection he was getting in our one-room womb.

I pull up to the parking gate, push the button to get a ticket. Pull forward to the first available spot. Dad gets out, walks two steps ahead of me. Treats me like a stranger.

There's a nurse in the room checking Andrew's vitals, switching out empty painkillers with fresh bags. Mel's asleep in a foldout chair in the corner, blanket hanging off to the ground. Anybody would be restless trying to sleep in a bed smaller than a baby's crib.

"How's he doing?" Dad asks the nurse.

"He's in pain. Had a fever through the night, but it's under control now." She looks back at Andrew. "He's been restless, so I gave him a little something to help him sleep."

Dad glances at me, then thanks the nurse.

I walk over to where my sister-in-law is laid out, rub her shoulder. She jumps at my touch nearly falling off the sleeper-chair. "Drew."

I motion my eyes to the man lying in the bed beside me.

Mel blinks a few times. "What are you doing here? Thought we told you not to come back."

"He *should* be here," my dad speaks up. He puts his hand on top his daughter-in-law's hand. "Why don't you go home for a while, get some real rest. If anything changes, we'll give you a call."

Mel stands up, adjusts her wrinkled clothes. "No disrespect, Mr. Carter. As long as Brandon's in here, I'd like to stay."

My father and his son's wife have had a good relationship up until this point. I refuse to let my indiscretions alter any more relationships than they've done already. "I'll leave."

"Son—"

I put my hand up. "It's cool. I'll get some coffee."

At this point, feels like I'm being shut out of everyone's life. Mom sent me away from tending to my wife. My brother's wife sent me away from tending to my brother. The woman responsible for me being in this position has even shut me out. After the act, she acted like she didn't want anything else to do me. I wish she would've just let me be on the treadmill. None of this would've happened.

*T*wenty-four hours later, Eric's condition hasn't changed. If he were awake, he'd see a lot about me has changed. I place my hand on top of his. Try to see if I can feel him through his bandages. Try to see if he can feel me.

Who am I kidding? We've both had bandages over our hearts for years and neither one of us have been able to feel each other. We've just been existing in a world that made sense until sense was no longer made. "How long were we going to lie to each other, Eric?" I sit on the edge of the bed and wait for an answer.

"Lie about what?"

Another voice in the room nearly scares me out of my skin. It's not that I was expecting Eric to answer me, but I wasn't expecting someone else to.

I slide off the bed and stand in front of my mother-in-law. "When did you get in?" I hug her.

She leaves me to go to her son's side.

Mr. Holmes says, "We came straight from the airport." He gives me a solid hug. "How are you holding up?"

"I have my moments. Just trying to stay strong for the kids."

"Are they here?"

I shake my head. "They're with my mom. I let them stay home from school today."

He nods. "How is he?"

Both of our eyes scan a bandaged man in a hospital bed, his mother shedding tears as she stands by his side.

"The swelling in his brain has gone down a little; not much, but enough for the doctor to feel like the worst is over." I pat my father-in-law on his back, say, "Go on over there. They say it's best for us to keep talking to him. Let him know he's not alone."

He takes my hand, squeezes it, then goes to his son.

Mrs. Holmes wipes at her eyes with a piece of tissue. Her husband reaches his hand across the bed to her hand. That makes her break down more.

I want to say something to comfort her. It's never a good feeling to see a mother watching her child in pain when there's nothing she can do about it. I'm the one who's caused her son to be in this pain. That makes my heart ache all the more. I can't take anymore. I grab my purse off the counter and slip out, give them time to be with their son.

"I'm stepping outside to get a little fresh air," I tell the nurse before stepping out of ICU. "If anything happens, please ring my cell phone."

"Sure will, Mrs. Holmes."

Before I can walk through ICU's double doors, I hear my name being called. I turn around, see my mother-in-law's crimson eyes approaching.

"Is there something you want to tell me?"

My bottom lip turns upside down, head shakes.

She stands firm. "You sure?"

I shift my weight to one leg, cross my arms. "Is there something you want to tell me?" I throw back at her.

"Let's not play games, Sydney. When Eric's father and I walked in, you said something about a lie. What were you talking about?"

I unfold my arms, adjust the purse on my shoulder. "Oh, that." I shake my head again. "Nothing."

Elaine Holmes and I have never really seen eye to eye. Not sure why. She's always seemed to have some sort of grudge toward me. Treats me as if I've never been good enough for her son. No matter how she feels about me, now is not the time for us to go there.

"How did my son end up in a coma?"

"I gave you all the details I had when I called you yesterday."

She just stands and stares at me as if my answer's going to change.

A man walks past us, cuts through our tension with his authoritative presence. "Ladies," he says and walks up to the nurses' station.

Elaine rolls her watch back and forth across her wrist with a nervous hand. "We'll finish this later."

As I'm about to walk off, I hear my name being summoned once again. This time a male voice calls for me.

The man who just walked past is now walking in my direction. "You got a few minutes to talk?" He reaches out his hand. "I'm Sergeant Lee. I work with your husband."

I shake his hand and nod.

Sgt. Lee pulls out a chair for me to sit once we make it to the cafeteria. "You been dancing lately?" he inquires.

I catch a glimpse of a platinum ring on his left hand. I look back up at his face. Just my luck. The guy who couldn't wait to get back to work to brag about my dancing skills to my husband would be my husband's superior. Mr. Platinum.

As if my mother-in-law didn't already have me on edge, this fool bringing up a night after one too many drinks is about to tip me off the cliff and I won't hesitate to pull him down with me. "I'm sure you didn't come here for unofficial business."

"You're right." He taps his fingers on the top of the table, the silver on his finger reflecting under the light. "How's Holmes doing?"

"He's still breathing."

"I'm sure if he wasn't you wouldn't be here, right?"

I get to the point. "Why are you here?"

A smirk crosses his face as he pulls out a notepad from his top pocket. He licks his fingers, flips a few pages. "Was hoping you could help me clear up a little confusion being that Holmes is unable to give his version of events."

I nod.

"Do you know this schoolteacher, umm, Andrew Carter?"

"He's my daughter's teacher."

"Have you seen or spent time with this teacher outside of *official* school business?"

"I have no reason to."

"Maybe not, but your husband seemed to think you did."

I lean back in my seat without losing my composure. "Is there something you want to ask specifically?"

Sgt. Lee puts the pad down on the table, scoots his chair closer to me. Almost gets in my face like I'm an uncooperative suspect under investigation. "Were you having an affair with Mr. Carter?"

"Nope." I let my lips pop when I say that.

"Well, what reason would your husband have to accuse an innocent man of sleeping around with his wife?"

"I don't know. Maybe that's something you need to ask him."

He scoots back in his chair. "I've seen the way you act when Holmes isn't around. Maybe this guy got the same lap dance you gave me."

"You know what—" I feel eyes beyond this table on me. I look around, do that to get myself under control. If this man wasn't a superior to Eric I would curse him from here to the Lake of Fire. "Are we done here?"

"I'm just getting started."

Saliva grows thick in my mouth. All of a sudden I want to spit.

Sgt. Lee flips a few more pages in his notepad. "Now, according to one report, you've been seen a couple of times outside of the school with this man. One time in particular inside your vehicle with a bloody hand. A minute ago you said you hadn't had any outside dealings with Mr. Carter."

"Michael told you that."

He doesn't respond. Just sits there like he has some secret info on me. One dance with this man and he wants to label me as the squadron's Jezebel.

"Michael had no right."

"So which is it?"

"I didn't lie. It wasn't the teacher in my car. It was his twin brother."

"Oh, and is that supposed to make it better?"

Everything inside begs me to jump across this table and strangle every last breath out of this imbecile. Again, Eric's career comes to my head and I back down. Not sure why he didn't consider his career while he was out proving his testosterone levels were up to par. "You have no right to judge me. You have no idea what's going on. Michael was quick to put me under the bus, but did you ask him why he was the one driving? Why isn't he being interrogated for putting my husband and somebody else's husband in critical care?"

I don't wait for an answer. I grab my purse and scoot my chair back so hard it screams against the tile. "We're done here."

My emotions are so heated I can barely see where I'm going. I bump into a few people on my way out. I'm so distraught I can't even apologize. My foot ends up kicking a chair, throws my equilibrium off. Somebody wraps their arm around my waist and catches me before my face hits the floor. I look up and stare straight into Brandon's face.

I saw it all.

The moment Sydney walked into the cafeteria a man with the word *Police* written across the back of his shirt and a silver badge hanging from his neck trailed close behind. Saw her sit with a frown on her face and fear in her eyes. Saw him laugh at her discomfort and her loss of control. Saw nurses and doctors gawking at the confrontation brewing at their table as voices raised. I'm sure if I were close enough to hear, I would've heard a lot of consonants and very few vowels. There was such ferocity in the way she backed out of her chair and moved toward the door, she nearly snapped my leg in half.

"You okay?"

She dusts off her ego. Looks at me briefly, then looks back at the table she was just sitting at.

The officer nods on his way out.

Again, I check to see if she's okay.

"This. Is. Too. Much." She rubs her hands back and forth on the sides of her neck.

I pull out a chair for her to sit in.

She shakes her head. "I'm tired of sitting."

"Need to run, huh?"

She sighs. "If I ran to Asia it wouldn't be far enough."

"Who was that officer?"

She digs in her purse, pulls out her cell phone. Checks the time. "Meet me at the park in an hour?"

From the way Sydney's falling apart at the seams, I doubt running will be the cure to what ails her.


After leaving Sydney in the cafeteria, I head back up to the room to check on everyone. As I approach the room I hear voices. My dad and brother are talking about me, I know that because I hear my name several times. I push the half-cracked door all the way open, make my presence known.

"He just doesn't get it," Andrew says, turning his head away from me.

"Hey, son."

I walk over to my father, hand him a turkey and cheese sandwich I got him from downstairs. Put the chips and coffee on the rolling cart next to him.

"You must've read my mind. My stomach was in here speaking in tongues."

"Where's Mel?"

He unsnaps the container to his sandwich. "She finally took my advice and went home. Had a bad crook in her neck. Told her a chair like that wasn't meant for sleeping."

The whole time my dad talks my attention is on my brother, the man I shared a womb with for nine months. The man who hid me for six, but made sure I got all the nourishment I needed to grow just as healthy as him. Before I knew what life was, he was looking out for me. And this is how I repay him.

I move around to the side of the bed where the window is, get down on my knees in front of Andrew. Look him in the face man to man, brother to brother. "I'm sorry." My voice shakes as those words come out.

Our father puts down his sandwich, puts feeding his hunger on hold. He stands up next to me, places a hand on my shoulder, the other hand on his other son's hip. "I don't like seeing you two like this. Never did like to see you two fight growing up. But I understand that's what siblings do. Look at Cain and Abel. They started sibling rivalry."

The more Dad talks, the bigger the fire brews behind Andrew's eyes. He's sending a message that this is not something he will be able to forgive me for. He tried to warn me off messing with a married woman, told me our parents didn't raise us that way. I failed to heed his warnings, failed to realize he could possibly pay the price for my consequences.

"And those twins, Esau and Jacob. They fought so bad in the womb, one held on to the other's heel on—"

"Dad, not today," Andrew says.

"Come on, son."

Andrew turns to look at our father. "Did he tell you how this happened?"

"I know enough."

"You know enough? So, how can you stand in here and compare this to sibling rivalry?"

"It's not Dad's fault, Drew. Don't take it out on him."

"You're right, it's not *his* fault." There is so much anger in Andrew's eyes when he looks back at me it scares me. "*You* did this."

Life has a funny way of reminding you that no matter how much control you think you have over your life, there's always someone who can take that control away from you.

My emotions made me lose control over my life. It was my emotions that made me feel like my wife was silently walking out of our marriage. Emotions led me into the arms of another woman, a married woman. Had I taken control over my emotions, I would've been able to get to the core of my wife's despondence probably while she still had a chance to fight cancer.

Emotions. The reason I'm driving to the park instead of going home to check on my wife.

I park a few cars down from Sydney's.

"Was beginning to think I was stood up."

"That's your job."

"I thought we let bygones be bygones."

"If that were the case, we wouldn't be here."

She moves her legs apart, bends over, puts her hands on the ground. Gives her hamstrings a good stretch.

There was a time where my wife and her husband were the main topic of discussion. Now that we've crossed the line into sin, we don't want to talk about the things that brought us to this point.

"Why aren't you stretching? Your legs'll cramp up."

I look down at my loafers.

"Wait, you're not running?"

I don't answer the obvious.

She goes back to stretching, tells me with her body language that she's not going to let me keep her from releasing what needs to be released.

I walk over to a lone bench by the beginning of the trail. I sit and wait for her to finish giving her muscles the attention they need before she tries to strangle them to death. I don't know how she can even think about running after the damage she just put on her legs less than twenty-four hours ago.

A lot has happened in twenty-four hours. A lot has changed.

She walks over to me, sits down. A second later she slides from the bench, grabs my hand, pulls me off with her. "Walk with me for a few."

I oblige.

Our hands are still intertwined as people run past us on the trail. Neither one of us say anything. We just walk holding hands. I'm sure we look out of place, awkward. I know I probably feel as out of place as I look.

Sydney stops in front of the restrooms when she lets go of my hand. "Be right back."

I debate running away from here while she's out of sight. I want to run away and not look back. When she walks out of the rest-room with an extended index finger calling me to follow her, I realize my mind didn't send the memo to my feet.

She locks us in the stall.

"What are we doing?"

Her voice a whisper. "You followed me in here. Don't you think it's a little late for questions?"

I let her lips touch mine, let mine touch hers back.

"I. Need. This." Desperation in her breath.

A few hours ago I needed her, but she left me in a hotel room. Naked. Hurt. Disoriented. It didn't matter to her what I needed because at that time she had other things on her mind. Priorities that didn't include me. I should've walked away from day one. I can't make up for what I didn't do back then. All I can do now is walk away.

I reach my hand behind her, unlatch the lock, and do just that. I walk away.

EJ nearly tackles me the moment I walk through the door. "Mommy."

I pick him up, give him a big hug. Feeling his little arms around me touches my soul in the best way right now.

"Is Daddy coming home?"

I put him down. "Not today."

"Can we go see him?"

Mom brought the kids home this morning so they could be around their own stuff since everything else in their life had become out of order. I look to her for some relief. I just can't do this right now.

On cue, she summons him back in the kitchen. "Help me finish making these cookies."

"Cookies," he yells and beats her back in the kitchen.

Kennedy's sitting in the middle of the living room floor. Her full attention devoted to the coloring book in front of her. Either she's working on a masterpiece or she's still pissed off at the world for hurting her favorite teacher, and in return, hurting her father.

"You still not talking?"

She digs out another crayon from the box.

I let her be. This just doesn't seem to be my day. Everyone has gone for blood today. My mother-in-law. Sgt. Lee. Brandon. My daughter. And in his silence, even my husband.

Brandon left me in the restroom horny and pissed. As much as I wanted to run, actually needed to run, I had no intentions of doing such. I needed to do wrong again to make me feel right. For just one moment I needed a temporary fix. Sex was going to be that. Sex with another woman's husband. Yep, that's what I needed to release all of this stress. I should feel bad about it, but I don't.

In my bathroom, I fill the tub up with heat. Since I didn't get the release I was going for, a hot bath will have to do. The moment my feet hit the water, something in me explodes. A wail crawls from my soul and crawls through my lips. I cry so hard I shake. Feel like I'm seizing.

All of this began with a lie, a lie Eric and I told each other, and ourselves, since our first date. Either one of us could've easily walked away. He could've gone back to the woman who kept his heart and I could've held on to my singleness until I met someone to give my heart to. Instead, we both tried to make something work that would eventually reveal our lies and fears. I made him responsible for my happiness and he failed. Failed because that wasn't his responsibility. Had I realized that way back when, life would be so very different.

Again, hindsight is everything.

A loud vibration rumbles next to my head. Feels like a woodpecker on crack is trying to drill a hole through my brain.

It takes me a minute to realize where I am. I'm still in the tub. Been in here so long, the water feels like ice. All of the crying I did must've sent me into a deep sleep. I unplug the tub, let the water drain. Wrap myself up in an oversized towel. Try to bring some warmth to my body.

Two short vibrations reminds me why I'm freezing. I grab the phone from the back end of the tub, see two missed calls; two new voicemails. Both are from my mother-in-law. I call her back.

"Is everything all right?"

"Well, hello to you too, Sydney."

"It's been a long day. Sorry if I seem short."

"If you say so."

"And what does that mean?" I put the lid down on the toilet, sit on top of it with the towel still wrapped around me. Don't know why, but it feels like a draft has blown through all of a sudden. Makes me shiver.

"I haven't forgotten what you said at the hospital."

Here we go again. "Maybe not, but you seem to have forgotten I also said it was nothing."

"Look, Sydney, I'm trying my best to get along with you for the sake of my son. You don't make it easy."

I lean my head against the wall, slightly bang it a couple of times hoping to bang out this conversation taking place. It doesn't work.

She continues. "I don't know why my son married you."

As much as I've tried through the years to be respectful, this woman has made it hard. A daughter-in-law can only take so much abuse before keeping the peace in the relationship between mother and son is no longer a concern. I've never wanted to cross the line of respect, never wanted to go off on my husband's mother like my mother didn't raise me any better. Today, she's caught me on the wrong day and at the wrong time. "Your son chose to marry me. He made that choice even after knowing how you felt about me. That says more about you than anything. So tell me, what's really the problem?"

After a deadening silence, Elaine says, "Eric is awake and is asking for you."

Nerves do a number on me as I walk through the doors to ICU. Feels like any minute I should be sitting on somebody's toilet. The last time my husband's eyes were on mine, they held more contempt than a judge toward an out-of-order attorney in court.

I stand in front of the window to his room. The blinds are open. I see him, see him looking at me. It's almost as if he felt my energy, felt me coming before I even arrived.

I nod.

He blinks slowly.

"It's a blessing," an approaching voice says.

I grab the familiar hand of my father-in-law as it wraps around my waist. Lean my head on his shoulder. "It is."

"Your name was the first thing he said. Called you before his eyes even opened."

Mr. Holmes' words make me raise up my head. I give him a kiss on the cheek, squeeze his hand.

He rubs his other hand on top of mine. "You know my wife means no harm. Eric is our only child and she can be overprotective."

"That's putting it mildly."

He sighs. "She just... We both want what's best for him."

I squeeze his hand again and move toward the door. As I walk into the room, Mrs. Holmes walks out. She says nothing, neither do I.

Eric studies the tension between our nonverbal exchange. Watches her walk out, watches me walk in. Takes notice of the space between us. His eyes close.

I shut the door once my husband's mother leaves. I nod at my in-laws through the blinds, then close them. Keep all outsiders outside of this room. My eyes focus in on the man I married. He's still bandaged up, face still puffy from the blow. I walk over slowly. As I approach, his eyes reopen. I sit in the chair his mother was sitting in by his side; place my hand on top of his. "You scared me."

"Thought you'd be here when I woke up."

"I wanted to be."

His hand moves underneath mine. "Where were you?"

"Went home to check on the kids. Had to make sure EJ wasn't driving my mom crazy. You know how he can get." I chuckle, both at our rambunctious son and to help calm my nerves some.

Eric looks through me, penetrates my thoughts. Searches for answers to questions I have yet to be asked. Questions I'm not sure I want to be asked or that he would want to hear the answers to. He slides his hand away from mine, reaches for his mouth.

"Wait, don't touch. Is it itching?"

"Yeah."

On the cart on the other side of the bed is some ointment and gauze. "Let me put some of this on to help." A piece of glass from the accident cut the side of his mouth; had to get stitches. I dab lightly at it. "That better?"

His fingers wrap around my wrist, pulls my hand down. Looks deep inside me again. "We're not okay, are we?"

I use my other hand to remove his from mine, place it on his lap. Take the gauze and throw it in the trash by the door. A shallow breath barely fills my lungs. Feel tears on the surface, but I exhale them away, turn back toward the bed. I look at my husband, press my lips together, and shake my head.

He says, "I can feel it."

My legs grow weak. I sit back down by his side. "Do you remember what happened before the accident?"

He doesn't look at me, he closes his eyes instead. "I remember more than I want to."

The door opens. A woman in blue scrubs enters the room. A clear bag in her hand. "How are you feeling, Mr. Holmes?"

"I'm alive. Guess that counts for something."

"Of course it does." She nods my way while checking his temperature. "You must be his wife."

"I am."

"Met his parents earlier. Such sweet folks. Good to see someone cared for. Sometimes people are in here for weeks without anyone coming to see them." She removes an empty bag and replaces it with fresh meds. Lowers his bed a little.

"Can't imagine what that feels like," I say just so she won't feel like she's talking to herself.

She writes a few things down on a piece of paper. "You think you're ready to eat, Mr. Holmes?"

"Not right now."

"Okay," she says. "I'll leave the menu with your wife, and maybe you'll be ready by the time I come back."

The moment she walks out, I tell Eric, "Why don't you try to get some rest."

"I've been resting for a couple of days now."

"I know, I know." I reach for the remote hanging off the back of the bed. "Want me to put on the news?"

"We can't keep skipping around our marriage, Syd."

He's called me Syd for years, but all of a sudden hearing it makes me think of Brandon. Damn these thoughts. "I'm not trying to. Just don't think right now is the time to go there."

A heavy gust of air bursts from his nostrils. Settles him for a bit.

"The kids want to come see you. When I told them you were awake, EJ was so happy he ran circles around the dining room table."

"How's Kennedy?"

"Confused. Hurt. Doesn't understand why her dad hates her teacher."

"That wasn't supposed to happen."

I hang the remote back up. "What were you thinking, Eric?"

He shakes his head, shakes it like he's trying to keep a bad thought from entering his mind.

I'm concerned about his head injury. "Are you hurting?" I reach for the button on his bed to call the nurse.

"It was Michael."

I pull my hand back. "That's what the reports from some of the people at the school said."

"I was standing with Kennedy and her teacher talking about how good she's doing with her math. I didn't know Michael had gotten out of the car until he started asking Mr. Carter all these questions. He mentioned you and the teacher being at Riverpoint holding hands and seeing you two riding in your car together."

"He had no right," I interrupt.

Eric reaches for his mouth again. This time I let him. He touches the stitches, touches around them. Feels around the rest of his face. Then plops his arm back in his lap. "Was it true?"

"No."

"Don't lie to me, Sydney."

I think about what I said. It was the truth. I wasn't at the park with our daughter's teacher. He's never been in my car. It was a case of mistaken identity, but Eric doesn't need to know all of that. I get up from the chair, give my butt some relief. Walk over to the window and look outside. I watch as the sun makes its descent.

My mind reminds me how Eric and I began with a lie. How we couldn't face our own insecurities enough to tell the truth of what we wanted. He denied himself of being with the woman he really wanted. I denied myself of loving me enough to know he wasn't the one for me. I couldn't love him out of his love for another woman just as much as he couldn't love me out of my fear of ending up lonely like my mother. These years have proven that. We've wasted all this time running from the truth and ended up running right into it.

"I don't want to live this lie anymore, Eric."

*L*ife as I know it changes the moment I walk through my apartment and see my mom bent over my wife. Mom's sniffles could be heard and her tears could be seen ten states over.

I came home to think, to have a moment to process everything that's happened over the past few days. Coming here was a far stretch for peace, I know, but I wasn't expecting this.

"Is she—" Can't bring myself to say it.

Mom comes over to where I'm standing at the foot of the bed, hooks her arm around mine. "She's still here."

Rene's eyes are closed, her arms clasped around Bear. I don't know what I was thinking bringing her here. Thought I could will her back to life with my love. But I couldn't do that before I knew about the cancer, so how would that work now? She didn't want to come here, didn't want me to be part of this part of her life. She knew I wouldn't be able to handle it. She pushed me away, made me pack up and move on with my life without her because she knew that ultimately I'd have to live without her.

I walk over to the bed, see Bear barely rise and fall against my wife's chest. I drop to my knees, plant my head against hers. "I'm not ready for you to go."

Mom gets down on the floor with me, her arms wrapped around

my shoulders. Does her best to comfort her broken son. "We talked after you left. She never meant for any of this to happen."

None of us ever mean for things to happen the way they do, but that doesn't stop them from happening. Rene tried to beat cancer once. It came back. No matter how much we try, it's impossible to change destiny. This is hers.

My lips touch her forehead, do the same to my mother's hand. I get up from the floor, look on table next to the bed for Rene's cell phone. Scroll through the contacts until I run across William's number. He doesn't answer. I don't leave a message. Told him I could do this on my own, told him I didn't need his help anymore. I was wrong once again. This is something I was never meant to handle alone.

My finger dials 9-1-1.


These are the final moments of my wife's life.

Soon as we made it to the hospital, I told my mom to go ahead and check on Andrew. There was nothing else we could do for Rene at this point. At least that's what the doctor told us. All they can do is pretty much make sure she's as comfortable as possible. It's only a matter of time.

A matter of time.

Time is everything. The thing is, we never know how much we'll have. Our son didn't have much time with us. We were just getting to know him, learn his likes and dislikes, qualities that would shape him in the years to come. Years we'd never see, years we'd never share with him. Just like we didn't know our time with him would be cut short, I never thought my time with my wife would be cut short. When we married, when we said those vows until death… You don't realize how soon that time could come.

A nurse walks in to check Rene's vitals and interrupts my thoughts. The avoidance of eye contact lets me know we don't have much longer.

When the nurse walks out of the room, I walk over to the woman I married nine years ago. All I can do is stand here and watch. Watch her clutch Bear as she sleeps. I pull the covers up over her shoulders. Tuck her and Bear in comfortably. A smile slowly spreads across her face; she grips Bear even tighter, if that's possible. Part of me feels she's nearing the bright light. Getting closer to reuniting with our son, her parents, those whose lives she touched once they reached their end. For a moment, those thoughts loosen the hold on my heart. They erase the anger that's built up over time for the only woman who's had my heart. A broken heart can only hurt so much before it becomes numb. She did the best she could.

So did I.

# 52
## BRANDON

Rene and I are at the beach in Destin walking hand in hand.

She's happy.

I'm happy.

It feels like it did in the beginning of our marriage, when we'd come and walk the beach every weekend and share our dreams with each other until the sun would fall behind the other side of the ocean. We were so in love, had so much hope for our future while living and enjoying the present. We'd talk about how we couldn't wait to have a house full of kids. Growing up an only child, she wanted ten kids. Having a twin brother, I'd only wanted two. But I'd give her as many as she could have. We had our whole lives ahead of us to make it all come true.

"Why did we ever leave here?" I ask.

"Hmm, seems like we haven't been good with making the right decisions."

Her tone catches me off-guard.

Rene stops walking, bends over, scoops up a handful of sand and resumes walking. With each step, she lets go of a pinch of sand. Not taking her eyes off the sand, she asks, "When were you going to tell me about her?"

It's my turn to stop walking. "What are you talking about, Rene?"

"C'mon, Brandon. Let's not play games."

I ask, "How'd you know?"

She drops another pinch of sand. "A woman knows when her husband has eyes for another woman."

I neither deny nor acknowledge her assumption.

"I have cancer not dementia. Neither am I blind." She turns to look at me. "I saw how you two looked at each other at the closing. More importantly, I felt more in that room than I actually saw. Felt enough to know lines had been crossed between you two."

"It's not what you think."

"Everyone always says that when they get caught cheating, only for it to turn out exactly how it *was* thought."

"That was weeks ago. Why didn't you say anything then?"

More sand falls from her fingertips. "I was hoping you'd be man enough to tell me."

"Just like you should've been woman enough to tell me about the lump in your breast."

"That's not fair, Brandon, and you know it." She tosses the rest of the sand from her hand, then picks up another clump. Tries to buy more time.

"It's the same thing, Rene. True, I should've told you. Just like I had a responsibility as your husband, you had a responsibility as my wife."

The sky turns from blue to a myriad of orange and pink as the sun begins to make its descent.

"Did you sleep with her?"

I tell the truth. "Yes, but not when you think."

"Doesn't matter when you go there. Just matters that you did."

"You shut me out of our marriage. What did you expect me to do?"

She drops another pinch of sand. "Do you love her?"

I don't have to think hard. "No."

That settles her for a minute.

We keep walking toward the edge of the earth. Neither of us share words. Both of us in our own thoughts. My mind on where we'll go from here. Something tells me her mind is on the same.

Rene breaks the silence. "Will you make love to me?"

That wasn't what I was expecting, but I nod. She drops the sand, dusts the remnants off on her dress. I slip out of my shoes, put my keys and wallet inside, toss my socks on top. I grab her hand and lead us to the water.

My wife kisses me with so much passion. It's a kiss she never wants me to forget. I slide my tongue in her mouth where it remains as we tread deeper into the warm saltwater. She wraps her legs around my waist. I enter her ever so slow, scared I'm going to hurt her, but also because I want to make this moment last until the end of time.

It's a little difficult loving my wife the way I'd like because my feet have no footing. I kick backward a little until I feel firm sand under my feet. "Better?" I ask.

She nods.

"I never stopped loving you," I say as I hold her close to me.

"I know." She holds my face in her hands, plants tender kisses all over my face, stopping momentarily on my lips. "I didn't make it easy."

"You were scared."

"That's no excuse."

I make love to my wife slow, give her the utmost affection. Whether she told me or not, this is the woman I chose to marry in sickness and health. She's all I've ever wanted. She's always been enough for me. With each stroke, I apologize for giving up so soon, for packing up and moving out of the home we shared together. I apologize for stepping into the arms of another woman for comfort. "I'm sorry, Rene."

I know this is the last time I'll ever be inside her. It's hard not to think about that as she moans in my ear. Moans I'll never hear again.

"It'll be okay, Brandon. You'll be okay," she says, reading my thoughts.

It's not what I want to hear. In ways, I don't want to be okay, don't want to get over our love nor do I want to love someone new.

Rene turns my face to hers, makes me look her in the eyes. "I forgive you and I need you to forgive me."

Deep in my heart, I know she was doing what was best for her. Selfishness and wanting to hold on to the anger would be the only reasons I wouldn't be able to forgive her. I don't know what it's like to watch close family members die. Nor do I know what it feels like to know you're about to die. I can't let her leave this life knowing I couldn't forgive her, or myself for that matter.

"I forgive you," I whisper against her ear.

She hugs me for what feels like two eternities. When she lets me go, she walks out of the water. For a moment, she stops in her footsteps, but doesn't turn around. She puts one foot in front of the other and walks toward the sunset.

A hand grasps my shoulder. I jerk to look behind me, realize I'm not in the ocean, not at the beach. Not in Destin. I wipe the fog from my eyes to see my brother in a wheelchair in front of me. My parents behind him. "I must've drifted off."

I get up from the chair to stand by Rene's side. The dream felt so real. She's still tucked under the covers, her face a look of peace. Bear's no longer clutched to her chest, though.

Andrew hands me the noseless bear. "She's gone."

My heart stops the moment I step back through the doors of ICU and hear a long high-pitched beep. It's the beep you hear in movies when someone's flatlined.

I rush to Eric's room with my hand pressed into my chest. The beep on his heart monitor is steady. He's still in the land of the living. I left his room a couple of hours ago after he fell asleep on me before my confession rolled from my lips. It takes a few moments before my heart calms down to a light pound against my chest. That was a close call.

The clock above my husband's bed reads close to midnight. I walk over to the blinds to close them, give us some privacy. As I get ready to close the door, my heart's pace picks back up as I see a nurse placing a sheet over a patient across the hall. Bent over the bed is Brandon. I can't take my eyes away.

Rene. Guess that's where the beep of death came from.

Oh. My. God.

Just a few hours ago, not only was I trying to have sex with her husband in a public restroom, everything in me at this very moment wants to run across the hall and stand by Brandon's side. Hold his hand, tell him everything's going to be all right. What kind of woman am I? My husband is lying in a hospital bed himself and needs me here by his side. What kind of wife am I?

The doctor and nurse walk out of Rene's room. Mr. Carter is pushed out by an older-looking version of himself. An older woman behind them. Everyone leaves a husband to spend the final moments with his wife.

"Why are you crying?"

As I'm watching someone else's husband, my husband's watching me. I wipe my face with the sleeves of my shirt, close the door. Turn to face him, hoping he can't see my tears in the dark. "I'm not."

"Thought you were done lying."

I don't say anything. What is there to say anyway? The truth's hanging in the air.

"Who's Brandon?" he asks.

My right leg goes weak, causes me to lose my balance. "Huh?"

"You said, *'I'm so sorry, Brandon.'* Who is he?"

Right then, right there in front of my husband, I have a break-down. Tears consume me like flames from a cigarette flicked in a puddle of gasoline. I fall to the floor and bawl worse than my five-year-old son when he's told no. I cry for my selfishness. Cry because I've involved two innocent, hurt men into my misery. Two men who deserved so much better than what I had to give. Two men who came to me because the women they loved chose not to love them anymore. I became their backup plan, and for my own selfish reasons, that was okay with me. In the end, every-one still hurts. Including me.

Today I lay my wife to rest.

The past few days have been the hardest days of my life, but they have no comparison to today. No matter how much I try, saying goodbye to my wife is the last thing I want to do. Rene handled every detail of her funeral before she left. There's no way I would've been able to make any arrangements. Doing so would have felt so final. I guess it is. I'll never know how she was able to do it.

Rene is gone.

I'll never feel her love again. Never feel her lips pressed against mine again.

I tried to tell myself I had lost her years ago. Tried my hardest to believe that lie. It was a temporary salve to a deep wound that never quite penetrated.

"How are you feeling?" The tender voice of my mother brings me out of my thoughts.

My lips can't form any words. I reach out to her, pull her close to me. Wrap my arms around her. Let her love comfort me the way only a mother's love can.

Our embrace is cut short by a knock on my hotel room's door. Couldn't bear staying in my apartment. Kept seeing Rene in my bed, clutching Bear as she faded from life. I open the door, let my father in.

"The limo's here."

I nod.

This is the part I hate, getting ready to head to the church. The time when friends and family gather to drive the streets with flashers on, cops holding up traffic to alert other drivers a family needs their consideration and respect for a moment, when everyone lines up in front of the church by position to the deceased to say their last goodbye. This is the time when you try to be the strongest, or at least look the part.

I grab my suit jacket from the bed. I don't put it on, just drape it over my arm.

Dad firmly grips the meat between my neck and shoulder as we file into the elevator. Does that to give me support without saying anything.

In the elevator's mirror I see my mom's red-rimmed eyes. She's had a hard time ever since they came into town. I hadn't told them about Rene. Saying anything would've only made things worse for me. I'm sure my brother filled them in, but I know they probably didn't think it was to the extent that it was. Mom's loved Rene since the moment I brought her home. They had a great relationship, the kind mother's dream of having with their son's wife. I pull her into my arms, hold her tight.

Once the elevator doors open, she pulls away. Looks up at me, "I'm okay, honey. I'm okay," she says and kisses me lightly on the lips.

I stop my parents from getting off the elevator. "I really appreciate you both being here."

"Son, we wouldn't have it any other way," Dad says.

"But you came for Andrew."

My father puts up his hand, silences my guilt.

Andrew is in his wheelchair parked in the middle of the lobby, Melissa wheels him our way as we approach. "How are you holding up?" he asks.

"Hanging in there," barely comes out.

Despite his feelings toward my situation with Sydney, my brother has been by my side since the day my wife passed away. He's been nothing but supportive, even offered for me to stay at his house as long as I needed to. I couldn't do that, couldn't have him looking after me while his wife looked after him because of my indiscretions. I've been selfish enough.

The sun greets us the moment we step outside. Once my eyes readjust from temporary blindness, I see a long row of cars lined up behind our limo. Though I wanted a small ceremony, seeing all the cars out front puts warmth in my heart. I'm amazed at the support for my wife. She was there for many of them during their time of bereavement. Feels good to know her work was greatly appreciated by the community.

Peter opens the door for me. He extends his hand toward mine. "Whatever I can do to make this time comfortable for you, just let me know. I'm here for you."

"Thanks, Peter." I shake his hand and draw him in for a hug. "You were a good friend to her, a good partner for the business. I'll always appreciate you for that."

He pulls me to the side, gets close to my face. "I know this is hard, but Rene made peace with everything. Shortly after coming to terms with this, she asked me to come with her to church. We prayed together. She'd asked God to forgive her for what she'd done to Reggie and what she allowed guilt to do to her and your marriage. She asked God to forgive her for what she made you do." He wraps his hand around mine, gives it a gentle squeeze. "She wanted me to tell you she doesn't blame you."

I do my best to let his words comfort me.

My dad and Peter help put Andrew in the limo while Mel folds up the chair. I wait for all of them to get in the car before I do. As we ride to the church, I'm saddened by the fact that not much of Rene's family is here. Most of them have already gone on. Knowing she's with them now gives me comfort. No one says much in the car. So much has happened over the past couple of weeks, I think everyone is traveling in their own thoughts.

"*Pass me not, oh gentle Savior, hear my humble cry,*" the choir sings as the church doors open.

The first thing I see is Rene's white casket staring back at me. My feet feel like they're sinking deeper into a bottomless pit as I make my way to the front of the church. Somehow I make it. I can't bring myself to look at her. I stand above her casket with my eyes closed until I feel my brother's hand on my back. I want to stand here forever, but I know I can't.

Scriptures are read, songs are sung, words are shared. Several times, I blank out, drift back to more joyful times. I remember a time Rene told me about driving to pick up a family who had lost both children in a swimming accident. Peter told her he was having stomach issues since that morning and needed to go home. They were shorthanded that day and she really needed him. Once he closed the family up in the car and got behind the wheel, the pressure from sitting down was so great a long fart ripped from his rear. Rene said it smelled like a camel on broil in the middle of a Las Vegas summer. Seconds later, she heard coughs coming from the back of the car.

When she told me the story, she laughed so hard she started snorting. Thinking about that causes me to belt out a laugh. I mean, a Miss-Sofia-rocking-back-and-forth-at-the-middle-of-dinner-in-*The-Color-Purple* kind of laugh. One of the ushers comes over and starts fanning me. They must think I'm on the verge of having a major breakdown. Makes me laugh even harder until tears begin to spring from my eyes.

A young lady and man approach the microphone. A few chords are played from the piano before voices begin singing. *"Sorry, I never told you, all I wanted to say. And now it's too late to hold you, cause you've flown away, so far away."*

Their rendition of Boyz II Men and Mariah Carey's "One Sweet Day" causes me to straighten up real quick. There's so much I still wanted to share with my wife, so much I wanted to tell her and hear her tell me. This is unfair, so fucking unfair. I want to run up to the casket, pull her out and shake her, ask her, "Why didn't you just go to the doctor?"

My emotions are betraying me. One minute I'm hurting, the next I'm ready to fight someone. It was so much easier to deal with her falling out of love with me than having to put her six feet under.

"Whyyyyyy?" I want to scream out.

My father puts his hand on my thigh, does his best to calm me before I erupt.

I put my hand on top of his, grip it like my sanity depends on it. I feel so much pain in my heart, so much pain I'm barely able to breathe.

*"Darling, I never showed you. Assumed you'd always be there."*

I showed Rene how much I loved her from the moment we met. Never did I take her presence for granted. She knew this. I knew it. I loved that woman. But my actions in her last days were everything but love. Only reason I moved out was to prove a point. Wanted to make her mad and come running back to me, beg me to come back to her. My plan failed and pushed me further away from getting my wife back. Now I've lost her forever. I don't deserve to be here. I don't deserve to mourn.

I'm no longer holding my father's hand, no longer am I sitting. I'm standing in front of Rene's casket.

"You want to do this?" Peter's voice shakes when he asks me that.

I don't nod, don't say yes. I just stand there.

Rene's body is lowered into the casket. I look at her for the first time. Peter granted her wishes and made her look exactly like the picture she gave him. She looks like the woman I fell in love with on our first date. Her skin glows as if she's standing in front of the sun. Her lips the color of kissing a thousand roses. I want to kiss her, kiss her like I did on that first date. I do. I bend over and place my lips on hers for the last time.

The fabric on the sides of the casket are folded over her body. Her lips are formed into a smile. I know she's up in heaven with our son in her arms. Her mother and father are with her, all of them beginning their eternal life together. She smiles because now she is at peace. No more worrying about lumps appearing in her breasts and traveling to other parts of her body, no more fearing the same fate as the women in her family who'd gone on before her. She's free from the guilt of feeding our son bad milk. She's free of having to push me away, free of making me hate her. She's free so I can be free. I do my best to tell myself that smile is for me.

Something is placed in my hand. I look down, see Bear in my hand. Andrew's next to me in his wheelchair. I didn't know he had brought my son's noseless bear with him. I bring the bear up to my face, rub my nose against the spot its nose used to be.

I uncover Rene's arm and tuck the only thing that brought her comfort in her final hours underneath. Put the sheet back over her arm.

Mel wheels Andrew back to his spot on the side of the aisle while I stand back and watch as Peter closes the lid. This is the last time I'll place my eyes on Rene. Feels like the sun's just gone down on my heart. Need someone to carry me back to my seat.

*Whyyyyy?*

"There are many times in life when things will happen that we can't understand. No matter what we do or who we talk to, things just won't make sense. Death is one of them. It's in those times where we have to look to the Lord. Philippians 4:7 reminds us that the peace of God, which passeth all understanding, shall keep your hearts and minds through Christ Jesus," the minister says in closing. "May God give you comfort now and forever more."

The bottomless pit is back as I fall in line behind the pallbearers carrying Rene to her final resting place. Feel like I'm about to lose the breakfast I never ate.

Before I make it out the door, Sydney's eyes find mine.

I'm not in love with my husband.

Being at the funeral put a lot of things in perspective for me. It caused me be honest about a lot.

I sat in my car at the gravesite for about an hour watching Brandon stand above his wife's final resting place. He stood as the cemetery workers tossed dirt on top of her white casket like they didn't have time to have any compassion for the man in mourning. Brandon didn't flinch. Just stood there and watched until the job was done. Until he was sure Rene wouldn't push open her casket, crawl up from the grave and kiss him one last time. He loved that woman without question.

Watching him made me finally admit to myself that I never loved my husband. I thought it was love in the beginning. I quickly learned love doesn't make you question if it's love. You just know. You feel it. That feeling never came for me. Part of me feels like the only reason I can say I love Eric is because he's the father of our children. Subtract that aspect from the equation, there'd be no us. Wouldn't be a him and me.

The only reason I married Eric was because he asked. He was the first guy I dated willing to take the plunge of putting a ring on my finger. I became emotionally invested in the idea of being someone's wife even when I didn't necessarily want to be *his* wife. For a man to find me worthy enough to pledge his life to gave me validation. I never got that growing up and didn't want to end up lonely like my mom, so I jumped at the opportunity without giving it much thought at all.

Now, I know that was a selfish move. He was right when he said I've wasted ten years of his life. But I was right when I told him he'd wasted ten years of my life as well.


Eric and I have just been existing since he was released from the hospital a couple of days ago. We've barely said more than three words to each other.

I tucked the kids in bed about thirty minutes ago. EJ usually calls out asking for something random like a piece of bacon or a sticker shortly after putting him to bed. I waited for him to make his usual request before letting Calgon take me away, but I guess tonight sleep took him under.

My body relaxes as I sink deeper in the hot water. Feel every muscle relax as the conversation I had with my mom the day of Eric's accident replays in mind. She was the other woman to a man who left her for another woman. I never intended to be the other woman. Never intended to develop feelings for another man. I have these feelings for Brandon I've never had for any other man. Maybe it's because we found each other at a time when we had no other choice but to be honest with each other and honest about how we felt in our marriages. I didn't have to hide behind any façade to get him interested in me and vice versa. It just was. We just were.

The bathroom door creaks open. Eric walks in with hesitation in his step. "Can we talk?"

I sit up, cover my breasts with the warm rag.

He sits on the edge of the bathtub. "You've been avoiding me since your breakdown in the hospital."

"Your parents have been here and I wanted you to have time with the kids. They've missed you."

"So, you're just going to run around the breakdown, huh?"

The rag grows cold against my breasts. I want to dip it back into the warmth of the water, but all of a sudden I'm ashamed to let my husband see my nipples. Just feels strange after all that's happened. "I slept with him," slips from my lips.

"Damn it, Sydney."

I swear if his arm wasn't bandaged up, he'd try to knock down a few walls.

I feel like Delilah. Feel like I've found out the secret to my husband's strength. All these years he's walked around with such confidence, like nothing could cause him to stumble. But I've found something. Found the one thing to shut him all the way down.

Eric gets up from the tub, leaves me in my bath of shame.

I kick my feet out of the water, sit them on top of the tub underneath the faucet. The water's caused all the calluses on my feet to become magnified. My feet look rough. Blisters under both feet. May be time for new shoes and socks. Then again, I just bought some. It's all the running. Running from my problems, running from my misery. At some point, all the running catches up with you. No matter how much or far I've ran, I'm still here. My problems are still here. I'm still in an unhappy marriage. As my mother said, I either need to walk away or learn how to make myself happy.

Eric marches back into the bathroom. "Please tell me you didn't violate our vows."

Back to the familiar I go. Want to lace up my sneakers and run away from here. But I can't. Can't keep running. "What do you want me to say?"

"Say something."

"I cheated, Eric. I had an affair." I let the water out of the tub, stand on the outside with a towel clutched tightly around me. "Yes, I violated our vows."

There's so much disgust in his eyes as they pour over me. "It's that Brandon guy, isn't it?"

I nod. I grab a bottle of oil off the counter and head into the bedroom. Eric follows, sits on his side of the bed. Both of our backs facing each other.

On cue, our bedroom door swings open. In walks a little person with eyes barely open. "Mommy, can I have a rabbit?"

I rub the top of his head. "No, EJ. You can't have a rabbit, but you *can* go back to bed."

"But Billy at school said he got a rabbit for his birthday." He walks around to my side of the bed.

"You're not Billy and your birthday isn't for another few months." I slip my robe on top of the towel still holding me hostage. "C'mon, let's go back to bed."

This kid is a work of art. The moment his body hits the sheets, all I hear are light snores. I stand at his door and watch him. I love this little guy. I love both of my kids. I don't see how parents can hate their kids because they hate their father. No, I don't hate my husband, but I do feel some kind of way about him that could affect how I feel about my kids. I could look at them as a mistake. They've been everything but. They're what has kept me sane most of the time. It's because of them that I've sacrificed my own feelings. If only I had sacrificed my desires. Instead of handling my misery properly, I've caused others to be miserable. The kids may not feel it right now, but in time, they'll reap the mistakes I've sown.

Back in the master bedroom, it's completely dark. Every light has been cut off. I'm not even sure if Eric Sr. is still in here.

I move to my side of the room with the familiarity of a blind person. I've trudged this same path for years. The carpet moves under my toes, molds to my feet like memory foam. I grab a pair of boy shorts from the dresser, a tank top. Resume my position on my side of the bed. Before I pull the covers over me, I slather my feet with Vaseline, rub so hard to bring moisture back to my parched feet that it makes my hands feel like they're on fire. I stop before my hands get all scratched up. Slip on some socks to seal the moisture in.

As my eyes adjust to the darkness, I see my husband is still sitting in the same spot on his side of the bed. His shoulders slumped, head hung low.

"I could've stopped Michael."

Moments ago I told him I slept with another man. Now he's admitting to nearly taking someone's life.

One confession warrants another.

"Why didn't you?"

"After the last conversation we had, I couldn't."

It's been weeks since the last time Eric and I said more than a few words to each other. It was right before the accident, after things had already fallen apart in our marriage. He admitted I was a distracting convenience to him. I admitted he was a cure for loneliness to me. Maybe I couldn't form my lips to actually say that to him out loud, but the letter I had written him said it all loud and clear. Neither one of us was strong enough to stop things from going too far back then, and we're in the same boat yet again. "Tell me what happened."

"On the way to pick up Kennedy, Mike mentioned he had been wanting to talk to me about you. I didn't think anything about it. Figured it was another case of Rachel making a major issue out of something minor. But then he said he'd pulled you over for speeding. Said you had a man in your car with blood dripping from his hand. Said he'd seen the two of you together before."

Everything in me wants to deny what Eric's saying, but all it would do is make the situation worse. I draw my legs in, sit Indian-style, chin resting in my hands.

"He didn't say any more after that because his phone had rung. It was his wife. As they talked, I tried to put what he had said out of my mind. You'd just told me how unhappy you were. I know what happens when a wife isn't happy with her husband."

"But you said you were unhappy too, Eric."

He turns around to face me. "This isn't about me. It's about you, what you did. Yeah, I was unhappy, but I didn't go out and sleep with another man." He says that, then turns back away from me.

There's nothing I can say, though, at that time, I hadn't violated our vows.

"When we got to the school, Kennedy was outside in her usual spot waiting on me with Mr. Carter. He was in the midst of shaking my hand when Mike came rushing up to us. His disposition was off. He seemed angry."

My thoughts drift to when Michael pulled me over and had me get out of the car when he recognized Brandon's face. His disposition had changed then.

"He made a reference to her teacher's hand, asked him how it was healing. Mr. Carter looked at him dumbfounded. The more the teacher denied what Mike accused him of, the more irate Mike became. I'd seen him like that before. Whenever we'd responded to a domestic call and it turned out to be a result of infidelity, he'd have the same kind of hatred brewing in his eyes. I should've stopped him then."

Again I ask, "Why didn't you?"

"Riverpoint Park."

"What does that have to do with it?"

"Mike said that's where he saw you and Kennedy's teacher the first time. I started thinking about all the mornings you got up before the sun to go there. You were spending more time at the park or the gym. If something came up when you couldn't get out there, you'd be different. It was like you'd withdraw from me. I'd shrug it off, throw myself into work. Started picking up more shifts so I wouldn't have to see it."

"So you knew?"

"I get paid to notice things that try to go unnoticed, Syd." He coughs, tries to loosen whatever's gotten stuck in his throat. "My job is to pay attention to my surroundings, to look for things out of place. Twelve hours a day I have to be on alert. Didn't want to do that in my own home."

Part of me wanted him to notice. I wanted him to say something about my late nights out and my early morning runs. Wanted him to stop me from the temptation of sin before I was too weak to give in.

"I also get paid to pay attention to the truth. I knew Kennedy's teacher wasn't lying. I felt it in my gut. I heard her yelling, screaming for me to leave her teacher alone, that he didn't do anything wrong."

Now I know why Kennedy is mad with her father. Hasn't had much to say to him at all since he's been home. Though she won't admit it, I know she's happy her father is okay and she's missed him, but I don't know if their relationship will ever be the same. A lot of relationships have been changed as a result of what I chose to do.

"Mr. Carter ran off. Mike ran back to the patrol car. Kennedy was still screaming, but something got a hold of me and I ran behind Mike. I got in the passenger side and let someone else drive my fate. As Mike swerved in and out of traffic, my conscience kicked in. This wasn't a high-speed chase. We weren't going after a criminal. What we were doing had nothing to do with me or you or that innocent man. I put my hand on the wheel, tried to steer us toward sanity."

Eric's right. That accident had nothing to do with us. When Michael threatened me after walking out of the hospital with his minor cuts and bruises, I knew it had everything to do with his bruised ego. Rachel had betrayed him, she had gone behind his back and brought filth to the bed they shared. He saw his partner, his friend, the father of his godchild heading down that same road. He saw himself in Eric, saw his pain. Reminded him of his own. No matter how good his marriage was, he'd never be able to forget the betrayal.

He doesn't say anything for a while; neither do I. The more we uncover what has become of us, the more it becomes evident that we need to right our wrongs and move on before we tear apart more lives.

"Why did you sleep with him?"

I don't have to think about my answer. "Because I wanted to see how it would feel to be without you."

*I* stood by Rene's grave. I kept hoping it was just a dream. As more dirt covered her white casket until it couldn't been seen anymore, it finally registered that she was indeed gone. It had began to rain, the ground grew mushy under my feet. I almost lost my balance and fell forward to join my wife six feet under. That didn't stop the workers from digging. Didn't stop me from standing. My mind was somewhere else. It had drifted to the last time I stood in that spot. Rain fell hard that day as well. Rene had come to clean our son's name, clean it of the residue that would cover it once again in a matter of days. Would she want me to do the same to hers? I imagined her extending her hand out and reaching Reggie's some six feet under. United again. She no longer had to live without him. When he passed away, we had to learn how to live without him. We had each other to help make it through the rough times. Life went on without him. How would my life go on without her?

When she told me about the cancer as she signed our divorce papers, I was so angry I couldn't see how scared she was. As we fought in the rain, she showed me her fear, showed me what she denied me seeing all those years I thought she had fallen out of love with me. She didn't want a divorce. She never would've wanted to live without me. I knew that woman like I knew my social security number, and I knew the only reason we were standing there in that moment was because she was scared. I'd wished I had grabbed her the moment I felt her slipping away. I would've reached my hand in her breast, taken the cancer and placed it in my own chest. I would have rather let the disease be my end than hers.

I stood at that grave and replayed every conversation. Every laugh, every tear. Every time we made love danced through my head like Baby when Johnny Castle pulled her out of the corner. I was willing to stand in that rain soaking in Rene's eternal love until the Rapture. I would have, had a hand not slipped in mine and pulled me to the waiting limo.

There's a knock on my hotel room door. It has to be one of three people. By the lightness of the knock, almost sounding unsure as if they're at the wrong door, I figure it could only be my mother. It's been a long day of keeping a straight face in front of everyone. This last hour alone has left me pretty numb and not in the mood for company. I open the door without looking through the peephole.

"Can I come in?"

I move out the way so she can walk through.

Mother hands me a plate with a napkin over it. "I brought you back a piece of cake."

Tossing the plate in the trash is my first instinct, but I don't want to disrespect my mother's effort of consideration. Not sure why people bake cakes and pies for a funeral in the first place. *Celebration of life.* Is it ever a celebration for those in mourning? I tell my mother that.

"I think it's all about the thought," she says. "Food, especially sweets, comforts us in a way that nothing else does."

My mother has never been a small woman. Not big, but not

small. She began picking up more weight after Andrew's accident back in college. Every holiday since it seems like she's a few pounds heavier. These past few weeks have been filled with emotions, many things to make one need serious comforting. I put the cake in the mini fridge. Mom's sitting on the sofa when I turn around. I sit in the chair across from her. "How's your diabetes?"

"I'm doing the best I can. It's hard sometimes, trying to eat right when your spouse is used to things tasting a certain way. I'll change one ingredient and your dad can tell. He doesn't say much, but his face tells me everything."

"He's never been good with hiding his emotions."

"Not at all. If he doesn't like something, you will know."

I do my best to keep the conversation light, keep it off of me. "What time is your flight tomorrow?"

"Not until six in the evening, but you know your dad will want to get there before the sun comes up."

"Humph, that he will." My dad invented the rule of being on time is being fifteen minutes early. He took it a step further, though.

Mom smooths out the bumps in her skirt. Does that over and over again while looking all around this rented room. Time for her to get out what she came to talk about. When her eyes connect with mine, she says, "You going to be okay, honey?"

Not wanting to get involved with this conversation, I simply nod.

She drops her hands in her lap, lets her eyes wander again. Moisture builds between her eyelids. "Who was that woman watching you at the gravesite?"

I don't answer. Not because I don't want to, but because I don't know. I barely even remember being there myself.

"Is she—is she the one Rene told me about?"

"What are you talking about, Mom?" I move forward in my seat. My attention fully alert now.

"Remember how I told you Rene and I talked after you left for the hospital with your dad? A lot of what she said wasn't making sense to me. I had to ask her to repeat a lot." She scoots to the edge of her seat, reaches her hand across the table until it touches mine. "The woman at the grave, is she who you're having an affair with?"

Sydney immediately comes to mind. Wish she hadn't come to Rene's service. Maybe she was paying respects to her client, having just sold her house. Or maybe she was there to support me. She had no right to be there. After leaving her in the bathroom at the park, I was hoping that would be the last I'd see of her. Seeing her again would make it that much harder to forget her. And part of me is not ready to. At least not yet.

I search my mother's eyes, look for judgment, disappointment. I see neither. All that's riding her amber eyes is concern for her son. Genuine concern. I squeeze her hand back, then release it. "Have I always needed more attention than the average kid?"

"It was only you and Andrew. I can't tell you about any other kids."

"What about him? Did I need more attention than him?"

She reaches her hand back over my way. "Where's this coming from?"

"See, this— This is what I'm talking about." I raise her hand off mine. "Why do you do this?"

"Ohh, Brandon. I'm so sorry. It's just that... I wasn't... We weren't expecting you."

"I know the story."

She twists her wedding ring around her finger as she talks. Her eyes avoiding mine. "We hadn't planned on two babies. I was scared. Your father was scared. We barely had money at the time to eat a full meal each day. Feeding an extra mouth was one thing. We'd accepted the challenge. But when we found out about you, I broke down. I was depressed. I think I gave all of that to you."

Without saying it directly, she answers my question.

"Felt bad once you were born. You were so small, so innocent. I couldn't be mad that you found your way into our family. God allowed you to be with us for a reason. I held you all the time. Sometimes your father had to remind me we had another baby." Her hand grazes mine again. "I've spent all these years trying to make up for those isolated months in my womb."

I don't blame her or my father for feeling the way I feel. I am who I am. In a lot of ways, I'm like my father. He doesn't hide his emotions. Why should I be any different? "Yes."

"Yes, what, honey?"

"I was having an affair."

"That *was* Sydney?"

Guess my mom and Rene *did* talk about a lot. I affirm what I've already admitted to with a nod. "For the last three years of her life, Rene made me grow to hate her. Our marriage was dead a long time ago. It was only a matter of time."

My mom's face grows flush. Can tell the son she raised has disappointed her beyond any disappointments I caused in my youth. "Don't talk like that, Brandon."

There's nothing I can say to excuse what I did. Having an affair while my wife was dying of breast cancer makes my soul feel empty, but my soul was already empty. Still, no excuse is good enough and no apology would be good either.

*I* pull my car in the garage next to Eric's truck. He hasn't been cleared to drive yet since coming home. While his parents have been in town, they've come over and taken him for rides just to get him out of the house since I'm at work during the day. Don't know why I was hoping to not see his ride this evening.

Instead of going straight inside, I shut the car off, let the garage door roll down, and sit in my car listening to the end of a song by the woman who declared she is not her hair. I just need a moment, a breather before walking into the chaos I created.

A loud miniature voice rudely disrupts my peace. Little feet come charging toward my car. "Mommy." EJ slaps his hands against my rolled-up window, his breath fogging up his view of me. There goes that.

"Watch out." I open my door and hand him two of the value meals I bought at his favorite fast food restaurant on the way home. "Take these inside."

He yells his joy as he runs back into the house. "Kennedy, look what Mommy got us."

Walking in the house feels like my feet are covered in molasses. This is my life. I toss my keys on the counter, and instead of making sure the kids aren't fighting over their meals or seeing if Eric needs anything, I march right upstairs to my sanctuary.

I pour unscented Dove body wash and Egyptian oil into running hot water. Drop a few drops of aloe and soft linen scented oil into an oil warmer, burn a tea light candle underneath. My clothes come off, robe comes on. I shut the water off and head downstairs to check on the kids, and to give the water a few minutes to lower a couple degrees to the perfect temperature.

Eric Sr.'s in the kitchen making a ham sandwich. Eric Jr. is talking to him, but he's not paying attention.

"Leave your dad alone and finish your food, EJ," I tell him.

Kennedy's picking over her food. She doesn't share the enthusiasm of her brother over the golden fries. I tell her to throw it away if she's not going to eat it. She doesn't hesitate.

I address their father. "When EJ finishes his food, will you give him his bath?"

He nods.

Once upstairs, I slip my robe off, let it fall to my feet. Dip my foot in to make sure the water doesn't boil off a layer of my skin. It's perfect, one degree below hot.

I submerge my body all the way to my neck, feels like I'm floating. My eyes close. Thoughts float in Brandon's direction. He left me hanging in a public bathroom. It wasn't the ideal place to be in the first place, but I needed to feel him again. Needed him to feel me. Needed us to feel each other so we wouldn't have to feel everything else.

"Are you thinking about him?"

I almost hit my head against the back of the tub when my husband's voice comes out of nowhere. "Eric."

"Haven't seen you smile like that in a long time."

I try to hide my warming cheeks. "Don't be silly."

He comes over to me, sits on the edge of the bathtub, stares at me with lustful eyes. There's a swell in his groin. The bulge lets me know where his mind is. A chill crosses over me. I realize when he scared me, I raised my upper body from the water and now my nipples are rock hard, making me slightly cold. Eric dips his hand in the water and rubs warm fingers over my peaks. That quickly warms my center. He licks his lips as he watches my eyes flicker from fearful to the same lustful look in his eyes. He leans over, puts his lips on my neck while his fingers steadily dance across my aroused breasts. Lips move to my shoulder, slowly trailing down my wet skin until the heat from his mouth meets the heat he created on my nipples. Fire burns through me as my husband's touches penetrate the warmness between my thighs. He stirs up a part of me I thought I had lost for him.

I step out of the water with his fingers still inside of me and wrap my legs around his lap. As his good hand makes love to the most tender part of me, I feel myself on the verge of tears. Not sure if it's because I let my weakened emotions lead me to another man or if having my g-spot hit repeatedly is almost more than I can bear.

Eric juggles my breasts back and forth in his mouth. At the same time, sliding his hand away from my sweet spot. I reach my hands to unbutton his pants, to move this party up a level. He moves my hands away, kisses me on my shoulder as he slides me off his lap and walks toward the door.

"Where are you going?"

"Changed my mind."

"You're joking, right?"

His hand is on the doorknob. "You said you wanted to see how it would feel without me. Let me know what you come up with."

And with that he walks out.

In a matter of nine years, I got married, had a child, lost a child. Lost my wife. None of it seems fair.

A widower, a title hard to swallow.

A fatherless widower, an even harder title to swallow.

After death, the survivors have the choice to give up and die as well or move on with their lives while holding on to the memories. It's a hard decision many have to make. A decision I didn't believe I'd have to make for at least seven decades.

But I'm here now. This is what it is.

People move forward all the time without moving on. They stay stuck in moments of time while time still moves on. They fail to fully process circumstances for many reasons, avoidance of pain being the main reason. When Reggie passed, I made the choice to move on. I mourned, I moved forward and I moved on. Rene moved forward. A big difference in moving on. She kept moving further in life, time kept ticking, but in her mind, she never left that space where she first found that lump in her breast. Her fears kept her stuck and guilt ate its way through her body. I truly think that's how a lot of folks end up with cancer. Avoiding what was, in any situation, has to come out one way or another, even if that means taking people out. I don't want that to be me.

As I dreamt of Rene as she was transitioning, I realized my life could end the same way if I held on to the anger not only of losing her, but of my son's departure as well. Her leaving brought up the pain from his leaving. She knew I was holding on to too much. She knew that if she didn't reach out to me in some way to bring peace, that anger would've taken me over the edge.

I don't want to be stuck being angry at the decisions she made. Don't want to lose me because I lost her.

It hasn't been easy since she left. After taking my folks to the airport, I went back to my apartment. When I walked through the threshold, I swore I felt Rene's presence. She'd barely been in the space before her illness got the best of her, but she was in there long enough for me to know she should be there. I tried sleeping in the bed she slept in a few nights. Flipped and flopped all night. Kept hearing Rene coughing. I jumped out of bed, stripped the sheets off, tossed them in a corner. Fell on top of them, where I sat for what felt like another decade. I went inside each drawer in the dresser, grabbed handfuls of clothes and flung them in the corner as well. Whatever I could get my hands on found its way on the floor. The place looked like the state of Alabama after a slew of tornadoes ran through it.

That was three nights ago. Haven't been back since.

Maybe the anger hasn't gone far at all.


Nearly two weeks have gone by since Rene's passing and it's still hard for me to wrap my mind around it. My father calls every day to check on me. Says to take as long as I need to, and that *"Back in the Old Testament, it was mandatory for people to mourn for thirty days."* I had to tell him we weren't in the Old Testament. I understand where he's coming from, though. In today's society, we're expected to bury a loved one and return to work the next day. It's as if the pain is supposed to stop the moment the last pile of dirt is tossed on their grave.

I'm still hurt and confused about all that's happened. Still pieces of anger floating around my conscience. I try to block it out, find something else to think about, focus on, then someone calls to check on me and it brings it all back up.

I don't seem to know what to do with myself anymore. Before I knew about Rene's illness, I spent most of my time outside of work trying to figure out what was going on in our marriage. Then when I found out, I spent all my energy trying to cure her. I took an indefinite leave of absence from my job at the accounting firm. Though they understood, it didn't take long before client demands took their understanding to another level. So with no wife, no job, life pretty much feels empty.

I'm sitting at the foot of the bed staring at the little pieces of my life littering the room. Frustration makes me kick at a bag on the floor. A few papers fall out, stacked up mail that I picked up at the apartment the last time I was there. I grab the mail and toss it on the desk by the window of my hotel room. Bills, condolence cards. Stuff I don't want to give any attention to right now. The one piece of mail I open is from my old firm. I rip open the envelope and pull out my severance package including all unused vacation time in dollars and cents. This is my award for seven years of service. I gave them more time than some couples give their marriage.

My cell phone vibrates on the bed. A sympathy call is not what I'm in the mood for. I grab it to decline the call. The face displayed across the screen makes me feel like I'm looking in the mirror. I hit the green button.

"How are you feeling?"

"Tired of people asking me that. How about you?"

"Same here."

Andrew and I have barely talked since the accident. The only words we've shared outside of the hospital were at Rene's funeral.

Our mother shared with me how things have been a little rough between him and Melissa. She's had to take a lot of time off of work just to help him get around the house. His leg hasn't healed all that well. With all of the extra stress in his household, I can't help but feel guilty being that it was my fault. I let him know just that. "I'm sorry about everything, Drew."

"Won't change what happened."

"And if there was something I could do to take it all back, you know I would. I didn't mean for any of this to happen."

His voice becomes muffled.

"Hey, man, I can't hear you."

"Hold on. Trying to move with this walker."

I give him a minute to get himself situated. Hear a lot of huffing and puffing on the other end of the phone. I know the tone of those huffs; he's not out of shape.

"I'm not calling to talk about what's going on between us. Just checking to see if you need anything around there. Mel can bring some meals over."

"The hotel has a lounge. I'm good on food."

"Oh, I thought you had gone back to your place when Mom and Dad left."

"Couldn't take being there. Needed to get away." I hear Andrew's voice going on the other end, but I can't hear anything he's saying. My attention is drawn to the TV. I don't remember cutting it on. It's a commercial with a couple on a plane. The guy is proposing and as the couple's celebrating, the flight attendant is trying to get them to sit down so the plane can take off. Maybe this is a sign. Maybe I need to do more than get away from my apartment. I need to get far away.

I'm on a flight to the Virgin Islands.

Chicago, Los Angeles, Paris, London, and the U.S. Territory of the Virgin Islands were all places on my list of options. Had a tough time making a decision so I flipped a coin to decide. St. Thomas was the last destination standing. I booked the next flight out. Had to fly into Ft. Lauderdale before hopping on a smaller plane to the island. Didn't pack nothing but a clear quart-sized bag of three-ounce toiletries, passport, and one change of clothes. The rest I'd get as the days go by.

The pilot announces we are within minutes of landing. I slide up the shade on the window, see patches of land sprouting out of the vast ocean the color of a rainbow made of blues. Looks like camels' backs covered by The Great Flood that Noah warned the people about. The closer to land the water gets, the lighter blue it is, almost looks clear. Reminds me of the beaches in Okaloosa County. Makes me think of Rene.

"Flight Crew, please prepare for landing," the pilot says, perfectly interrupting my thoughts.

Underneath my feet I can feel the plane's wheels coming out from hiding. I glance back out the window, feel my eyes widen at the sight of the landing strip. So small looks like we're about to land on a stick of gum. My heart rate quickens. I close my eyes until I feel the wheels brake against concrete. I'm not able to open my eyes until the plane comes to a stop, and when it does, I don't hesitate to grab my bag and deplane.

Stepping off the plane, I'm glad with my decision to wear shorts. The heat is no joke. First on the list to buy is a hat, a pair of shades, and sunscreen. And something cold to drink is a must.

I walk past baggage claim and right out the doors to a swarm of taxis. I hop in the first one with an open door. I tell the driver, "Frenchman's Cove."

He tells me the fee is eight bucks since I'm without luggage, then says to give him a few minutes for a few more passengers to arrive.

I nod.

The ride to the hotel is quick. Was afraid for my life riding up and down narrow roads at ninety miles per hour and no seatbelt. Not sure I would've felt any safer being secured to my seat. Thank God, we arrive unscathed. I give the driver a onceover to make sure if I ever see him again, I run in the opposite direction.

After checking into my room, I head downstairs to grab a bite to eat. It's happy hour. Half price on drinks. I order a piña colada with double rum, a jerk chicken wrap and a side of fries.

I sit back and take everything in. It's not crowded, but enough people to know vacation can be any time you take it. Two couples are playing volleyball in the pool; guys against the girls. Others are standing at the edge of the infinity pool, looks like they can walk straight into the ocean. A few are in the hot tub even as hot as it is out here. People are sunbathing. Women, men, kids. There's a live band playing. One local on a keyboard, one beating hand drums, and another one does double duty with strings and the microphone. They've definitely set the island atmosphere.

The waitress brings my drink. As pineapple-coconut-flavored rum travels down my throat, a smile crosses my face. In this moment, I feel everything is going to be all right.

"My parents are coming over for dinner to spend a few hours with the kids before flying out in the morning."

"I'm not in the mood for company, Eric."

"Just said they're coming to see the kids."

"And who's supposed to feed them?"

He struggles to pull a T-shirt over his head. His motor skills haven't quite been the same since the accident. When he finally gets it off, he tosses it in the laundry basket. "Look, nobody's asked you to cook or entertain. I was just telling you *my* folks are coming over. You can stay up here, or better yet, you can go for a run."

It's been like this since I told him about the affair. Two weeks with him taking jabs at me whenever he can. It probably wouldn't bother me as much if I were still sleeping with Brandon, but I haven't talked to him or seen him since the funeral. Not that I haven't tried. Been to his apartment, the gym, the lake. Even went to the hotel where our sin stained the sheets. No luck.

"That's what I thought."

"Whatever, Eric."

He shuts the bathroom door with a little too much aggression. I wait a couple of minutes before busting into the bathroom. Wait for him to get good and wet, let the heat from the shower steam up the space. I pull the shower door wide open.

"Hey, what are you doing?"

I don't say anything as I stand with my arms folded.

He tries to reach the door to close it back. Each time he reaches for the door, I move, block his way. "Come on, Syd. Quit playing."

My left foot steps in the shower. My right foot behind it. I step in the shower with my work clothes still on, pull the door shut behind me. "Is this how we're going to be?"

"You made that decision."

He's right. I made that decision just like I have so many other decisions through the years that I'm not proud of. Most recent, soiling this marriage. It was never my intention to have an affair, to go against the vows I made before family and God, but I knew what I was doing when I got in bed with another man. Another woman's husband, at that. I knew there was a possibility that decision would lead Eric and I to this point. It was a consequence I was willing to risk.

My husband stares at me, begs me to apologize for something I'm not sorry for.

Ego against ego.

Husband against wife.

It shouldn't be this way. We have to come to an equal understanding. Compromise. He has to give a little and I have to give a little. Can't be any other way.

The fresh-scented green bar of soap drops from his hand, hits the tile floor and slides between my feet. I kick it as I move toward my husband. My eyes don't leave his and his don't leave mine. He wraps his good arm around my waist with a question. I move forward with an answer. Our lips touch for the first time in months with the unfamiliarity of a first kiss. Our tongues try to find a familiar rhythm. When they don't, they create a new rhythm.

I help him lift my soaked shirt over my head. I reach behind me to unzip my skirt. It clings to my wet skin. Takes effort to get it fall. My bra comes off next. Eric watches as I remove my panties.

Both of us stand bare.

My womanly parts wetter than my skin.

His manly parts harder than his heart toward me.

Husband and wife ready for what comes next, but not sure what to do next.

I'm not sure what I was hoping would happen by intruding in on Eric's shower. Guess I wanted him to get mad, yell at me. Keep blaming me for what I did to our marriage, to his career, his friendship. After he awoke from the coma, he gave Sgt. Lee every detail of the accident. His version of events were consistent with the reports from the witnesses, including Mr. Carter's. Although he wasn't the one behind the wheel or the direct cause of the accident, his involvement in the altercation, which sent an innocent man into panic, warranted a suspension. Mr. Carter chose not to press charges for harassment. He wanted to move on with his life. But lines were crossed and it created a bad image for the department and Eric's and Michael's unit. Thirty days with no pay for Eric. Michael, on the other hand, had been terminated. He wants nothing else to do with his ex-partner or this family.

As my husband reminded me moments ago, it was a decision I made. Though I didn't choose none of this, I chose something. Everything else is a consequence.

His lips on my ear summon me from thoughts of disaster and reignite my desire. He nibbles on my neck, draws me closer with his arm still on my waist. I feel his manhood throbbing against my womanhood. It taps at me with a new beat. Not sure where the music will lead, not sure where I want it to lead, but as I once heard in a song, I'll take passion over pride.

Laughter greets me the moment I reach the bottom of the stairs.

Eric Jr. is sprawled out in the middle of the living room floor being tickled crazy by his grandfather. He laughs like everything is all right in his world, like he has not a single care. My father-in-law has so much joy in his face, like this is what living is all about. Watching them brings a smile to my heart. I feel like a voyeur in the lives of adolescence and history.

Meowing and purring is at my feet. I look down, see Forrester in all his furriness looking up at me. "Hey, buddy." I grunt as I pick him up, rub him on his head. "I know you don't agree, but it's time we put you on a diet, sir." He yawns in my face, breath smelling like The Dead Sea. I put him down by the fireplace.

Mr. Holmes stops tickling his grandson long enough to give me a snug hug. "This guy doesn't stop, does he?"

I wrap my arms around his shoulders, give him a kiss on the cheek. "Never."

"Come on, Grandpa. Lemme show you the fort I built in my room."

"EJ, let your grandfather breathe for a minute."

Mr. Holmes grabs EJ's hand and winks at me. "Can't disappoint my favorite grandson, now, can I?"

I nod. "Be careful."

EJ pulls his grandfather's hand so hard up the stairs I see my father-in-law jerk, and he looks back at me. I shrug. He was warned.

Light chatter from the dining room trickles into the living room. Kennedy's at the table talking with her grandmother about school. I can see Eric in the kitchen, putting slices of pizza on plates. I wink at him and quickly divert my attention to his mother. After what her son did to me upstairs, I'm willing to call it a truce. "It would be nice if we lived closer to each other. The kids love spending time with you all."

She glances up at me with no words coming from her lips, then diverts her attention back to Kennedy. "You get your smarts from your father. He was good in school," she tells her granddaughter.

"My mom is smart too," Kennedy says in my defense. I swear, kids are a lot smarter than we give them credit for. They have a sense almost stronger than animals.

A smirk crosses my face. I want to say, "That's right, my daughter has my back," but I don't. So much for that truce.

Eric Sr. comes out with two plates for the kids, puts them on the table. "You want juice or milk?"

"Mom, can I have some soda?"

My eyes are on my daughter, but I see my mother-in-law look to her son.

"Soda's not an option tonight, Kennedy. Juice or milk. Better yet, how about some water?"

The little miss gets up from the table, her chair screeching against the hardwood. "I'm not hungry."

"Young lady, that's not the way you talk to your father."

I put my hand up. Say, "I'll handle my child."

"Doesn't seem like you've done much handling as is."

"Excuse me?"

Eric marches off back into the kitchen. Leaves his wife and mother to war between themselves. Same thing he's done since the day he introduced us. He knew right off the bat his mother wasn't a fan of me. He's never tried to get us to an equal ground. Just lets us fend for ourselves. Maybe he's waiting on one of us to reach a breaking point. I'm past that point.

"Why do you have such a problem with me?"

"I don't have a problem with you. I only wish my son had made a different decision."

"Why? What makes me such a bad choice?"

She reaches her hand over, pinches at my shirt. Flicks a piece of lint to the ground. "Do you even love my son?"

I step back, run my hands down my shirt. "Why does everyone keep asking me that?"

"Because everyone can see the truth but you. Or at least we're willing to call you out on it."

"That's ridiculous."

She scoots back from her chair so hard it bangs against the wall. "You want to know what's ridiculous? I knew the day Eric first introduced you to us that he was making a bad decision. The only reason he ended up with you is because Abigail broke his heart. Had she not taken that job overseas, she would be my daughter-in-law, not you."

I do all I can to keep my simmering blood from boiling over. The name of the woman who Eric wanted to marry instead of me has never been mentioned in this house until now. Both he and I did our best to pretend she didn't exist. But as much as she didn't to us, she existed to Elaine.

"Well, as I told you before, he chose me. It was his decision to marry me." I point to my chest, do it so hard almost feels like my fingernail broke skin.

The mother of my husband takes her seat, sits down with a Mona Lisa-smirk dancing across her face. She's angered me and she knows it. "By the way, did he tell you they saw each other the night before your wedding?"

Those words chop down my pride of being the *chosen one*, they quickly deflate me from the high her son inflated me with twenty minutes ago when he put something good on me in the shower.

I go into the kitchen to find Eric fumbling with an unopened bottle of apple juice. He struggles to twist the cap off with his good arm, which is his weak side. His doctor says it'll be months before he gets full strength back on his right side, his strong side; his gun hand. I watch him struggle with the bottle out of the corner of my eye. I know he needs help, but I won't step in unless he asks. But the way he fumbles with the jar and avoids my eyes, I know it's more than his weakness.

"I didn't sleep with her, if that's what you're thinking."

"Obviously we've been lying to each other all these years, no point in changing things now." I look behind me to make sure no one else is involved in this conversation. "And since we're lying, the shower was just a fuck, right?"

"You came in the shower with your nipples hard. I'm a man."

"And you're also my husband."

"You weren't thinking about that when you were laid up with another man."

I grab the juice from his hands, twist the cap until it loses its suction to the jar. I do that, slide the jar back over to him, and dismiss myself from the conversation. As I walk past Mrs. Holmes still sitting at the dining room table, I tell her, "Safe travels back to Denver."

*M*y eyes are closed, head leaned back. Feel mist from the ocean spray against my face. Hear the sounds of life flowing through my ears.

I'm on a boat with fifteen other people. We're cruising between the Caribbean Sea and the Atlantic Ocean on our way to Virgin Gorda. A tour of the British Virgin Islands arranged by the hotel resort. The Baths is our first stop. I remove my flip-flops and slip into a pair of water shoes I bought at a shop back at St. Thomas last night. It was advised when I registered for this excursion, as we would do a little bit of rock climbing in the beginning of the tour.

"You look like you needed this trip."

I peer into eyes the color of the ocean at sunrise. "You just don't know."

She points her thumb to the boat behind us, says, "Didn't want to interrupt your moment back there."

"Was just enjoying the ride. Never been to the islands before."

"Same here. My girls and I take a trip every year. Last year was London. This time we wanted bikini weather."

I eye her without eyeing her. She has on a fuchsia top moderately covering above-average breasts, bright green shorts lowered slightly to see the top of her bikini bottom. Colors to assure she'd be seen if lost at sea. "You ladies enjoying yourself so far?"

"Minus these mosquitoes, I'm having a blast."

I laugh. "They are aggressive out here." I reach my hand out to help her down a rock as the group travels the path of Devil's Bay.

"Hilda," one of the girls ahead calls out.

My companion for the moment yells, "I'm coming."

I say, "You don't look like a Hilda."

She stops walking, turns around with a hand on her hip. "And exactly what does a Hilda look like?"

I throw my hands up, throw in the towel before this battle even gets started. "No offense."

She laughs. "No offense taken. I actually get that all the time. Thought about changing my name to Kendra or something, but then I'd be denying half of my roots. My mom's German; it was her grandmother's name."

"Interesting."

"My dad hated it, but had a lot of love for my mother and her mother, so that's what went down on my birth certificate."

I say, "I'm Brandon, by the way."

An older couple from the boat catches up to us. Lets us know our chatter has slowed us down.

"You better catch up to your friends," I tell her. "This *is* a girls' trip after all."

She smiles and moves with a quickness to catch her friends.

The Baths is unlike anything I've seen before. Feels like I'm in another world after being hidden behind trees for the seven-minute hike. Makes me think of the movie *The Goonies* at the end as they watch the pirate ship of One-Eyed Willie drift to the unknown in awe. That's how it feels now. Life's perfect perfection.

"Hey, Brandon." Hilda calls me over, hands me a camera. "Can you take a picture of us?"

All five of them stand inside what looks like a lovers' cave, an upside-down V formed by volcanic rock cooled by the ocean. The tour guide mentions something about Tyra Banks taking a picture here for *Sports Illustrated* many years back.

I snap a few pictures of the ladies in different spots before we make our trek back through nature-made pools, dirt paths, and trees to our open-air safari bus taking us to our next destination. Somehow, I've become the designated carrier of Hilda's camera. I make sure I'm relieved of the responsibilities once we're all situated on the taxi, though it does feel good to have a camera back in my hand.

"Oh, I'm sorry about that."

"No problem."

She takes the camera from my hand, letting her fingers linger on my skin a little longer than her eyes in mine.

Climbing through The Baths, snorkeling in Diamond Reef, eating at Marina Cay, swimming to Soggy Dollar Bar at Jost Van Dyke Island, an all-day adventure that left me drained. Had to come back to my room, shower and climb in the bed for a few hours. My stomach woke me up a few minutes ago. I ate a lot from the treats they had on the excursion and at Pusser's for lunch, but I burned just as much calories in all the water and land activities.

I rinse my face off and mouth out with water, gargle some Scope, and head downstairs. Take hotel transportation over to the adjoining resort for dinner at Havana Blue.

All their drinks sound appetizing. I've been in a coconut mood since I've been here. I stick with the theme and order up a Lychee Heaven: Cruzan Coconut Rum, lychee juice, lychee fruit, toasted coconut rim. For starters, I munch on shrimp and lobster tostadas and finish my meal off with mojito skirt steak.

I pay my tab and head down to the beach, order another drink at the bar. I roll up the legs of my khakis to my knees, sit my shoes next to a lounge chair. Drink in hand, I walk the edge of the shore. Without much control, my thoughts drift to the dream I had with Rene the night she passed. Feel my heart sink. I would give anything to make love to her in the waves of the ocean right now. Would love to hold her in my hands and hear her whisper in my ear how much she loves me. I shake away the thoughts. No matter how hard I try, that's one wish that will never come true.

The night's sky is crystal clear, a billion stars glisten above me. Looks like a million pairs of eyes looking down on me. For a moment, I wonder if a set belongs to Rene. Wonder if she's up there having the same thoughts about my dream that she starred in.

"Brandon."

The glass falls from my hand. I turn in every direction in search of my late wife. She's nowhere to be found. I pick the glass up from the sand. Maybe it's a good thing I dropped it, because it's got me hearing voices I don't need to be hearing.

"Brandon."

There it is again.

I pick up my pace, grab my shoes. When I take the glass back to the bar, I see a woman running toward me with more waves in her hair than the sea. "I thought that was you," Hilda says nearly out of breath.

I tell her, "You almost had me looking for the nearest psych ward."

That goes over her head. I can tell when she takes a quick pause. "My girls and I were eating upstairs and I thought I saw you walking out."

I say, "Your friends are gonna have a bone to pick with you if you keep ditching them for me."

She lets out an embarrassed chuckle. "I, umm, told them I'd catch up with them."

"Where are you heading?"

"Came to see what you were up to." Her eyes do that lingering thing again.

"Just walking the beach."

Her tone is bold. *"Let's* walk."

I put my shoes back down. Hilda flings hers in the dirt on top of mine.

Soon as we begin walking on wet sand, she says, "Okay, so I have to ask. Why every time I see you, you're alone?"

"Came alone."

"Where's your wife?"

"What makes you think I'm married?"

Her eyes travel down to my left hand.

I touch my gold band. Haven't taken my ring off my finger since the day Rene put it on. Guess I'm not ready to part with it just yet. "She couldn't come," I say and stuff my hand in my pocket.

"If you want to talk about it…" She leaves the door open.

I don't walk in. Instead I spin the wheel in her direction. "Are you married?"

She runs her hands through her hair, fluffs it until it starts to frizz a little. "Yesterday was my wedding day. He called the wedding off a few days ago, said he wasn't ready to make such a commitment."

"Ouch."

"My thoughts exactly. You'd think he would've figured that before putting a ring on my finger or investing thousands in a destination wedding."

"That's why you're here?"

She sighs. "Yeah, this was where we were to pledge our lifetime to loving one another."

I try to add a little positivity to the air. "Well, at least all the money wasn't lost."

"That is the only, I repeat, the *only* reason I'm not totally pissed. My girls had already bought their tickets, so we just used this as our yearly trip. I would've hated for them to waste their money. I couldn't care less about his."

"Understandable," I say.

She waves her hands in the air. "Enough of that. This weekend is supposed to be—" She stops moving forward and takes big steps back. "What the heck is that?"

I follow her eyes, see a huge something walking out of the water. "Whoa, I think it's an iguana."

It stops moving when it senses us. Not sure if it wants to hide back under the water or continue with its plan of walking the land.

I take a few steps back as well, grab Hilda's hand. "That thing's the size of the Incredible Hulk on his hands and knees."

"I didn't know those things could swim." Her hand trembles in mine. "I'm so not a creature person."

"That makes two of us. Let's head back to the restaurant."

We continue walking backward, but turn around when we realize there could be another oversized lizard walking behind us. Gotta stay focused on what's in front, not behind.

When I feel we're in the clear, I release her hand.

She doesn't let mine go.


We're in my room.

Hilda's standing on the balcony looking out at the pool. "This was supposed to be my honeymoon."

I walk up behind her, hand her a glass of water. "I'm sure you don't see it now, but it was probably for the best. I once heard rejection is God's protection."

She sips nature's best gift. "Thanks." Puts it on the table.

I stand next to her, take in the moment. Hear light splashes and flirty giggles coming from the pool. Says, "Sounds like a private party."

Both of us stand on the balcony, watching and listening. Voyeurs in the dark.

All of a sudden, I feel eyes on me, someone's trying to peep in on my thoughts. I turn and look over at the Peeping Tom. Hilda's eyes are intense, sends me a message I'm not sure I want to or am ready to decipher. Her hand grazes mine, intertwines her fingers with mine. Leads me back inside.

We're standing steps away from the bed. Neither of us are prepared to make the first move, but we're here and a move has to be made.

In the darkness of the room, for the first time in ten years, I remove my wedding band. It doesn't come off easy. I close my eyes and picture Rene standing in front of me, her fingers pressed against my band keeping it from budging. I open my eyes, see she's not in this room, only in my conscience. I ask her to forgive me as the ring comes off and I place it on the table next to the TV. My hand feels lighter and that makes my conscience feel even lighter.

I step forward, gently place my hands on her face.

She puts her hands on top of mine and steps forward until our lips touch.

"You know you've made my life hell, right?"

"Stand in line."

"I'm here now."

The woman I once considered my best friend stands in front of me with no intention of stepping down anytime soon. I'll stand here with her all night if I have to. "Rachel, you need to take this up with your husband. Michael was the one driving the car."

"You just had to do it, huh? Just had to cross the line."

I was wrong. I won't stand out here all night and defend my actions. I chirp the alarm to my car, reach for the door. Rachel shoves her body in front of the handle, makes it hard for me to go anywhere. "Really now?"

She folds her arms across her chest. "Why'd you do it?"

I toss my portfolio and purse on top of the car. Since she's determined to get in my business, I do the same to her. "Why did you?"

"This isn't about me right now, but since you want to know. It's as I told you. I cheated on Michael long before we got married."

"Cheating is cheating."

"Gosh, Sydney." She pushes herself off my car, leans on hers. "Don't you see you've messed up my life?"

I feel myself on the verge of being belligerent right along with her, but I'm in front of my office. This wasn't the time or place for a confrontation. She's here now, said what she's had to say. I lower my voice hoping she'll follow suit. "How was I supposed to know? I've tried to reach out to you. You won't return my calls, you won't reply to my texts. I don't know what you don't tell me."

She runs a hand through her blonde hair, holds a lock at the tips. Picks at split ends, then folds her arms back across her chest. Her voice now a whisper.

I strain to hear, so I move closer to her. Lean against her car next to her.

"We were so happy when we found out. Now I just don't know."

I'm lost. "What did you find out?"

"Michael's termination sent him over the edge, he's started drinking. He's out late at night at these random bars, keeping company with random people. He's a different man. He comes home drunk, throws stuff all around the house."

Though I don't feel like any of Michael's misfortunes or the amount of beers he has at night has anything to do with me, I tell her I'm sorry anyway. Apologize to her, because that's what friends do when the other is hurting.

Her eyes meet mine briefly. "How am I supposed to raise a baby around that kind of behavior."

"Hold up. You're pregnant?"

"Michael was so happy when he found my positive pregnancy test hidden in his lunch box. He ran around the station holding it in his hand. Eric videotaped it with his cell phone, sent it to Michael. He sent it to me. I cried when I saw it." Her eyes well up as she reminisces.

"When was this?"

Her hand grazes her still-flat belly. "A couple of months ago. I'm ten weeks."

"Eric never told me."

"He probably forgot. It was the same week they lost Bragg. I'm sure it wasn't intentional."

I try not to let my hurt show. She's my best friend, at least she used to be. Outside of her husband, I thought I would've been one of the first ones to know. "Why didn't you?"

Her mood changes, she loses the joy in her voice. "Don't make this about you."

"I'm not. I'm just surprised you hadn't told Katrina or me."

"She knew."

Okay. Seems like everybody knows everything but me. Was I so distracted with whatever was going on with Brandon and me that I wasn't paying attention to what was going on around me?

"Here's something else I bet you didn't know. Kat went back to her ex-husband."

"Why on earth would she do that?"

"Because of you."

"Wait, now. I may be to blame for a few things, but that, I will not take credit for."

"Well, it's the truth. She said he may have trouble being faithful, but he's a good father. Her son needs him on a consistent basis. She knows him, is used to him. Bringing another man into the home to help raise her son wouldn't be right. She said your cheating showed her that there really isn't much better out there, so why not take him back."

"That's stupid. I'm not going to accept that."

"Of course you wouldn't, Sydney. You know, all these years I never realized how selfish you are. You have a good man, but that isn't good enough. You have a good job, two healthy kids. A mother and father who love you. You've got a lot that a lot of us don't have, but the moment you feel unfulfilled in your marriage, you go out and ruin the lives of everybody else."

"Don't. Don't do that." I move back across to my car, and hop inside. Shut the door so hard it sounds like it caves in. I feel myself shaking as I try to put the key in the ignition. How. Dare. She.

Rachel knocks on my window as I put the car in drive. In her hands is my portfolio and purse. I roll down the window just enough for my things to fit through. Before pushing them in, she says, "You don't have to take responsibility now, but at some point you will have to face the consequences of your actions."

If only she knew, I already am.


Kennedy greets me with a tear-stained face the moment I walk through the door. I swear someone has a hit out on my sanity.

"Mommy, Mr. Carter's not coming back to school." The pout on her face tells me this has changed her world, even though there's less than three weeks of school left. "I have to have a new teacher."

I run my hand down her disheveled ponytail. "Aw, honey. I'm sorry."

"It's all Daddy's fault. I hate him and Uncle Mike."

"You don't mean that." I squat to her level, turn her to face me. "Sometimes things happen that we don't have any control over. Don't blame your father or your uncle." I want to tell her to blame me. That would only make matters worse, though. I pull her into me, give her a tight hug, rub her back, comfort her any way I can.

Through sniffles, she asks, "Can I have some ice cream?"

"Sure, honey." Lord, it's too early for this child to be an emotional eater. "Where's your brother?"

"Daddy's giving him a bath."

"Put one small scoop in a cup for him."

On my way out of the kitchen, I trip over Forrester's water dish. Water tips out, spills into his food dish. Now I'm jacking up the cat's life. I bend over, pick both dishes up. Pour the food in the trash, the water in the sink. Rinse them both out. Dry the food dish. Instead of more hearty nuggets, I grab a can of tuna from the cabinet. Before I can get half the can open, he comes running in the kitchen. As fluffy as he is, his belly beats him in here. His deep meow sounds like he's gargling hairballs.

Once I finish giving our fur-child his dinner and fresh water, EJ nearly tramples over the dish as he slides into the kitchen in socks and Spiderman pajamas. "Mommyyyyy."

If I hear "Mommy" one more time tonight... "Watch out, EJ."

Kennedy sets his cup of ice cream on the island and scoots the barstool out. "You have to sit here and eat it."

His eyes light up. "Ooooh, we should put some chocolate chips in it."

Kennedy goes to the pantry. Before she can add the extra sugar to her brother's dessert, I intercept the bag.

He hops down from the barstool, slides over to me. "Noooo, Mommyyyy."

Why me, Lord? Why me?

"What's all this ruckus down here?" Eric Sr. shows up just in time.

Our daughter grabs her bowl of ice cream and huffs out of the kitchen.

"You really need to talk to her," I tell him.

"And say what?"

"Something." I shut the pantry door. Glance at EJ sitting at the island digging in his ice cream, apparently no longer concerned about chocolate chips. "You've got five minutes, then upstairs you go."

I don't bother saying anything else to my husband before walking out of the kitchen.

His steps follow close behind mine. "You go somewhere after work?"

I take my heels off before I hit the stairs. My feet thank me as the coolness of the hardwood brings them back to life. "No, why?"

"Thought you would've been home earlier."

"Had an unexpected appointment." I peep in Kennedy's room to make sure she's okay. She's sitting on the floor, her ice cream melting away on the floor next to her. A notebook nestled in her lap, pencil moving at a steady pace. Again, I say to Eric, "You need to talk to her."

"Were you with him?"

My stomach knots up. All of a sudden I have the urge to hurl, let everything come up out of me like it did weeks ago as I ran through my mother's neighborhood. A few hours ago, my best friend blamed me for screwing up everyone's life. Now my husband wants to pin every missing minute on me being with another man. Is this the world I've created?

"I take that as a yes," he says as he follows me into our bedroom. I close the door behind him. "No, Eric. It's a no. I was at work."

"You should've called."

The expression on my face scares me. Can see myself in the mirror in the corner of the room. One of my eyebrows is raised so high my head throbs. If I get any more tense, it might just attach itself to my hair line. "I was a few minutes late. Don't make something out of nothing."

I grab a nightgown from my dresser, take it in the bathroom behind me. Cut the shower on, let the water rinse me from head to toe. Rinse today's stress from me.

Eric's standing by the window in our room when I make it out of the bathroom. The moon has his attention. He doesn't hear my footsteps. Doesn't hear me walk out of the room to check on the kids. He's in the same spot when I come back in.

I pull the sheets back to the bed, proceed with my nightly ritual. Slather petroleum jelly on my feet, slip on a pair of socks. Cut the lamp off next to the bed.

"Mom says I should divorce you." My husband breaks the silence, his eyes still on the moon.

"Your mom says a lot of things."

His exhale lets me know I'm right. The last time his mom said something, I found out about a visitor he never wanted me to know about.

I close my eyes, search my thoughts. Don't have to delve too far. Seems like every thought, every feeling is on the surface. "You know, we both had plenty of opportunities to turn away from each other. We never misled each other, we just chose not to acknowledge the truth, like it was going to disappear." I let my words do their best to saturate the thickness in this room. "Now we're presented with another opportunity. Tell me what you want to do."

"My mom said we need to call it quits."

"You've already said that. I want to know what *you* have to say?"

"I don't like the way I feel. When you're gone, I think you're with him. I'm here all day until I pick up the kids. All day, my mind is on where you are." A hint of aggression mixes with insecurity.

I release an annoyed sigh. "At least your suspension is almost over and you can go back to work."

He turns in my direction. "That's not the point, Sydney."

The moon peeps through the blinds and casts its blue glow against his skin. His brows are furrowed, lips balled up like tiny fists on his face. There's nothing I can do to reassure him I'm busy selling houses when I'm not here. If I had a video crew following me around all day, he'd continue to swear I was up to no good. Infidelity plants a seed that absence makes grow.

"I have one of the most dangerous jobs there is. When I strap that gun to my belt every morning, I need to be focused on what I'm paid to do, what I swore to do. I don't have the luxury to think about what's going wrong in my marriage, who my wife is with, what she's doing when I'm in these streets. If my thoughts wander, that's it. If I make the wrong move, I can lose my life or cause one of my brothers to lose theirs. You put the wrong number down on a contract, that can be fixed. Can't bring a life back once it's gone." He flexes his gun hand. Opens and closes his palm, spreads his fingers. Does that over and over. "It shouldn't be like this," he says.

I flip the covers off, swing my legs to the side of the bed. Cut the lamp back on. Sit up straight and look my husband in the face. "You're right, it shouldn't be like this. It never should've been like this. We were scared to do anything about it before. What are we going to do about it now?"

He breaks my stare, lets his eyes roam the room. He walks into the bathroom. Warm water mixes with cool water. The toilet flushes. He comes back out. "My parents have been married nearly forty-two years."

"You keep reminding me."

"I only wanted to get married once."

"So you've said." I look down at my feet. Think about a question I've asked him before but never got an answer to. "Why'd you marry me, knowing your mother didn't approve?"

"I'm her only child. She's always wanted to dictate my life and have control over the things I did, the schools I attended, the women I'd dated. I was tired of that. I knew how bad she wanted me to marry Abigail. I married you to spite her, to let her know I was man enough to make my own decisions."

This conversation is going deeper than I have the energy for tonight. He dated me because I was a convenience in his life and married me to show his mother he was the boss. I take a deep breath, put my feelings to the side otherwise I might say something I'll regret and I don't have a lot of regrets in my life. Don't regret stepping outside of my marriage for happiness. "Eric, we're just existing in this marriage. Is that what you want?"

"It's been working all these years."

"We shouldn't be working this hard. It's starting to feel like a second full-time job."

This time he goes in the bathroom and cuts the shower on. Stays in there longer than a shower takes. I contemplate going in to check on him, but the last time I went in while he was under the water, I ended up under it with him creating our own steam. Tonight's not the night for that.

As sleep begins to pull me in its trance, I feel pressure on the other side of the bed. "What about the kids?"

I rub my eyes, clear my throat. Do my best not to slur. "We'll figure something out. All I know is we can't keep living like this. The kids will adjust. We'll adjust."

"You make it sound so easy."

At this point, everything is easier than this marriage.

What happens in the Virgin Islands stays in the Virgin Islands.

Hilda and I agreed not to exchange contact information. Our moment would forever stay on that island, in that room. We were both vulnerable from hurt and abandonment and anger, and in need of the kind of validation only a stranger could provide. Someone who didn't know enough about our situations to stop us from crossing that line.

Everything about St. Thomas was what I needed. Even Hilda.

As we watched the moon trade places with the sun, I told her about Rene. She cried. There she was, grieving over the loss of a marriage that should've been and a fiancé she loved since she was sixteen, while I was in mourning over the end of my wife's life. It was his choice to leave, and in all honesty, it was Rene's choice to leave me. Hilda comforted me through it all, she held me and wiped away my tears. And before she left, I did the same again for her.

For the first time in a long time, I was able to just be, to be in the moment. Didn't think or worry about anything out of my control. Didn't think about the future or how I was going to put the pieces back together once I got home. I breathed in the present. No what ifs, only what was and what is.

Now it's back to reality. Hopefully, I can maintain my newfound mentality.

Traffic is no different than any other Monday. Bumper to bumper, people falling asleep on their brakes, and others blowing their horns like they have Tourette's. Driver after driver pressing buttons on their cell phones, trying to occupy idle moments in time, neglecting to look up in time to see the pileup of cars in front of them. Another accident caused due to spectators of another accident. Looks like a Suburban tried to run a car off the interstate. Makes me think about my brother's accident for a minute. I shake that nightmare out of my head. For every brake light that flashes in front of me, another thirty cents is added to the meter on the cab. Good thing my exit is less than a mile up.

Though it's part of his job, I tip the taxi driver a few bucks extra for the trouble, grab my bag with nothing more than what I left with, head up the stairs to my apartment. I left the extra clothes I bought for the weekend with a local who looked down on his luck. Seemed to be really appreciative, so I gave him a few extra dollars as well. Made the man's day, made mine as well. It's not like I'm hurting for money, so I'll help who I can, when I can.

Money had never been a problem for Rene and me. We had a very good life insurance plan, though I hate using that money for anything. We never touched the money we got when Reggie passed. Rene had no siblings. There was no one to squabble or share the profits from the sale of her parents' house with; because of that, a hefty five-figures went into our bank account at closing.

Feels like I've been gone longer than a few days once I stick the key in my apartment's door. The moment I do so, my vacation runs from my memory like it was just a dream, while the pain and anger of what I left behind floods back in. I have to shake this feeling off.

After a quick shower, I throw on some gym shorts and a tank top. In the kitchen, I fill a cup with water and put it in the microwave for three minutes. Add some instant coffee mix to it and hazelnut creamer. I plug my drained phone up to the USB connected to my laptop. Once my phone receives enough juice, it powers on. There's a steady green light flashing as incoming messages roll through.

Next to my computer desk is my room. I peer inside and see all the destruction I left before I left. The mattress is still hanging on the floor. I see Rene lying in it. Her eyes are closed, her skin clammy. I see a sheet being pulled over her face. A chill runs through me.

I dreamt of her before she passed. She wasn't the first one to come to me before transitioning to the next life. My grandmother visited me the night she passed away. She had a message too. Told me to take care of my brother. He was born minutes before me, weighed more than me, but she wanted me to look after him for some reason. We were ten at the time. I never knew what she meant by that. After his car accident in college, I thought that's what she was trying to warn me about. When I was in St. Thomas that dream came back to me. Made sense then. She wanted me to protect him from me.

I'm at the hospital again.

One of my voicemails was from my brother. He needed a ride home. That call came in yesterday. When I went up to where he said he'd be, a nurse told me he was discharged last night.

I pay the parking attendant five dollars for all of five minutes and drive toward my brother's home.

My parents had called while I was gone. I didn't tell them or Andrew that I was going out of town. Was on the phone with my brother when I made the decision to leave, just didn't share that with him. Packed what I had in the hotel room and went straight to the airport. Hadn't talked to any family since.

I pull up to Drew's house, ring the doorbell. No one answers. I knock a few times. Still no answer. I walk around to the side of the garage, peer through the window. Two cars are parked inside. Back at the front door I ring the bell again. When no one answers, I take out my spare key and let myself in. "Drew," I call out.

A woman comes down the stairs with her finger pressed to her lips. "He just went to sleep."

I look around the house, look for my sister-in-law. "Where's Melissa?"

She reaches out her hand. "I'm Laura, one of the teachers at the school with Andrew. You must be Brandon. You look exactly alike. Wow."

"We're identical." I refrain from shaking hands with her until she tells me why she's in my brother's house.

"I know this looks crazy, and to be honest, I'm not sure what's going on. All I can tell you is that Andrew called the school yesterday to see if someone was available to pick him up from the hospital. He said there wasn't anyone else he could call. I picked him up last night after our school's end-of-the-year program."

None of this makes sense. I was only gone a few days and it seems like the world has turned sideways. "Where's his wife?" I ask again.

She shrugs her shoulder. "No one's been here since I brought him home last night."

To be clear, I ask, "You stayed the night?"

"He just had surgery and can't walk. I wasn't going to leave him alone."

I grab my wallet out of my back pocket, remove a few twenties, hand them to her. "Thanks for all your help. I've got it from here."

She puts both hands in the air as if my money offends her. "I won't take your money. Andrew's a good person, a good friend. I'm glad I was here for him, since he obviously couldn't call on anyone else." She grabs her purse from the sofa, picks up a few books from the coffee table. "He'll need another dose of pain killers in a couple of hours."

Once Laura vacates the premises, I walk up the stairs to check on my brother. The way his face is smoothed out tells me he's in a deep sleep. No emotion is riding his face. His coworker made it sound like he was up here in distress.

I pull up a chair next to his bed and wrack my brain trying to figure out what the heck happened while I was gone.

"What are you doing here?"

"What's wrong? Are you in pain?"

"Man, calm down."

I realize I'd fallen asleep in the chair. Forgot where I was. After watching my brother for a little while, I decided to walk through the house to see if there were any clues. The one thing that was consistent was the absence of Mel's things. Her side of the closet was empty, drawers were bare. No makeup in the bathroom, no trace of feminine toiletries. Pictures of her were gone. Even pieces of furniture were missing.

I sip from the bottle of water I brought up after my tour, let it moisten my throat. "I met Laura."

"You say that like it's something to it. At least she was there for me."

"Are you cheating on Mel? Is that why all of her stuff is gone?"

"You've been snoop— Damn." He moves too quickly, grabs at his leg.

I reach for the pills next to the bed. "How many of these are you supposed to take?"

He snatches the bottle from me. "It's too late to care."

"How was I supposed to know you'd have surgery while I was out of town? I went to the hospital as soon as I got your message."

Two pills and a glassful of water go down his throat. He leans his head back on the pillow slowly. "Where'd you go?" The pill container snug in his hand.

"We can talk about that later." I watch the tension grow in his face. "Are you in pain?"

"Won't feel much once the Oxycodone kicks in."

The way he popped those pills makes me think he's trying to take himself out. I take the container from his hand. His strength is too weak to fight me. "Where's Mel?"

"Look around. You tell me."

"Stop with the mind games."

Andrew stares at the ceiling, a tear glides from the corner of his eye.

"Talk to me, bro. Both of us can't fall apart."

"She left."

That much is obvious. I dare not say that, though.

"She took me to the hospital, kissed me before I went back to surgery. When I came out, no one was in the recovery room. No one came to my room for two days. I called her phone; she changed her number."

I know my sister-in-law and brother had been having a little trouble lately with trying to have a baby. Had no idea it had gotten to a level where she was willing to walk away, and at a time when Drew needed her the most. "Was not being able to have a baby that serious?"

He reaches underneath the pillow next to him. An envelope is in his hand. He passes it to me.

I unfold the letter, read its words.

Melissa couldn't handle the pressure of taking care of him. The way the first accident paralyzed him was one thing. This accident and the second knee surgery was too much. She wanted to be free to enjoy life and felt like she'd be stuck in the house with a crippled man. She realized how much of her life she sacrificed by trying to live up to the life he told her they were going to have. Since none of it happened, she took the accident as her way out. She'd recently come in contact with a man from her past. The love they once had for each other resurfaced. He was worth her leaving her marriage for. They had history. In high school, she had been pregnant with his child. They were too young to be parents. They gave the child up for adoption. Giving the baby up caused them to grow apart. They resented each other and couldn't handle the pressure of being together. When their paths crossed recently, because she and Drew hadn't had luck in the child department, she took the opportunity to run off with a man she already had a child with. They wanted to go on a search to find the child they gave up. She knew all of this when she married Andrew, but didn't feel any of it was important to share with him. She'd never been able to stop thinking about this guy and the life they would've had had they kept their child and stayed together. She felt like this was the perfect opportunity. She didn't want to be tied down to two broken men, her husband and his brother, so she left. She dropped eleven years with her husband in the trash like it was the wrong piece of mail.

Born minutes apart, and again, both of our lives falling apart.

I want to pop some pills, lie in the bed, and forget it all right along with my brother.

After picking the kids up from my mom's, we stop by Publix on the way home to get a few things for dinner. Kennedy wants tacos. EJ wants tacos, too, just because that's what his sister wants. I tell them both, "No tacos tonight. We're having spaghetti."

Frowns appear on both of their little faces. "But, Mom," Kennedy starts.

"But nothing. Now grab your brother's hand and get us some garlic cheese bread, please. I'll be right over in the produce section," I say as I push the cart toward the right.

Before I can even bag up tomatoes for the sauce, Kennedy comes running in my direction holding a man's hand. "Mom, look who I found."

He's shaking his head trying to find a way out of being mistaken for somebody else. "I guess your daughter gets her eyesight from you."

I blush at the memory of how we first met and also from seeing him again for the first time in months. "Kennedy, this isn't your teacher."

Still holding his hand, she declares, "I know that. Mr. Carter has a worm on his chin. This is his twin brother. Don't they look just alike? He used to always tell us about him."

Who am I to take away her joy? This is the happiest she's been in a while. "A worm on his chin?"

"Yeah, a scar from a car accident some years ago," Brandon shares.

Oh great. No telling what scars he has from the car accident our affair caused. My eyes search his for any indication of… "Kennedy, where's your brother?"

She looks around the vicinity and comes up short. "He was right behind us." She lets go of Brandon's hand and runs back to the freezer section. I'm right on her heels.

He's not where she left him. We scour the aisles, yelling out his name. Causing a panic all around. Brandon is with us. Both of us were so caught up in our brief reunion that everything else was forgotten, including my kids.

"Is this who you're looking for?" a young guy in black pants and a green shirt asks shoving a four-foot something in our direction with chocolate smeared across his face.

"Mommy, look what I got." He holds his hand out with remnants of what was once a candy bar.

"Thank you." I nod at the grocery store employee.

I reach inside my purse and pull out a pack of hand wipes. "Clean your hands before you get any more of that goo on your clothes."

"And get it off your face, silly," his sister adds.

"That's why you didn't get any candy, silly," he retorts.

Brandon watches us without saying anything. His eyes stay on EJ. I'm sure his mind is on his son, probably on the family he should have. He blinks away the memories.

"Mr. Carter, is Mr. Carter still going to teach?"

Her teacher didn't make it back by the time school ended for the year. There was talk that he was supposed to be coming back when the new year started. From the frown that crosses Brandon's face, I guess that was just talk.

"I'm not so sure, young lady."

"I hope he does. I want him to be EJ's teacher."

EJ chimes in. "Yeah, me too."

I can see discomfort in Brandon's face. I mouth the words, "Are you okay?"

"Well, it was nice meeting you, Kennedy and EJ." He reaches down and gives both of them a handshake.

"Will you tell Mr. Carter hi for me? Tell him I'm sorry for what my daddy and Uncle Mike did."

Brandon looks up at me, "Yeah, I'm sorry too."


Seeing Brandon flooded me with emotions I thought had long gone. Just as innocently as my daughter brought him over, what him and I shared began as an innocent gesture. We helped each other fill the empty spaces in our lives. Made each other laugh, made each other feel needed. Seeing him again brought all of that back, brought back why his presence in my life came to be.

Soon as I get the kids settled in, I head up to my room. I dig my work phone out of my purse, scroll through the contact list until I come across Rene Ortiz. I hit send. It rings twice.

"Was hoping you'd call."

My insides feel like I've climbed to the top of the highest roller-coaster and am on my way down the longest descent. I had saved Brandon's number under his wife's name. Had to make sure if my husband was ever inclined to browse through my phone, he'd find nothing. "Hi." I take a breath, wait for my heart to make it back to base. "How've you been?"

He doesn't say anything, makes me think he's giving himself a minute to gather his bearing as well. "What we did, we shouldn't have."

I close my eyes, let his words sink down to my soul. "I know."

A season ago, I slept with a married man and defiled my marriage. Just like the seasons change, a lot changed in my home as well as a result of my actions. Life didn't just change for me, they changed for him, and they changed for others who didn't make the decision we did.

"We can't take it back. This is what we have to live with."

"I'm okay with that, Brandon. I wouldn't want to take it back."

A shallow breath escapes his lips. "Me either."

I put my hand on my chest, try to slow my heart from beating so fast. "Can I see you?"

"Sydney, I'm not going to lie, I haven't stopped thinking about you. I care about you, but—"

"No buts. It's not right, I know, but—"

"No buts."

What am I doing? Seeing each other again—on purpose this time—wouldn't be good. Wouldn't be right. He's got to move on with his life. Being with me would only be a reminder of a void I couldn't fill and never would be able to. "Are you still running?"

"Nope." He chuckles. "Only did that to try and get close to you."

"Oh, and now you're pushing me away?"

"I didn't mean it like that."

"I was just messing with you." I press my lips together. Do that to give me pause before I say too much. "I'm sorry for all the chaos I brought into your life."

"No need. It was a mutual effort. If you're sorry, then I have to be. And I'm not. I did what I wanted to do."

It's what I wanted to do too. I didn't want what all came with it, though. Don't think any of us ever do. All we want is to have a moment when we feel nothing but the pleasure of that moment. We deal with everything else afterward.

I was his mistress.

He was my should've, would've, could've.

That's the reality.

Another reality is I ran from ending up like my mother and ended up just like her. I've become the lonely woman. My heart aches for the man on the other end of this phone, but there's nothing I can do to mend his pain. I tried once. What good that did. Sleeping with each other didn't do anything about our situations. Continuing it would do the same. Nothing. I can't do this.

I hold the phone close to my ear, my other hand pressed against my chest. "You take care of yourself, Brandon."

*I*t's funny how we always talk about communication being important in a relationship, but the reality is, none of us are communicating.

Sydney couldn't talk to her husband. I couldn't talk to my wife. My brother's wife couldn't talk to him. And so the story continues.

A few days ago, after running into Sydney and then getting a call from her, I did entertain the idea of continuing what we had started. Her ending the call was the best thing she could've done, done for her and for us. Seeing her with her kids put it all in perspective. She had a family and needed to put her focus on them. If she was going to end her marriage, it wasn't going to be because of me. I was going to tell her that, then the conversation started going in a different direction. For a moment, I again put my needs at the forefront of my mind and got off track. I don't know what was going on in her mind, but it was a thought we both needed.

"Remember this?" My father hands me a box.

Inside is my old camera, the one he took from me in high school that caused me to get in lots of trouble for going missing in action. "Man, do I."

"You were more attached to that thing than Linus to his blanket."

Going back to those memories brings a smile to my face. Holding the camera in my hand also makes me think of Hilda in St. Thomas.

Brings another smile to my face. Maybe we should've exchanged info after all. Who am I kidding? We'd just be two broken people trying to put the wrong pieces together. I think about Sydney. As with everything else in life, she'd soon become a distant memory. A faded picture in an old album. I glance at the top of the camera to see what the number is. I'd only taken fourteen pictures when the camera was taken from me. I cut it on, aim it in my father's direction, press down on the black button.

"There you go again."

Funny how he took it from me years ago because it was a distraction. Gave it back to me now only for it to be another distraction. "Doesn't take long for an old habit to be revived."

"Speaking of…" He removes the camera from my hands, places it back in the box. Takes a seat on the chair next to me in the basement, puts the box behind him. Out of reach and out of sight. "You and your brother need to work this thing out. As you've both been witness to, people come and go, but you two will always be there."

Andrew and I made the drive to our parents' home in Houston— the home we grew up in—a couple of days ago. After Mel left, I stayed with him at the house. Helped him nurse his knee back to where he was able to stand with only the need of a crutch. His pill-popping count was decreasing, though his drinking increased. That was when I threw some clothes in a suitcase and dragged him into my truck. He'd have plenty space to stretch out and elevate his leg when needed. It was a thirteen-hour drive we both needed, at least as far as getting out of a place where too much pain existed. The only time he talked to me was when he had to use a restroom or wanted something to eat. Other than that, my conversation went ignored. We weren't okay as brothers, but we were working on being okay with our circumstances.

"Dad, that's going to take some time."

He reminds me again of what I've been witness to as of late. "Time isn't always on our side."

It was true. I thought I'd have forever to watch my son grow up. Thought he'd be the one to bury me. Thought I'd have forever to love my wife. Thought we'd die together. I'm sure my brother thought the same about his wife and the kids he promised they'd have.

"The peace of God, which passeth all understanding, shall guard your hearts and minds through Christ Jesus." He repeats a familiar scripture in the Bible. The last time I heard those words was from the minister at Rene's funeral. My father grabs the box from behind him, stands up, hands the camera back to me. He grips it tight, not allowing me to take it. "Make peace, son."

There's been a lot over the past few months, and even over the last few years that I don't understand and probably never will. One thing's for sure, though, I'm slowly learning to have peace with where I am at this very moment. And sometimes, that's better than understanding.

I tell him, "I will."

"Love is patient and kind. Love doesn't demand its own way."

I put a hold on my nightly ritual, stop rubbing lubricant into my feet. Give Eric my attention. "Where'd you hear that?"

"You don't remember?"

My headshake confirms what he already knows.

He slides a picture across to my side of the bed. It's a picture of us. I was in a white gown standing next to him in a white tux. Our lips in a smile, misery in our eyes. "The minister said it that day."

I stare at the picture, wishing I could rewind time. Wish I could go back to that first date and listen to my intuition. I'd be singing a different song now, had I just been real with me. He could've kept lying to himself, could've found someone else to tell that lie to. Put a ring on her finger, put seeds in her belly. Could've let him be some other woman's boredom. But I let fear overrule. Fear of my biological clock ticking until the clock wouldn't tick anymore. Didn't want to sing the song my mom continues to sing. I was so desperate for a different song that I buried my soul.

Eric takes the picture back, sits it on his nightstand. "I did sleep with her that night."

If I had the capability of stopping my heart right now, I would reach inside my chest, wrap my fingers around it and squeeze until it ceased to beat.

"She'd flown in from Europe the night before. I wasn't going to see her. I had finally gotten over her. We were just friends. She'd moved on, was engaged as well. Said she just wanted to see me to close that chapter for good. I knew what her definition of closure was, so I planned to give her the runaround until after the wedding."

My heart defies my desire to stop beating and increases its speed. Feels like I've downed a whole bottle of Metabolife. "How could you?"

"The same way you could sleep with that dude. Doesn't feel so good, does it?"

My jaws are clenched so tight feels like my gums are rubbing against each other. "Don't go there."

"I wish I could say I did it because you did something to piss me off or I found out you'd lied to me. I can't say you did anything, because you didn't. I slept with her because I wanted to. Because I was still in love her."

The bed we've slept in for the past six years, the bed we made love in, created our kids in all of a sudden feels like a mattress tossed by the trash. I feel dirty. Feel like bedbugs are making a new home in my pores. If I had some matches, I'd set this bad boy on fire. Burn it, ashes to ashes and dust to dust, just like everything else has been in this marriage.

"Are you going to say something?"

"What is there to say?"

"Tell me I'm a bastard, tell me you hate me. Say something."

As much as I want to say those words to my husband, I can't. I'm as much to blame in all of this as he is. He knows it. I know it. We've both made our mistakes and seems like we keep making them. It all started from day one. I get up from the bed and leave him in this room where too much has been said and a lot more has been done.

In the hallway, I catch Forrester trying to scratch his way into Kennedy's room. He looks tired, like he's been digging away all night. The closer I get, the louder his breathing sounds. Poor kitty's winded. "Tomorrow you're going on a diet, buddy. I mean it this time." Not sure why my daughter's door is closed to begin with. The kids know their doors are to stay open. I crack the door open slowly, but Forrester nudges it all the way open with his big head, and announces his entrance with a deep meow.

Kennedy stirs in the bed, her journal hits the carpet. I pick it up, flip through it without looking at anything in particular. She's almost seven. I'm sure there's not much for her to vent about. It's evident she's still mad at her father, can't see too much else going on with her. I close her privacy up and put it next to Forrester at the foot of her bed. Before walking out, I give her a light kiss on her head. Make sure I leave a wide gap in the door.

"What are you doing up?" I ask EJ when I enter his room.

He slams his face in the pillow. "I'm sleeping, Mommy," says a muffled voice.

Toys are tossed around all in his room. It was not like that when I sent him to bed nearly four hours ago. I sit on the bed next to him, put my hand on his back. "You're something else, you know that?"

He giggles, then flips over and puts his head on my lap with a serious look on his face. "Mommy, I don't like it when you and Daddy fight."

I rub by hand across his hair. "Aw, honey. I don't either."

"Then you should stop. Fighting's not nice."

"You're right; it's not."

"Okay, I wanna go to sleep now."

"Can Mommy have a hug first?"

He wraps his growing arms around me as best he can. I melt in his arms.

On my way out his room, his father's words rush through my thoughts like runners at the beginning of a race. *Love doesn't demand its own way.*

The moment my kids were born, they came out loving me. There was nothing I had to say or do for them to love me. It was natural, instinctual. Love should be that way. No one should have to do anything or treat someone a certain way to deserve love. If that's the case, love is one thing it isn't. Eric and I both tried to make ourselves love each other. It didn't come natural for us. And when we tried to force it, we felt the pull making us pull away. What would happen if we just let each other be?

Instead of going downstairs to catch up on some TV, I turn around and walk back in the master bedroom. It's time I stop lacing up my sneakers and taking my mark, get set, go. I'm tired of running from the consequences of bad decisions. I've been running for far too long. Running from fear. Running from the mistakes I've made. Running from the mistakes I didn't make. Tonight, right now, I'm going to face this for what it is.

I cut the light on and position myself right in front of my husband. Just like I told his mom he chose to marry me, I chose to marry him. It's time we stare truth in the face.

I search his face, search his eyes. Look for any indication that he's ready to call it quits. I come up short. "I had an abortion before we got married."

Now his eyes study me. "I know."

My knees buckle. Eric catches me, ushers me to sit on the bed. All these years I thought that was my secret, thought it would follow me to a very deep grave. "Why didn't you say anything?"

"You want the truth?"

"It's time we start telling nothing but."

He bends over, elbows on knees, chin in hands. "Because I wasn't going to marry you. I knew if I went along with your act of everything being normal that you'd terminate the pregnancy."

I pull my feet into my lap, fold them like a pretzel. "How'd you know I was pregnant?"

"You always talked about being bloated when it was that time of the month. You'd talk about all the gas you had. It was clockwork every month. One day while at your place I needed to look up a date on the calendar. I noticed you had a date underlined. I looked on the previous month, saw the same underline on a different day, but that day had a circle as well. Kept flipping through and saw the same thing in all the other months except for the month we were in. That line had been two weeks ago." He rubs his hands up and down his face.

"You get paid to notice things."

"That's the real reason Abigail came to town. I had told her I wasn't going through with the wed—"

"You weren't going to marry me." I cut him off. "Uh yeah, I get the picture."

After a pause on both of our ends, a pause long enough for our thoughts to circulate, Eric's hand slides over on top of mine. "We didn't marry for love, we've both admitted that. But over time I've grown to love you. We have two beautiful kids together. I can't make you love me, that's something you have to want to do on your own."

I think about what he's saying as I slide my hand from under his. I run my fingers through my hair, give my head a light massage. I had no idea how my life would change after allowing my heart, mind, body and soul to tiptoe out of this marriage. Had no idea how it would change if my husband ever found out. The last two weeks of Eric's suspension, he flew out to Denver to visit his parents. He needed time away to think clearly without being in the heart of the situation. We both needed the space to think without having the other to distract the process. I was able to put things in perspective. Though I didn't love him when we married, I, too, have grown to love him as the father to our children and as a man. Not *in* love with him, but love is there.

Eric interrupts my thoughts. "Is this it for us?"

I repeat his words back to him. "Love doesn't demand its own way." I don't know what that means in this moment, but it makes me feel better about any decisions I have to make in the future.

He moves his lips to speak. "We can't go back from here, you know that, right?"

He's right, we can't go back from here. I had an abortion because I didn't want to be with him for the long haul. He knew about it and didn't say anything for the same reason. If I *could* go back, I would put the egg he fertilized back in my womb and let it have a life of its own. Instead, I took matters into my own hands and made life worse for all involved. Maybe Eric and I didn't talk about it, but all these years, it was talked about in our silence. I killed for him and he let me do it. I let me do it. Ultimately, the decision was all mine. A piece of me I'll never be able to get back. Peace, I'll never be able to get back. That's something I'll never be able to move from as long as I'm in this marriage.

I get up from the bed and stand in front of my husband. I look him in the eyes. Again, I see the truth he refuses to speak. I will no longer play this game with him. Just like the last exhale—when the lungs release all of the air in its capacity—this marriage has released all of the lies it's used to keep it alive. I twist the engagement ring and wedding band off my finger. Release the weight. Grab his hand, open his palm. Place the rings inside. "Yes, Eric. This *is* it for us."

# ABOUT THE AUTHOR

Julia Blues is a storyteller on a mission. That mission is to help better lives univerSOULly every story. Living several years of her life on different sides of the globe, she's able to take her cultural experiences and plant them into the souls of the characters in her stories. *Parallel Pasts* was her first novel of many more to come. She is expanding her storytelling to television and film. After years of the gypsy life, she has finally found a home in Austin, TX. To read more of her story, visit www.JuliaBlues.com.

# REFLECTIONS FROM THE AUTHOR

February 1, 2014.

It's 11:47 a.m. and I'm somewhere between thirty and thirty-four thousand feet in the air on my way back to Jacksonville, North Carolina, after a short visit to Austin, TX. I'm sitting next to my father whom I have not flown with since he retired from the Air Force two decades and some change ago. Sitting next to him, I am reminded of how far back a moment can seem in your mind but how close it can stay in your heart.

Speaking of my dad, since I began writing this book, I've been asked what makes me an authority to write about marriage having never been married. This is a valid question, one that my only answer continues to be, "My parents have been married for thirty-nine years. I've experienced marriage through them." Their story of meeting makes my heart smile every time I think about it. A friend of my dad's was taking a gift to his girlfriend's house for Valentine's Day. My father decided to ride with him. Guess who answered the door? Yep, my mom. My father slapped his friend across the shoulder, chastising him for not letting him know Wanda had a sister. None of that mattered because from then on, my father would be very aware of my mother's existence. At fourteen, he knew she would be a constant in his life. They married four years later after my father joined the Air Force. He went back to his hometown to join forces with my mom as husband and wife as she was completing her senior year of high school. They've been together ever since.

Stories like theirs don't come around too often, so when they do, I cherish them. In the thirty-odd years I've been a witness to my parents' union, I've learned a lot about love, sacrifice, respect, devotion and effective communication. My parents welcomed me in their very early twenties. I grew up just as they had. And I've experienced their evolution, fully understanding the commitment involved when you agree to "for better or for worse." Even as a grown adult living with them now, I continue to learn. I have so much respect for the institution of marriage, of what it means 'til death do us part. It's because of them that I believe marriage works, no matter what statistics say. It takes work, and when two people are equally yoked, love each other, and are willing to do what it takes to honor their commitment, we will begin to see more successful marriages.

Though I've learned a lot through watching my parents, this novel is not about them at all. What it is about is an exploration of what happens when the truth is kept from the person you've pledged forever to, and often times, yourself. I've been in a couple of relationships through the years, some in which I've spent way more time in the relationship than I should have. Like Sydney in this book, I knew this from the beginning. But just like her, I stayed for the wrong reasons. I stayed because I felt time slipping away from me. Stayed because I thought I was happy. Stayed because I convinced myself I wasn't settling. Stayed because deep down inside, I doubted that someone whose pieces fit my puzzle, and mine his, would ever show up. Fortunately, we realized we were wrong for each other and walked away before walking down the aisle. I wanted to explore how those relationships could've been had I stayed. As a result, *The Last Exhale* was birthed.

Sydney married the wrong man. And as we found out, her husband knew she was the wrong one, too. Yet, they married for their own reasons instead of for the right ones. Originally, I wanted their story to be something completely different. I wanted them to fall apart because he was a workaholic. He spent more time taking care of responsibilities instead of taking care of the ones he was responsible for. Not that that wasn't interesting enough, I felt the story was too familiar. I didn't realize that until after I had written half of the story. Sydney spoke up. She was miserable and it was by her own doing. She had to get honest with herself in order to make the changes needed to have a different experience. What she wasn't expecting was her husband to feel the same way. Their lives could've had different outcomes had they both been honest from the very beginning.

How many times in life does this happen to us? We dig a hole, throw the truth in it, and toss dirt on it hoping it'll stay there. But the longer we keep it there, the more dirt gets piled on top until it's buried so deep, it'll cost us more to dig it up than it would have had we just been honest from the get-go.

Brandon's situation was different. He married the right woman. They had a wonderful, truthful marriage until an unforeseen wrong turn took place. The death of their child. Though that unfortunate event took place, it wasn't the cause of the breakdown in communication. Guilt crept into the marriage and ate its way through Rene's body. Could Brandon have pushed harder for his wife to talk instead of moving out and into the arms of another woman? Quite possibly. But that wouldn't have healed Rene from cancer, though; it would have helped Brandon from living with the same guilt that took her life.

When I began writing this story, I had no intention of having Brandon and Sydney have a physical affair. I wanted it to be emotional only. They had different plans. As Sydney's friend told her, "What y'all are doing is building a relationship." That wasn't what I wanted for them. It actually left me stuck for a while. For Brandon to cheat after finding out his wife was ill, left a bad taste in my mouth for him so much so, I couldn't write his parts anymore. He'd stop speaking to me because I'd judged him. I'd judged his story, his situation, his journey. Thanks to a conversation with my aunt (thanks, Miriam), I was able to free the judgment. Sleeping with Sydney made sense to him. I got it. Once I accepted it, I was able to finish the story.

The same was for Sydney. In my head, she was supposed to stay married to Eric. As the story began to unfold more, there was no way she could stay. The kids would've been her only excuse. In the end, everyone would've felt the misery. And who wants to feel like they're being smothered by a hundred pillows? She wanted me to know that nothing good would come of staying Mrs. Holmes. I had to honor her decision and her experience, and wrote what I was told. I actually exhaled right along with her.

The lessons I've learned in writing this story will follow me into any relationship I enter. One thing's for certain: Idle chitchat can turn into a lot more than you can handle when you're unhappy in your relationship and vulnerable. You don't even have to know that you're unhappy and vulnerable for the chatter to grab hold of and take over your conscience.

I hope *The Last Exhale* has opened your eyes in some way, whether you're single, involved, or married. Tell the truth to yourself and to those you're with. It's never too late to make things better.

And with that, it's time for some gratitude.

God, I thank You for placing this story in me. I may not fully realize the reason You chose this path for me, but I am grateful. You never do anything without purpose, and I know these stories You place in me will fulfill that purpose. Thank You for your reflection of love and your blessing of marriage.

Mom and Dad, thank you for being a wonderful example of a union. I know it's not your intention to set some mark or standard in your marriage. All you did was found the one you wanted to share your life with and chose to honor those vows through it all. As long as you two have been married, it seems as though you're just getting started. May God continue to bless your union. Here's to another thirty-nine years and then some.

Strebor Books Team: Zane and Charmaine, thank you for affording me the space to tell my stories.

The Sara Camilli Agency: Sara and Stephen, thank you for all you do to help my stories make their way from my head to my fingers to the world.

Orsayor Simmons of Book Referees, thank you for joining me on this journey. You've been a blessing.

My Social Media Family: Kelly Grover, Tammy Stewart, Larnell Baxter, Nadira Abdul Quddus, Kimyatta Walker, Stacy Campbell, Robin Hardeman, Chad Tomme, Christy Turnquist, Tracy Hunt, Jordan Jones, Kyle Dowling, Ms. Niko, Marquita Olive, Tiffany Tyler or Tiffany Talks Books, Concetta Burns-Ramsey, Yolanda Long, Leigh Mohr, Marquita Davis, Sheora Harris, Alisha Gordon, Melody Frederick, Nicole Burgess, Javania Webb, Toshii Cooper, Shauna Clarke, Kimerlin Spencer, Craig Wilson, Kebia Bellamy, Candice Robinson, Monica Tolbert, Monica Rogers, Olivia Henley, and Will Dawson, thank you all for posting pictures of *Parallel Pasts* on Facebook, Twitter, Instagram, Pinterest, and other social media platforms, and for getting involved in the conversations about it. Your support, interactions and excitement about my firstborn novel was joy to my soul.

Book Reviewers: Mary Rhone, Viviette L. Carr, Tiffany Craig, BridgeFresh, Stacy Lawrence-Campbell, OOSA Online Book Club, Barbara1216, Ms. Niko, Amazon Fan, Teresa Beasley, Orsayor Simmons, John P. Young, Kimyatta Walker, Kristina, and Chris, thank you for being the first fifteen people to post reviews on Amazon. I never realized how much anticipation goes into seeing that number go up. Thank you, Johnathan Royal, for doing the first video book review of *Parallel Pasts* on YouTube. You definitely put a smile on my face.

Medu Bookstore: Sister Nia and Brother Dub, thank you for hosting my first book signing. From the time I began writing, I'd always visualized myself sitting behind a table, greeting readers, and signing their books. You made that a reality. And a huge thank you to all who attended: Miriam Pollock, Craig Wilson, Mr. and Mrs. Campbell, Reuben Griffith, Eric Griffith, Kimerlin Spencer (Niya), Kim Bright, Jasmine, Susie, Markeida Evans Hicks, Mary McCarter, Kebia Bellamy (Kiyon), Kimberly Reese, Monica Tolbert, Diane Dorce, Deborah Dorce, Toshii Cooper, and Jaha Knight.

Music: Anthony Hamilton, Jill Scott, Ledisi, Joe, Chrisette Michele, Avery Sunshine, Boyz II Men, Eric Roberson, Mariah Carey, Jagged Edge, India.Arie, and John Legend, thank you for your gift of music. This book would not be what it is had it not been for your songs. They helped me get through the hard parts.

If you have not seen your name, do not think I've excluded or forgotten you. Here's a big THANK YOU. Nothing you have done has gone unnoticed. Thank you for picking up *Parallel Pasts*, and this book, *The Last Exhale*. Thank you for reading these stories, for telling others about them, for posting about them on your blogs and social media pages. Thank you for rooting me along, and for joining me on this journey.

It is my hope that the story of Sydney and Brandon will help relationships all across the board. Let us learn to live, learn, grow, and love. We have to be willing to open the lines of communication in honesty and not in fear of the results. Marriage should be a lifetime commitment, not until you don't feel like being married anymore. Let's all work together to make the right choices in the partners we choose for life, because after all, it is our decision.

I'd love to hear from you whether it's about this book, something else I've written, or if you just need someone to talk to. Email me at juliasblues@gmail.com. You can also find me and all of my social media links on my website, www.JuliaBlues.com.

Thank you again for taking out the time to read this book and for your contribution in bettering lives univerSOULly every story.

Until the next book…

Abundant blessings and peace be unto you!

Julia Blues


*"Love is patient and kind. Love is not jealous or boastful or proud or rude. It does not demand its own way. It is not irritable, and it keeps no record of being wronged. It does not rejoice about injustice but rejoices whenever the truth wins out. Love never gives up, never loses faith, is always hopeful, and endures through every circumstance."*

—1 Corinthians 13:4-7 (NLT)

If you liked "The Last Exhale" and "Parallel Pasts," we hope you enjoy this story.

# Heated Waters

By Julia Blues
(Writing as Jewells and Featured in
"Zane's Z-Rated: Chocolate Flava 3" anthology)
Available from Atria Books

The pool mirrors the moon in its stillness.

I dip the tip of my foot in and watch the moon's reflection break into tiny pieces just as my life has shattered within the last twenty-four hours.

*"I'm filing for divorce."*

My eyes sting as a fresh batch of tears form. I do everything I can to prevent them from falling. Clear my throat, swallow, cough. Nothing helps.

His familiar scent of Sicilian citron, apple, and cedarwood tickles my nose and betrays my emotions.

"How did we get here?" I ask as I feel him standing behind me.

He doesn't answer right away. Instead he sits down next to me, rolls up the legs of his pants, and sticks his feet in the water right along with mine.

I look over at him; beg for answers with my liquid emotions.

He wipes away a tear just before it falls from my chin. "I think this is something we've both been wanting for a while. Why prolong the inevitable?"

I sigh. "It doesn't have to be this way. I...I don't want you to leave."

Trevor looks up at the sky, says, "Full moon. Emotions always get the best of folks on nights like this."

I lean my head against my husband's shoulder. The shoulder that has carried the weight of my infidelity for the last two years. His love for me kept him around all this time despite my indiscretion. It wasn't intentional, wasn't planned. It was a moment of weakness. I was lonely. Married and lonely. Two words that should never be used in the same sentence. His job kept him away more than a husband should be away from his wife. Seemed like the more I spoke up about it, the more business trips he would make. One trip lasted a week longer than planned. When he came back, I had already broken my vows.

"It wasn't the way you think."

His shoulder tenses under my head when I refer to that night. He tenses and shuts down every time I try to talk about it. "It doesn't matter anymore."

"Are we really over?" I want to know, though I already know his answer. I just need to hear him say it again to make it official.

"The papers are on the dining room table. Movers will be here in the morning."

My eyes begin to burn again.

Trevor leans his head down and places his lips against my forehead. "You'll be okay. We both will."

Maybe a full moon does get the best of people because as hurt as I am, another feeling between my thighs won't let me break down the way my heart wants me to. Been fighting my hormones since he walked out smelling all good.

I lift my head; turn it in the direction of the lips that were just on my skin. I close my eyes and kiss my soon-to-be ex-husband.

"Let's not—"

"Shhhhh," I say as I try to gain some control over what happens in my life.

For a second, neither of us moves or says anything. Contemplation is in the air. Him debating if he should oblige my offer.

Me wondering if I should take it off the table.

He wins.

He removes his legs from the pool and walks back in the house.

I cover my face with my hands and tremble as the floodgates of my heart break open.

Footsteps entering the shallow end of the pool silence my sobs. I open my eyes to see Trevor walking toward me. He stops right in front of me, looks me in the eyes as if to ask if I'm sure I want to go there. With my irises, I tell him yes.

He moves in between my parted legs, reaches his hands behind me, and scoots me to the edge of the pool. Scoots my heat closer to his face. Long, slender fingers creep underneath my skirt and trace the edges of my thighs and the curve of my hips until they reach the top of my panties. I raise my torso up slightly for smooth removal. My panties are tossed to the side just like this marriage after eight years, but I refuse to think about that right now.

His eyes are intense as his face nears my warmth. He licks his lips, kisses each thigh softly. Again he grabs my rear and pulls me closer than close. His tongue navigates its way around familiar territory.

My head leans back, glazed-over eyes staring up at the moon as his tongue swims to depths only his tongue can go. My inner walls tighten around his thick tongue, trying to pull him in deeper, causing me to close my eyes and bite down on my lip at the same time. A moan trembles from my lips. He's always been a gifted eater. I run my fingers through his locs, pull him closer than close.

His moans make my love below vibrate, tickle my pearl in the worst way.

I feel his eyes on me.

I put my eyes on him.

We stare.

He wants me to know this last time is personal.

I want him to know this last time is personal for me, too.

He flips me over on my stomach, throws my legs across his shoulders. Devours me from the back. His lips against mine, tongue flicking in between my folds. Smacking noises loud enough to wake up the whole neighborhood. His tongue moves in and out of me as I ride his face like Secretariat going for the Triple Crown.

My trembling makes me lose my balance. He helps me turn back around and yanks my shirt above my head. Tosses it and my bra over where he tossed my panties a while ago. He doesn't take my skirt off for whatever reason, and refrains from removing any of his clothes.

He submerges under the water, swims to the stairs on the shallow end of the pool. Sits and waits for me, pants pulled down to his ankles. I know what that means.

I go under the water and come back up with my face right in his lap. His firmness stands at attention waiting for me to salute. I lick its girth; let my tongue linger in the juices on the tip for a second before I let half of him disappear in my mouth. I know how he likes it; not too much at first. I flick my tongue up and down his shaft; take his cleanly shaven sperm holders into my mouth, let my moans vibrate against him like his did me moments ago. This time I take him all the way in my mouth, feel him slip down my throat.

He massages his fingertips against my scalp as I massage his manhood with my mouth. He thrusts deeper down my throat and then nudges my head away. The hunger in his eyes is now a look of revenge. He grabs me away from the stairs and pulls me to the wall of the pool, turns my back to him. He prefers it that way. Hasn't been able to face me as he enters me since my moment of weakness.

His hardness enters my soft spot without hesitancy.

I scream in torture and in pleasure.

"Is this how he did it to you?"

Trevor's question catches me off-guard. I don't know what to say.

My silence takes him to another level as he grabs my breasts with both hands and fills my insides in a way he never has before. Pumping in and out like a drill trying to reach the bottom of the earth. If I said it didn't feel good I'd be lying.

I toot my butt out to push him outside me. I want to stare at his wrath face-to-face.

He understands.

I reach in the water and escort him back into my fiery dungeon. I shiver as he enters me again.

They say to never look an animal in the eye because they will be able to see your fear. At this moment I wish I had listened. Fear is in my eyes. Looking in Trevor's, I can see my fear of being alone. And if I can see it in his eyes, I know he can see it, too.

Alone.

The reason we are here.

I rock my hips hard; try to ride him back into this marriage.

He makes short, hard thrusts, tries to get my mind off the matters of this marriage.

We're going at it like animals. Bucking like kangaroos and howling like wolves. Going at it so hard I feel my flesh scraping against the edge of the pool. Trevor sees my pain. Without removing himself from me, he moves us back over to the stairs. He's on top of me, growing inside me, the tip of his penis trying to knock my cervix out the ballpark. I bite down on his neck until I taste blood. That excites him all the more. He puts both of my nipples in his mouth, sucks hard like he's trying to suck a thick milkshake through a too-small straw. It hurts and feels good at the same time. My fingernails claw at his back, his drill digging deeper into my earth. He's trying his damndest to leave a lasting impression in my womb.

My legs shake. Not from ecstasy. I'm in pain.

Trevor's too far gone to even realize this is no longer pleasure for me.

This is too much. This is vengeance. Not the way I want to remember my final hours with my husband.

Again, emotions get the best of me, and I lose it. I cry like I did when I confessed my adultery and saw how thin the line was between love and hate.

He wipes away my tears, wraps his arms around me. I realize it was no longer pleasurable for him either. Again he pulls me closer than close. My inner walls throb against his manhood as my outer walls crumble against his chest.

"Are you sure we can't work this out?" I hear myself plead.

He looks at me, kisses me with the love he's always had for me, the love he had before everything changed.

My answer is in his kiss. Nothing else is to be said.

I loosen my legs from around his waist. Feel life escaping from me as he withdraws from between my legs for the last time.

Going in the house is the last thing I want to do. I want to stay in the pool until the water doubles over with my tears and drowns me in my apology. Doing so would be insane. It's my fault that life has come to this point. Nobody made me do what I did. Can't blame Trevor. Can't blame circumstance. It was my actions.

I let my body drift to the bottom of the pool, but my damn skirt acts like a life preserver, refusing to let me sink.

What the hell? This is futile. I walk the floor of the pool toward the steps. With each step, the weight of my emotions decreases as less water engulfs me. My nipples harden as the air lays kisses on my wet skin. I take off my skirt and wrench the water from it, grab the rest of my clothes from the ground, and enter the house of loneliness.

"I thought you were going to stay out there forever."

I use my clothes to cover my exposed flesh. "Trevor? I thought you left."

"I did. Came back."

"Oh" is all I'm able to say.

Neither of us look at each other, both of us probably feeling a mixture of shame and remorse from where we let our emotions take us a couple of hours ago.

"Come here," he instructs with an outstretched hand.

Still holding on to my clothes, trying to cover as much of my private parts as possible, I take his hand and move to where he is.

He grabs an orange envelope from the dining room table and

walks us over to the fireplace. He removes papers from the envelope, takes our ending in his hands, rips it to pieces. Tosses it on top of wood. Clicks the remote to the gas a few times until the hum of gas kicks in and fire slowly begins to burn what would have been our demise.

Our hands tighten around each other's as we watch those divorce papers turn to ashes.

Trevor turns to me, says, "This is our beginning." He clicks the remote again to shut the gas off.

Though the light from the fire diminishes, the light in my eyes glows.

Hand in hand we walk upstairs. When he opens our bedroom door, several candles are lit. Sheets are pulled back on the bed with rose petals sprinkled over it.

"Remember our honeymoon?"

I feel my cheeks spread from ear to ear. "I do."

On my pillow, petals form a heart and a letter with my name on it is in the middle of it.

"Read it," Trevor says. "When you're done, join me in the bathroom."

We decided not to write our own vows when we married. But my husband surprised me on our wedding night by putting his written vows on my pillow for my eyes only. I thought it was the sweetest thing ever. I went to a printer and had them overlay the vows over one of our wedding pictures. It's been on my nightstand ever since.

I unfold the paper to see a resignation letter to his job.

With the letter in my hand and tears streaming down my face, I join my husband in the bathroom. "You did this for me?" I ask him.

He helps me in the tub, gets in behind me. Says, "Couldn't imagine doing it for anyone else."

We settle into the tub together. His legs straddle my body. I lean my head back on his chest. "I can't believe you're letting your job go."

"It needed to be done. In order for this marriage to work, it had to be done."

Nothing else needs to be said. I understand him and he understands me.

He rubs his soapy hands up and down my arms, rubs my neck. Takes a few suds and teases my nipples. He smoothes my curls to the side, whispers in my ear, "I miss making love to my wife."

"I miss my husband making love to me."

He kisses behind my ear. His lips make love to my burnt-almond skin. He turns my face up toward his and our lips connect. My mouth opens, his tongue greets mine. I can still taste my love on his tongue from earlier. Can feel him hardening against my back as my love below coos.

"Wait," Trevor says. He fumbles in the water for a washcloth. He pours my favorite black orchid and velvet hibiscus body wash on it and lathers me up from my neck to my toes. He leaves no skin unclean. I take the washcloth and do the same to him. We jump in the stand-alone shower to rinse the suds off and run water through our hair to get rid of the chlorine. I hand him a bottle of lavender oil for him to rub me down before I pat myself dry. I take the bottle and do the same for him. He squeezes as much water out of his locs as possible, then carries me back into the bedroom.

Everything about tonight reminds me of our honeymoon. He did the same exact things the night we married.

He lays me on the bed ever so gently. "Turn over."

I do as told.

He warms oil in his hands and places them on my back. He's careful around the scratches I got from the pool. Soft kisses apologize to my tender spots. His hands work out every worry in my body, every fear, every doubt. His lips do the same thing to the opposite side of my body, starting with my face. He kisses my forehead, my eyelids, my lips. We stay mouth to mouth for a while, slowly tonguing each other with so much passion. He sucks my bottom lip before heading further south. Locs tickle my skin as his tongue traces the roundness of my nipples. He does one then does the other. Goes back and forth before putting both breasts in his mouth at the same time. He does that and I swear the rivers of life flow from between my thighs.

His lips continue down to the land of milk and honey. "Baby, you are so wet."

"You did that," I say.

Instead of draping my legs over his shoulders, I spread them wide, placing one foot on each side of his rib cage. Opens me up something serious, allows him to dive face-first into my heated waters.

He licks and sucks like I'm a double scoop of ice cream melting down his cone. Surely my juices are dripping down his chin and he doesn't want to lose one drop to the sheets.

My husband holds my hips in his hands as my freshly waxed folds grind against his face. He holds me to keep us going in the same pace. His tongue flicks my swollen clit and for a minute I lose my breath. I can't moan, can't yell, can't scream my infamous, "Shit." I fight to find air, yet I ride his face until he comes up for air.

On his way up, he stops at my breasts again and perfumes them with the scent of my love.

I feel my sweet spot revving up again, ready for round two... three...four.

He kisses me; damn near tongues me down. I try to eat my flavor off his palate. Feel myself grind against his pelvis until I find what I'm looking for. I draw him in like quicksand; feel him hit the bottom of my pit. He makes slow, deep strokes, and enters my soul in a way he never has before.

Every stroke is an apology to what went down earlier this evening. Saying, *"I'm sorry for treating you as anything less than my wife. Sorry for pushing you into the arms of another man."*

He pulls all the way out to the tip and then glides back in. Every time he does that he promises to never leave me lonely, to always listen to what my heart says, and to be a better husband.

With every rock of my hips, I apologize for not trusting in his position as the head of this household. Every tilt of my pelvis begs for forgiveness for stepping outside of this marriage for comfort and validation.

I open my eyes and see my husband's on me. I tell him, "I promise to never leave your side again."

He kisses my tears and reminds me, "This is just the beginning."